Y0-EKR-894

SAINT —'S SECOND SEASON

Raleigh Bruce Barlowe

MINERVA PRESS
ATLANTA LONDON SYDNEY

SAINT —'S SECOND SEASON

ISBN 0 75410 512 1

First Published 1999 by
MINERVA PRESS
315–317 Regent Street
London W1R 7YB

Printed in Great Britain for Minerva Press

SAINT —'S SECOND SEASON

Chapter One

'Her brother? No. No, he can't be! They are both dead. One of Edward's bastards maybe?'

Henry's eyes narrowed and his voice rose as he shrilled, 'He can't be! He can't be! A bloody thieving bastard, that is what he is!'

Henry Tudor was suddenly seething inside. The unwelcome news his counsellor had brought was enough to make a man's blood boil. As he laboured to regain his normal composure, he asked himself: 'Who is this pretender? Could he be one of the Queen's brothers? No, they died in the Tower a good thirteen years ago. Could he be another of Edward's bastards? No, he must be a fraud, another roguish adventurer who would try to turn a resemblance to Edward into possible fortune.'

John Morton, a cardinal of the Church, Archbishop of Canterbury, and Lord Chancellor, waited calmly for the King's surge of anger to subside. Henry, the seventh of his name to wear the crown of England, was never an easy person to counsel, particularly not on occasions such as this. Almost any unwary action or comment could unleash the royal wrath during Henry's not infrequent outbursts of temper.

The Archbishop had no illusions about the King's probable reaction to the news he brought. But someone had to tell Henry about the appearance of another pretender to the throne, this time a fair-haired young man who insisted he was the Queen's younger brother.

'Get rid of him and quick!' the King barked. 'We want no more pretenders questioning our right to rule.'

Morton nodded his head in agreement. Henry had had more than his share of challenges from pretenders. In recent memory, first Lambert Simnel and then Perkin Warbeck had appeared out of nowhere with their claims that they were the rightful heirs of Edward IV.

Simnel had been discredited and condemned to serve as a scullery lad in the King's kitchen. Warbeck, a more noisome nuisance, had voiced his claim and then fled to Scotland where he stayed for several months making plans to lead an uprising in England. Unknown to him, Morton's agents had learned enough about his movements to alert Henry's guards and make it easy for them to seize him and his co-conspirators when he slipped back into England in 1497. Henry had honoured his plea for mercy and committed him to the Tower where he had now languished for almost a year.

'Should I instruct your guards to get rid of that Perkin chap too?' Morton asked.

'No, we made our mistake with him. We should have taken your advice and hung him last October. Now the world knows of our act of mercy in just sending him to prison, we cannot rid ourselves of him without more provocation on his part.'

'It could easily be arranged, Your Majesty.'

'What are you suggesting?'

'Should he try to escape, you would have every reason to charge him with treason.'

'Maybe so, but we must think of what people both here and on the Continent would say.'

'We can handle that by getting a full confession from him and publishing it for all to see.'

'Captain Mason can get the confession. But will it say what we want?'

'It will if we write it.'

'How can we be sure he will sign it?'

'He will gladly sign it if you give him the choice between being drawn and quartered or signing the confession and staying in prison.'

'He might go for that, and even agree to humiliate himself by repeating his confession in public.'

'An excellent idea, Your Majesty. Two or three public confessions should convince even your critics of his guilt.'

'But if we promise him life imprisonment, we will be back where we started.'

'True, but you could keep him in prison for another year or two and then hang him for some new crime such as bribing his jailers or trying to escape.'

'Morton, you are the devil's own genius. You have hit on a strategy that can work without tarnishing our good name. While we are about it, let us have young Warwick join him in a plot to escape from the Tower. This may be the best chance we'll have to rid the kingdom of that feeble-minded brat.'

'That can all be arranged in good time, sire. Back now to this new pretender – should I get the constabulary to arrest him?'

'We said, get rid of him. Arresting him will only draw attention to him and his claims. We do not need any more of that. This is a job for Mason's crew. Tell the Captain to arrange for his quiet disappearance, and the sooner done the better. And while you are about it, make certain the men who do the job keep their mouths shut. Let us have no more wagging of tongues than is absolutely necessary.'

'I'll have Captain Mason attend to your orders at once, Your Majesty. He is one man we can trust to do a thorough job.'

'And a clean one too, we hope.'

Morton rose from his chair in preparation for leaving,

but Henry raised a hand to stop him. 'Before you leave, tell us again if there is any doubt in your mind about the deaths of the Queen's brothers?'

Bishop Morton stroked his chin and bristled internally as he recalled the many times Henry had asked that question. He was a faithful supporter of the King and had probably done as much as any man in England to put him on the throne. Yet there were times when he could not help but wonder about this man who sat across the table from him.

Henry could be so self-assured and decisive one moment and so seemingly insecure the next. There was little about him or his personality to commend him to others as a king. Unlike the princes of Plantagenet blood, he lacked both the bearing and the handsome visage to fit the popular image of a great king. He was of less than average height with gaunt features and a homely face. True, he was shrewd and sly but he had shown no skills as a warrior.

His subjects could credit his reign with bringing an end to the years of warfare between the houses of Lancaster and York. But the nobility were restive because his plan of vesting more authority in the crown undermined the power and prerogatives of the barons. And the common people had little love for him because his greedy taxes had gone mostly to fatten his own tightly guarded coffers and were seldom used for enterprises that excited public enthusiasm.

In answer to the King's query, Morton said, 'You can rest your mind on that point, sire. The two young princes died years ago.'

'Did you see their dead bodies?'

'No. I was not there, but I have never had reason to question the veracity of the report I had of their deaths.'

'Is it possible that Edward left some bastard sons who are not known to us?'

'That is a hard question to answer. Your majesty has

recognised two of his bastards and given them places at your court. I do not know of any others. But it is always possible he had other children. From early on, Edward was famed for his many mistresses. Unfortunately no one, not even Edward himself, paid close attention to whom he was sleeping with, or what happened to them.'

'Women talk, some even brag about such things. You must have some idea whether he had other bastards.'

'If supplying stud service to half the willing women he knew was the only criterion, I would say he had dozens. The real question though is how many of his unions led to pregnancies and births. We can be fairly certain there were no other bastards born of the women he had at the royal court. The problem is that he also slept with numerous women he met during his travels about his kingdom. I would be rash if I told you that none of those couplings resulted in the birth of royal bastards.'

'We say this is a good time for us to put an end to further speculation. Put this down as a new law. Anyone from this day on who claims to be Edward's royal bastard or the bastard of any of his brothers will be treated as an impostor. We will speedily stamp them out before they can make public spectacles of themselves. Those people with Plantagenet blood who are now known to us can live in peace if they swear allegiance to us. Should any of them speak of possible claims to the crown, it will be off with their heads! We will have no questioning of the primacy of the House of Tudor.'

'It is decreed, Your Majesty.' Morton spoke his agreement almost by rote. In his mind he was thinking that here was a man of remarkable determination. He might lack many qualities that could endear him to his subjects, but he had no doubts as to his right to rule. He believed he was picked by God to govern England, and he would brook no opposition to that conviction.

Perhaps it was a mistake to encourage him in that belief. Now after years of practice, he no longer sustained doubts about his status or self importance. He adopted the royal 'we' with relish, and had long since stopped using the terms 'I' and 'me'. More than that, he had claimed pre-eminence over his forebears by insisting that he be addressed as 'Your Majesty' rather than 'Your Grace'. Yet for all of his self glorification, he was still troubled by a suspicion that his self-image was no more than a fragile figment that could be dashed to naught like the bursting of a bubble.

Morton sensed a break in his audience with the King. As he started to hoist his bulky figure from his chair, he said, 'If you have no other need of me, sire, I will be about my meeting with Captain Mason.'

Henry watched him without comment until the Archbishop had walked to the door. Then quite suddenly, he said, 'Wait a moment, Morton. There is a matter that has been troubling us on which we need your counsel.'

'Yes, Your Majesty.'

While Morton was returning to his chair, Henry observed, 'We have ruled England for more than a dozen years now. During that time we have done much to consolidate power in the hands of the monarch.'

'That you have, sire.'

'And compared with other kings, we are probably past the middle of our reign.'

'I would never say that, Your Majesty. You will be England's king for many, many years yet.'

'Maybe yes, maybe no. The point though is that with our tenure on the throne being as secure as it is, we think it is time to give serious thought to the future.'

'How so?'

'We want to be known both now and in the future as a great and noble monarch.'

'You are that already, sire.'

'Perhaps in your eyes and those of others who profit from our favour; but it is plain even to us that we are not a popular King.'

'But, Your Majesty—'

'No "buts" about it. There are no crowds shouting their acclaim when we ride in the streets. We see their sullen expressions. Tell us, Morton, tell us truly… what do our subjects think of us?'

'They wish you long life, sire. After all you are God's anointed choice. True, there are some dissidents, but they are few and unimportant. It makes no differençe what they think of you. Most of your subjects realise that you have made us and England what we are. We love and honour you for it.'

'That is what you think. Now tell us and tell us truly what your spies report that others think of their King.'

For a fleeting moment, the Archbishop felt himself trapped. How could he tell the King that most of his subjects thought of him as Henry the Pinchfist, as Henry the Unloved? How he answered this question would really test his talents as a diplomat.

'All but a few of your subjects are satisfied with your rule, My Liege. They like the security and stability your years of peace have brought. Of course, there are always some whiners and malcontents who want lower taxes, fewer regulations, more spending from the royal purse. There are even some who would have you fighting a war in France. But most of your people love you in their hearts and would fight for you.'

'If there is love in their hearts, they have a queer way of showing it!' Henry retorted. 'And if they are waiting for a reduction in taxes or for the crown to spend good money on frivolous parades or celebrations, they will have to wait. As for another war, we think it best to keep their sons at home until we have good reason to fight, or until we can be sure of winning.'

The King paused for a moment before continuing. 'What can we do to be a more popular monarch? And more important how can we make sure that our subjects' grandchildren will cherish good memories of us?'

'Those questions call for thoughtful consideration, sire. There may be some things we can do to that end; but we must weigh their likely consequences before taking any action.'

'We are not asking for advice on these issues today, Morton; but we want you to give them serious consideration. You have a stake as big as ours in this matter. Our reputations are intertwined and will ride into the future together, so let us devise a programme that will cause people to look on us with favour.'

A few moments later, Morton left the royal chamber and went directly to the royal guardhouse where he asked for Captain Mason. The Captain showed neither surprise nor concern when the Archbishop instructed him to send some trustworthy fellows to seek out and apprehend the pretender.

'Should we arrest him and bring him back for trial?' he asked.

'No, the King wants him silenced for good.'

'We will have no trouble with that,' the Captain assured him. 'Should we have him die in a tavern brawl?'

'It would be better if he just disappeared and his body buried in some forest or bog. The King wants him to disappear without a trace.'

'We can do that too.'

'And make doubly sure your men are sworn to secrecy. Public knowledge of this could be embarrassing.'

'Never fear, Your Grace, my men are professionals,' Mason growled. He hesitated, and then snapped, 'They will do the job right as they always do.'

The change of tone in Mason's voice reminded Morton that he was talking to the often surly commander of Henry's little publicised execution squad. He knew Mason had a temper which exploded whenever his personal pride was pricked, and hoped he had not been offended by the bluntness of the request for secrecy. Mason was privy to some of Henry's ugliest secrets and most certainly was not a man the King or Morton wanted to cross or offend.

'I am sorry Captain,' he apologised quickly. 'I spoke without thinking. Not for a moment would I question your competence, or that of your men. You have always done your job quickly and well, and the King and I are grateful to you for your faithful service. King Henry speaks fondly of you as his Minister of Nuisance Control, because of the expertise you have shown in eliminating potential pests before they could do him harm. How many years is it now that you have served Henry in this capacity?'

'Thirteen, Your Grace – ever since we lifted Richard's crown at Bosworth Field.'

'Thirteen years, and in that time you have used your unique talent quietly to remove a good many thorns that could have torn his majesty's flesh. Yes, indeed, the King has much reason to value your service.'

'Thank you, Your Grace,' the now smiling Captain replied. 'And don't worry about that pretender. You will hear no more of him.'

Back at the building he called at the Chancery where he had his official office and also maintained his living quarters, Morton was met by Father Gregory, the priest who had served for years as his deputy, chief clerk and confidant. The good Father was a tall, thin man with a kindly countenance. Ordinarily, he would have been calm and would have waited for the Archbishop to give him any necessary instructions. Today though, he was curious about the King's reaction to Morton's news.

'He took it about as we expected,' Morton told him. 'Why, were you concerned?'

'One of the guards reported that there was some shouting. I feared he might be blaming you,' Gregory answered.

'Oh that! Yes, Henry did raise his voice for a bit. He was hot and bothered again about the royal bastards. He fears them like the plague because they pose possible threats to his sovereignty. I shouldn't say this, even to a trusted friend like you Greg, but I find it hard to justify his vehemence. After all, the father and the great-grandfather who gave him his double claim to royal blood were both royal bastards!'

Chapter Two

John More was not a regular patron of The Grey Horse tavern. Unlike many of his fellow barristers, it was not his usual practice to stop at an alehouse for a pint of brew at the end of his working day. On those occasions when he did, it was ordinarily at a tavern along a street that led directly to his house. But today was different. He had just left a client's shop and was feeling jubilant. He wanted to celebrate. This had been his most successful day in well over a week. After a long spell of negotiations, he had worked out an agreement between his client and another merchant that promised to be of benefit to both parties.

As he entered the tavern, he was startled by a voice that cried out, 'Over here, John!'

He peered intently about the public room of the tavern as his eyes adjusted to its semi-darkness. The room was large but noticeably lacking in adornment. Shadowy alcoves that offered a measure of privacy lined two walls. Four small, smoke-darkened windows on a third wall provided the only source of light, save for that which came from the brisk blaze that glowed in the huge stone fireplace.

'Over here!' the invitation was repeated.

John focused his gaze on the corner alcove and sauntered towards it with a smile of recognition on his face. 'Good day to you, Ned!' he exclaimed as he grasped his friend's hand and slid on to the bench beside him. 'It's been ages since I've seen you.'

'It has been a long time, too long. As two blokes who

put on their black robes together, we should see more of each other.' Edward Barnes paused a moment and then added, 'John, I want you to meet Sir Francis Musgrave. Sir Francis, this is John More, my one-time law partner.'

John half rose from his seat and offered his hand to Sir Francis. 'It is an honour to meet you, sir. I've known about you and admired your service on the King's bench for years even though I have never practised in your court.'

Barnes turned to Sir Francis and explained, 'John and I go back a long way. We read law together some twenty-five years ago, and then were partners in practice for a few years. The honest truth is he is a better barrister than I ever was. But my connections at court were better than his. You know what that means.'

Sir Francis snorted. 'So you parlayed your father's knighthood into an appointment to the King's Bench, while your friend is still a practising lawyer?'

'Yes, and an envious one too,' John added. 'But I'm not shedding any tears in my ale over it. For a baker's son, I've prospered and done well. But let's not talk about me. With your years of experience, Sir Francis, I want to hear about you.'

'That is a dull topic. What can I tell you?'

'Is it true what they say about you and the Battle of Agincourt?'

'Agincourt! The rumour that I fought there is totally false,' Sir Francis chuckled. 'But it is true that my father was there with Henry V on that glorious day while my mother was here in England giving birth to me on the same day.'

'Why, that was eighty years ago.'

'25th October, 1415, to be precise. So you can see I'm just a shade short of being eighty-three.'

'A lot of water has passed under London Bridge since then. Why, you have seen the reigns of a half dozen kings!'

'Five, I would say. Six, if you insist on counting that uncrowned son of Edward IV as Edward V. Henry V died while I was a wee lad. Then there was Henry VI, Edward IV, Richard III, and now Henry VII.'

'How would you compare them?' John asked.

Sir Francis gazed intently at his two companions; looked about the room, and then responded in a hushed voice. 'I don't think we should get into that today. Comparisons between kings, at least the more recent ones, are not something one shouts from the rooftops these days. I will say this though. I've seen a full gamut of them. Henry V was a great warrior who conquered half of France. He died early, and Henry VI, who started as a boy king, managed to lose almost everything his father had won. Richard of York and his son Edward IV stirred things up for the Lancasters for several years, and we had a running war as they played a game of musical chairs with Henry VI and his Queen to see who would get to sit on the throne. That finally ended when Edward's brother, Richard III, was killed at Bosworth Field and our present King took the throne.'

'I'd like to hear more of your memories,' John remarked.

'Some other time maybe, in a less public place,' Sir Francis answered.

'You are right,' Barnes observed. 'It is best not to talk about our present King in a place like this even among friends.'

'There is no good reason for me not saying what I want,' Sir Francis continued. 'Henry does not look as much like a king as York's sons did, but he has one good thing going for him. He has given England the longest stretch of near peace we have had in this century.

'On the bad side, he is greedy and uses his taxes and fines to squeeze every last shilling out of us. This Morton's fork business is terrible. It is a most unfair means for raising money for the crown.'

'Morton's fork?' John interrupted. 'I've heard the term, but I'm not clear how it works.'

'It is a simple device invented by our Lord Chancellor and Cardinal, John Morton,' Barnes responded. 'The good Bishop told the King he could fatten his purse by levying fines on selected owners of property who were spending money.'

'That is only the first prong of the fork,' Sir Francis interjected. 'Comparable fines can be levied on property owners picked out by the King's agents who aren't spending money, the theory being that if they aren't spending money they must be saving it.'

'It sounds like an arbitrary tax on incomes.'

'It is arbitrary, all right. It is also illegal because it amounts to taxation without the consent of our burgesses in Parliament. But it is a levy on net worth, not on incomes. More than that, it taxes property owners at different rates. The King's agents decide on the amount of every fine. If they like you, you are passed over. If they have some reason to dislike you, you may find yourself an unwilling contributor to the fattening of the royal purse. Selection for that dubious honour comes easy when one says or does something the royal agents do not like.'

'Are you saying we could be fined for just talking as we are today?' John asked.

'We could be fined for even thinking about it; so be careful what you say or do. Any day now you could be fined fifty or a hundred pounds or more, for what seems like no reason at all,' Barnes advised.

'Back to what I was describing as Henry's weaknesses,' continued Sir Francis. 'I could excuse his taxes and fines if he would only spend what he takes so we could get the money back in circulation. Edward IV had his taxes and his wife's family, the Woodvilles, managed to get their claws on more than their share of the revenues; but they were big spenders and we soon saw the coins back in use again. Henry squirrels his surplus away in some secret chest while our merchants suffer from the lack of money in circulation.'

'I agree that our King is tight, but it seems to me he has done us a good turn in clearing up the question of the royal succession,' John observed.

'You are right on that count,' Sir Francis continued. 'Someone must have told him of the Turkish practice of strangling all of a sultan's brothers at the time he comes to power. Henry has solved the problem of claimants to the throne by simply beheading everyone with a respectable claim who dares to remind us that he too has royal blood.'

John and Ned nodded their heads in agreement. Before anyone could say anything more, the relative quiet of the tavern was broken by an outburst of scuffling outside. A cry of 'Stop! Stop thief!' was followed by several shouts and a babble of many voices. The three men nursed their tankards of ale whilst waiting for the tumult to subside.

When quiet returned, John asked, 'Is there anything to the rumour that another pretender has surfaced?'

'It is more than just a rumour,' Ned responded. 'I've been told on good authority that another candidate who claims he is the missing Edward V has turned up in Kent. No one is taking his claim seriously. Some people at court are even placing wagers that Henry will let him off as he did that scullery lad Simnel.'

'He is a foolish lad if he expects to escape with that punishment,' Sir Francis drawled. 'Henry has run out of patience with pretenders. He regrets his decision to let Warbeck off with life imprisonment. I doubt he will ever be that lenient again. More than that, I suspect he is just waiting for a good excuse to send Warbeck to the gallows. The same goes for his genuine royal cousins such as the

Earl of Warwick.'

'Warwick? Is he the heir to the old Earl of Warwick?' John inquired.

'He is his grandson. His father was George Duke of Clarence and he is a nephew of Edward IV and Richard III.'

'I surely have not heard much of him.'

'For good reason too. Henry has had him penned in at the Tower since he was a boy of eight. They say he is muddle-headed, but what else could one expect if he has been there without teachers or playmates for a dozen years?'

'What was his crime?'

'Crime? It is one of the worst. He is guilty of being the last surviving direct male heir of Richard of York.'

'Well, at least he was not murdered like his cousins the two little princes.'

'Speaking of the two princes, does anyone know for sure that they were murdered?'

'Most people think they were,' Barnes replied, 'but we have never had an official report on what happened to Edward IV's two sons. One or both of them could still be alive somewhere. When you stop to think of it, it is really surprising we have not had more pretenders, or maybe even genuine princes, coming out of the woodwork.'

'I wouldn't give a pretender much of a chance.' John said. 'I'm convinced the two little princes were done in back in King Richard's time.'

'What do you think really happened to them?' Barnes asked, looking at Sir Francis.

'That is not a topic most people dare to talk about,' Musgrave replied. 'Of course, there has been a lot of whispering. Buckingham put out the word that the boys had been murdered when he was stirring up his rebellion against Richard. A lot of us dismissed the report at the time, thinking it was just a ploy to gain the support of the noblemen who were calling for the crowning of Edward's eldest son as King.

'After Buckingham's death, Bishop Morton told Henry's supporters that the princes had been murdered in the Tower. But Morton was Buckingham's associate and again there was no proof. Richard III never gave a hint that they were dead or missing. There were no dead bodies on display, no funerals, no orders for saying prayers for their souls.'

'I think Richard got rid of them,' John interjected. 'After all, they were an embarrassment to him. As long as they lived, they were a threat to his claim to the throne.'

'No, you have it wrong,' Sir Francis corrected him. 'You have forgotten the law of "Titulus Regius" that Parliament passed when the facts about Edward IV's prior contract of marriage to Eleanor Talbot became known. That law proclaimed the illegitimacy of Edward's children by his wife Elizabeth. With that proclamation, the young princes no longer had claims to the crown.'

'I am surprised you dare to remember that unmentionable law,' Barnes snorted. 'Isn't that the measure Henry VII had rescinded and wiped off the books? All references to it in any records were supposedly destroyed, and it was made a criminal offence for anyone to discuss or even mention it.'

'Kings can act to destroy written documents and hush the tongues of their subjects. But they can not go so far in rewriting history as to blot out memories of things I cannot forget,' Sir Francis answered. He then turned to Barnes and asked, 'What do you think happened to the two princes?'

Ned pressed a forefinger to his lips as he answered, 'I shouldn't say this, but I've suspected for some time that Henry found them still alive in the Tower when he came to power, and quietly arranged for their elimination.'

'That is a terrible accusation, Ned!' John half whispered. 'How can you justify it?'

'Several details point to that conclusion. The two princes had claims to the crown that were far superior to Henry's, especially after he had that law rescinded.

'His conduct during those first few weeks after he seized the crown and came to London has always puzzled me. He had full access to the Tower and must have known whether the princes were still alive. Yet when he sent that message to Parliament in which he detailed the list of Richard's crimes that justified his taking the crown, he made no mention of Richard's complicity in the murder of the princes. The omission of a charge he most certainly would have made if they were dead tells me that they were still alive.

'His being responsible for their murder after that date could account for those weeks of delay after Henry seized the crown when there was no announcement about his wedding plans, even though half the people of London were clamouring for his marriage to Princess Elizabeth. And the fact that thirteen years have now passed without any explanation from the court about what happened to her brothers suggests a guilty conscience on his part.'

'So I say that Richard was responsible and Ned sees Henry as the guilty party. Who do you blame, Sir Francis?' asked John.

'Me, I say there are too many loose threads here for any clear answer. You have pointed fingers of suspicion at Richard and at Henry. Some people say Richard sent the boys to a northern castle. If he did, they could still be imprisoned there. One or both of the princes could have escaped and be living somewhere in England or on the Continent. They were not without friends both in and around the Tower, friends who could have acted on their behalf. If they escaped by boat, they could have fallen overboard and been drowned.

'Then too, it is possible people have gone too far in discrediting the possibility that Perkin Warbeck is Edward's second son, Richard. According to his account, his older brother Edward died and he, the Duke of York, is the logical claimant to the crown. To the best of my knowledge neither the Queen nor any of her sisters have been allowed to see or talk with him. Several people who have seen him say he has the bearing and the looks of a Plantagenet. His aunt Margaret, the Duchess of Burgundy, saw him, and is said to have accepted him as her nephew.'

'But hasn't he admitted that his claims were all a hoax?' John protested.

'That is what the King's agents say. Unfortunately, that is what they always say. If Warbeck really did confess, did he do so in writing? We need to know if his confession was witnessed and if it was given voluntarily or under some threat of reprisal or torture.

'Getting back to the other possibilities, we should remember that Richard left London on a progress after his coronation. While he was gone, Buckingham or someone else who had access to the Tower could have murdered the princes or taken them off somewhere. Richard was naive if he ever thought he had Buckingham's sincere support. The Duke was always looking out for his own interests. He hated the Woodvilles, but he also had reasons to hate the Yorkists. His grandfather, the first Duke of Buckingham, his father, the Earl of Stafford, and his uncle, the third Duke of Somerset, were all killed fighting against York. More than that, Margaret Beaufort, the aunt who raised him, must surely have told him that the princes of the House of York were the only ones who had stronger claims to the throne than he had.'

'Do you have any reason for denying the possible guilt of either Richard or Henry?' John asked.

'Judging from his actions, I would say that Richard either assumed that the two boys were safely tucked away in the Tower or, if they had disappeared, hesitated to speak of their absence because he did not know where they were. As for Henry's innocence, I have some troublesome questions, questions that will likely remain unanswered during my lifetime.'

'This has been really interesting,' Ned ventured as two men who had just entered the tavern crossed the room and took seats in the adjoining booth. 'We've said more than we probably should have. On another subject, do you still have that property in Dorset where you used to hunt?'

The conversation shifted to other topics. As it lulled and they made preparations for leaving, Ned asked, 'How are things going with your boys, John? Tom went to the University didn't he?'

'Yes, Thomas went to Oxford. He finished his work there four years ago. He studied the next two years at the New Inn and has been reading law at Lincoln's Inn these last two years. He is still at Lincoln's Inn, but is also working as an intern at the Chancery with Bishop Morton.'

'Tom always was a bright lad. Is he going to join you in the law?'

'I doubt he knows what he really wants to do yet. One day he talks of going into the priesthood and the next it is law and public service.'

'Well, at least he has a choice. Lawyers have some prospect of getting ahead in the King's service these days. It is no longer like it was when Morton was young. In those days our kings seldom looked beyond the Church and their own families for their administrators.'

'And for a very good reason too. The clergy had a near monopoly on learning in those days,' John said.

'So your boy is working with Bishop Morton,' Sir Francis said thoughtfully. 'A few years in the Chancery could be good experience for him. Tell him to be careful though. The Lord Chancellor has a reputation for using people.

Henry didn't make Morton the Archbishop of Canterbury and then get a cardinal's hat for him because he had a reputation for saintliness. Morton is where he is because he is the slickest politician in all England.'

Chapter Three

'Augustine! St Augustine! Holy Christopher, Tom, is reading one of St Augustine's sermons your idea of fun? This is Saturday night for goodness sake! Come with Henry and me. We've worked hard all week. Now is time for us to go out and have our toot.'

Will Givens stood in the half light of early evening looking down at Thomas More who was seated on a stool wiping his goose quill pen while waiting for the ink to dry on the still opened page of an office ledger.

Thomas smiled and shook his head while Henry Abel, the third young clerk in the candlelit work-room of the Chancery, rose from his excuse for a desk, put aside a pile of government billings, and stepped over to Thomas's table with its neatly stacked pile of books and papers.

'Yeah, Tom. St Augustine was your excuse last week and the week before that. Why spend your time reading another sermon? We have some real living to do!'

Thomas looked at his two colleagues with a mirthful glint in his eye. 'You lads talk of living, but you really know you are just wasting your lives with frivolous, sinful pursuits. The time you spend drinking and carousing could be far better spent in improving your minds.'

Thomas More, a young man of medium stature and cheerful countenance, and two of his fellow interns in the office of the Lord Chancellor were engaged in another round of their frequent banter. The Chancery was the most important of the several buildings over which Bishop

Morton exerted control. It was here that he had his office and administrative headquarters. It also provided residential quarters for him and some of the priests who assisted him.

As Lord Chancellor, Morton held the top administrative post in the realm. He presided over the Chancery Court and was the foremost member of King Henry's royal council. He was responsible for such varied functions as the conduct of foreign affairs, enforcement of the crown's laws, and management of the King's estates.

Just a few weeks short of his twentieth birthday, Thomas More was a serious-minded young man, a student of human behaviour and at the same time a zealously pious person much devoted to his religious beliefs. From earlier discussions he was well aware of the deep chasm that separated his view of life from the carefree attitudes and behaviour of Henry and Will. It was not a barrier he intended to bridge. With cordial goodwill, he was inclined to tolerate their many differences from himself, and to accept their right to live their lives as they wished.

He was very much aware of the fact that if he took a different attitude their differences could cause contentious conflicts, conflicts that could lead to harsh words, hateful behaviour, and a disruption of office morale. This was a threat Thomas was determined to avoid. Henry and Will were jolly good friends with whom he enjoyed occasional bantering. With them, he could carry on merry discussions with the tacit understanding that no one would take or mean offence in anything that was said.

'Why don't you drop that line about what we ought to be doing,' Henry chortled, 'and come with us to a place where we can show you what is missing in your virtuous life?'

'Tell me again what you and Will plan to do?' Thomas asked with a twinkle in his eye and a half smile.

'Do? We'll do what we do every Saturday night. We go

to the Red Rose, have our tankard of ale, eat some bread and maybe a chop, and then see if we can get some action.'

'And what will that be?'

'Who knows? We'll sing, talk to people, tell jokes, maybe argue a bit, and if we are lucky there will be some buxom floozies there who will want to dance and pet and maybe even beg for some swiving.'

Will slapped Henry on the back and added, 'Now that is real living for young bucks like us.'

'It certainly is,' Henry went on, 'and if any of them say "Please" or even "Yes", I'll say "Why not?"'

Thomas recoiled. 'Be serious now. Is that what right thinking men should do? Why should any of us talk or even think of tarnishing our souls with the pursuit of such lustful debauchery?'

Will started to laugh. 'Tom, quit talking like a bishop. You are a law student and an underpaid intern in a government office, not a priest. At least not yet. And until you are, there is nothing wrong with us enjoying some real fun.'

'What you are suggesting reminds me of the parable of the three torches.'

'Oh good. Another parable. Are you sure this one had only three torches and not four or five?' Will chided.

'What is the lesson this time, Your Reverence?' Henry asked.

'There was a father in a far country who had three sons. One morning he gave each of them a torch and said, "Guard these well for you will need them after night falls. Tonight a great feast will be laid out for you in yonder house and you will need the light from your torches to enjoy it fully."

'After their father left them, one son complained, "I am hungry now. Why wait until darkness falls? Come with me and we will sample the cakes and wine and return later for the feast." The second son said, "No, we should stay and follow our father's advice." But the third son said, "Why wait when we can use our torches and enjoy the feast twice over."

'Two of the sons then went to the house where they found the dining chamber dark and only part of the food and drink laid out on the tables. They ate and drank but came away still hungry and thirsty. When night came, the obedient son went to the feast where he was royally received and came away much satisfied. The two who had gone earlier returned to the feast with high expectations but their torches soon flared out and they had to be content with the scraps they found on the floor.'

'That would never happen to Will and me!' Henry snorted. 'We would have more sense than to leave the feast without having had our fill.'

'Yeah. The moral to that story is for us early birds to stay on at the feast until all of the food is gone!' Will added.

'Better still, a man needs an eternal flame like mine that never burns completely out,' Henry boasted.

'No. The real answer would be for us to take our father Thomas with us. You wouldn't leave your sons in the dark if you had the only torch that worked would you, Tom?'

'With two blowhards like you for friends, I probably would not,' Thomas confessed. 'Putting your humbugging aside though, you should know that for me real living calls for safeguarding my eternal soul.'

'Glory be man, you aren't St Thomas yet!' Henry interrupted. 'Young blades like us are in our prime. This is the time when we are supposed to live it up and spill our oats.'

'Where did you get that idea?' Thomas queried. 'Sodom and Gomorra, that's where. True believers should follow the path of righteousness their whole lives through.'

'Yeah, that is what they tell us in church, but there are plenty of people, even some bishops and cardinals, who get their taste of life and have their fling before asking the church for its blessing and settling down to a life of prayers and giving advice to others.'

'That part about bishops and cardinals is a lie and you know it,' Thomas snorted as he rose from his seat.

'Oh no, it isn't,' Will insisted. 'Take your St Augustine, for example. He had a mistress, another man's wife I've been told, before he settled down to saintliness.'

'Yes, and our eminent Lord Chancellor, a cardinal of the Church, is another example,' Henry added.

'Bishop Morton! I don't believe it.'

'Well, I wasn't there, but my father's brother read law at the same time that Morty was starting his practice here in London forty-five years ago. Uncle Henry told me that our good Bishop used to go out with students almost every weekend just like we do. He was a conscientious priest during the day who took off his cassock and raised hell at night.'

'There must be some mistake. He couldn't have, not Bishop Morton,' Thomas insisted.

'Holy shit, Tom, what's so impossible or wrong about the Archbishop acting for once like a normal red-blooded Englishman?'

'Henry, much as I like you as a person, I must protest when you use blasphemous language here in the Cardinal's house.'

'Sorry if my street language upset you. Anyway, what I said was not blasphemous. I am careful not to take the Lord's name in vain.'

'Maybe I overspoke, but you did use a lewd gutter term that has no place in polite conversation.'

'Tut, tut! Clean living, clean thoughts, and now you want us to clean up our language too?' Will snickered.

'Is what I am asking for too much here in the Cardinal's house?' Thomas retorted.

'No, you are right and I apologise for my language. That

word just slipped out. It was one thing they did not undo for me at Oxford. I was a child of the streets picking up a gutter vocabulary while they had you learning how to speak politely in the Bishop's house.'

'Oh quit rubbing it in!' Thomas rejoined. 'I'm not saying I am any better than you.'

'Holy Christopher!' Will chimed in. 'We know that. Sure we ride you pretty hard about your priestly attitude. It's not that we want to get under your skin. But when you refuse to go out with us, we enjoy trying to get a rise out of you.'

'A rise? A flare up of temper! Of all the people around here, you and Henry will be the last to provoke me. There are lots of things we will never agree on, but you are my best friends and I intend to keep it that way.'

'Even though you are headed for sainthood while we are dancing our way to damnation in hell?' Henry smiled.

'I'm not sure who is going where or who will get there first. I try to be broadminded and recognise that each of us has ideas about what is right and proper for us. As for me, I could not live with myself if I did what you do. I have a genuine fear of hell that you do not seem to share. I know what I must do if I am to live up to my standards. That does not mean I am always right nor that you are wrong. We are different, but that should not interfere with friendship.'

'We see things differently, that's for sure,' Will agreed. 'But there is one big question about you I wish I could figure out. How can someone like you who is such good company and so enjoyable to argue with be so opposed to having fun?'

'It is because each of us has our own definition of fun. We all like a good joke and having a lively discussion. Beyond that, having fun for me calls for exercising my mind, not debasing my body.'

'You mean you operate on a spiritual level, while Henry

and I are driven by our animal instincts.'

'Quit it, quit it. You are too earthy for me but that does not mean I look down on you. Askance maybe, but not down. Anyway there is no chance anyone is going to win this argument. Each of us will always be charmed by the thought that his fart smells less foul than those of other people. The best thing about arguing with you is that we can talk plainly about our differences without anyone losing his temper.'

'I'm all for that,' Will answered. 'But tell us, how do you justify your priestly attitude?'

'No one ever asked me that before,' Thomas answered.

'I suppose I am a sincere Catholic who is one hundred per cent committed to his religious beliefs. I accept and try to follow the doctrines of the Church without reservation. More than that, I accept the teachings of St Jerome and St Augustine and the other Church Fathers who insisted that we can best show our submission to Christ's rule by practising chastity and piety.'

'I follow you to a point,' Henry observed, 'but as I recall the Church Fathers emphasised the need to accept poverty and humility along with chastity and piety. Those qualities make quite a package when they are accepted together. I question whether we should accept any of the package if we do not take all of it. Why should we be concerned about being chaste or pious if we do not choose to live lives of poverty? As for me, I'm not ready to settle for a life of being poor and I doubt that Thomas More is either.'

'Your reservations trouble me, Henry, but let me ask you and Will how you justify embracing the worldly life?'

'You should narrow your question, Tom. We do not have to justify our preference for singing, eating, even some drinking. The Scriptures have plenty of that. What you are really asking us to justify is our association with what some call "loose women".'

'Fair enough,' Thomas agreed. 'How can you claim to be good Christians and yet go to an alehouse on a Saturday night in the hope of finding women for your swiving?'

'Good question, Tom. Before I give you my answer though, you tell me why I should not.'

'Why? Because that was the original sin for which Adam was turned out of the Garden of Eden and for which we all must die.'

'Yes, I can agree with that. Everything was pure bliss in the Garden until Eve was tempted to play around with that part of Adam that most resembled a serpent. When he found out what it was for, he frigged her under an apple tree and they found themselves kicked out of the Garden into a world where they had to earn their living. But that was Adam's sin, not mine. I accept the need to work for a living; and anyway if Adam and his sons had not done it, there would be no people to populate the world.'

'God allows for that, Will. Sex is permissible between man and wife when the object is procreation. But it is not to be indulged in for simple pleasure. The Church Fathers have always condemned promiscuity as being sinful and immoral. Acceptance of God's authority and full obedience to his laws calls for self-denial and chaste behaviour.'

'Self-denial! Come on, Tom, we all know that God made Eve to provide Adam with a companion and help-mate. She was supposed to serve him and give him support and pleasure. I'll bet he enjoyed cuddling up with her as much as we enjoy our women; and he didn't go in for self-denial either. Thank goodness for that! We would not be here if he had.

'More than that. God later commanded Noah to multiply and replenish the earth. Now that is an order to have sex if I ever heard one. He did not specify that we men had to marry our women. And another thing for sure, He made our women different from the female animals that mate only during those limited periods when they are in heat and are almost certain to get pregnant. Women can swive with us for years without getting with child. Whether a man wants her to become a mother has no effect on her getting pregnant. So if my woman and I enjoy a bit of swiving and stand ready to accept what happens, I say we are doing our Christian duty.'

'Great answer, Will!' Henry hooted. 'That is the best defence of your lustful appetite I've heard. It's a fishy answer but it is good enough for me!'

'Are you sure you won't come with us, Tom? We would really like to show you the ropes. A face like yours could bring us luck!' Henry tried one last time as he and Will prepared to leave.

'Not this time,' Thomas answered. 'I would only spoil your fun and probably lose my soul while trying to save yours!'

Chapter Four

Father Gregory came into the Chancery workroom just as Will and Henry were leaving. As the Lord Chancellor's chief assistant, he was the person responsible for supervising the work of the interns and scribes who handled the routine functions of the Chancellor's office. He greeted the three interns in a cheerful voice and asked Thomas to stay on for a few minutes.

'His Eminence expects to see me a little later,' he explained, 'and he will want a report on the attainder of Lord Cornfield's estate.'

Thomas supplied the information he wanted and tarried to discuss some items of office business. As they talked, he noticed that Gregory was less stiff and formal and seemed more relaxed than he usually was in his dealings with his staff. When Gregory complimented him on the thoroughness of his report, Thomas sensed some breaking of the ice that until now had kept them apart. On impulse he asked, 'You have been with His Eminence for many years, haven't you, Father?'

Somewhat to Thomas's surprise, Father Gregory welcomed the question. 'Yes, I've known Bishop Morton since my student days. You probably did not know that he was the Principal at Peckwater Inn where I was a student in 1453. He was one of my teachers and it was there that he came to know my family. My parents and my sister were very fond of him. I've felt close to him because he was my early patron. It was he more than anyone else who stirred my interest in going to Oxford, taking holy orders, and later reading law.'

'Have you worked with him all the years since?' Thomas asked.

'Not all of them. We saw a lot of each other while I was at Oxford, and then again while I was reading law. He used his connections to get me an appointment with Cardinal Bouchier's staff when I was ready for an assignment.'

'Henry Abel says his uncle Henry was a colleague of His Eminence's when he first practised law here in London. Did you know him?'

'Henry Abel? Yes, I know him, but I did not meet him until sometime after I finished my legal studies. As I recall, he was a few years behind Bishop Morton and some years ahead of me.'

'How did His Eminence get his start in government service?'

'He rose to the top because of his talent and skills; but he had important help along the way. Like most of us, he had a patron. Bishop Bouchier took notice of him while he was still a young priest. The Bishop was a man of power and influence. He was a great grandson of Edward III and his father and two of his brothers were earls. With a family background like that, he enjoyed preferences that opened the way for him to become Archbishop of Canterbury and a cardinal.

'Richard of York recognised his ability and picked him to be Lord Chancellor during one of those times when Henry VI was out of his mind. Queen Margaret hated Richard, so she booted him out of the Lord Chancellorship as soon as the King regained his senses, but the King kept him on as one of his advisors.'

'How did the Archbishop help Bishop Morton?'

'Bishop Bouchier had an eye for identifying talented men and then showing them preferment. John Morton handled several sensitive assignments for him. That led to more prestigious duties. Thanks to the Cardinal, he was soon working with the Privy Council, and enjoying grants of income from some church-owned estates and from the revenues of Lincoln and Salisbury cathedrals.

'Queen Margaret took a liking to him and asked that he supervise the education of her son, the Prince of Wales. He guided the ceremony for knighting the young Prince when Edward was only seven. My career was just starting at that time, and I recall that the Bishop spent much of every day with the Prince.

'He shielded him and loved him as though he were his own son. It was during those years that he became much attached to the Lancastrian cause.'

'Did his position regarding Margaret and her son get him into trouble with the House of York?'

'Indeed it did. He was with the Queen when her army defeated York's forces at the Battle of Ludlow in 1459. Richard of York fled to Ireland after his defeat but was soon back in England where he assembled a new army. With Warwick's help, he marched to London where he claimed the throne. He could have become king but settled for less when Parliament designated him as Lord Protector and as King Henry's heir.

'A few months later, Richard was surprised and killed along with his second son by Margaret's army at the Battle of Wakefield. York's eldest son Edward then took command of the York forces. He routed one of Margaret's armies at Mortimer Cross and marched to London where he seized the crown for himself. Only a few weeks later, he met and again defeated Margaret's principal army in a major battle at Towton.'

'Did the Bishop travel with Margaret's army?'

'Sometimes yes, sometimes no. He was with her party at Towton. After that débâcle, the Queen was fortunately able to escape to Scotland. But Bishop Morton was captured and would have been massacred along with most of her defeated troops had he not been dressed as a priest. He was released and escaped to Flanders. All of his property was attained. He stayed on in Burgundy and France for the next nine years, during which time I had occasional letters from him.

'Bishop Morton was extremely busy during those years. Once Margaret and her son had come to the Continent from Scotland, he again served as the Prince's tutor. He also acted as the Queen's agent in seeking commitments of money, men and arms for the Lancastrian cause. Around 1468 or 1469, he worked out the plan that brought the Earl of Warwick and Queen Margaret together. Prince Edward was betrothed to Warwick's daughter Anne and Warwick agreed to invade England and restore Henry VI as King.'

'Was this the same Earl of Warwick who fought for York a few years earlier?'

'Yes. He was one of Richard of York's closest allies. He had a big reputation as a military commander and was a power to be reckoned with. He was popular with the people, he was the wealthiest baron in England, and he had the support of many other noblemen.

'Warwick had been Edward IV's chief supporter for several years, but they drifted apart for some reason. People say Warwick fancied himself as a kingmaker and that he expected Edward, the son of his old ally, to lean on him for advice. Edward showed more independence than he cared for, and the two men found themselves in opposing camps.

'Warwick knew he could not be king himself, but he saw a prospect for becoming a grandfather of kings. His eldest daughter Isabel was married to Edward's brother George, the Duke of Clarence. Warwick conspired with Clarence to put him on the throne. When nothing came of that scheme, he reacted favourably to Bishop Morton's suggestion that he support the Lancastrian cause and marry his second daughter to the Prince of Wales.'

'Then Warwick led the invasion that almost toppled Edward IV from his throne?'

'Yes, Warwick showed real genius in his military strategy. He got some friends to stir up an uprising along the Scottish border. While Edward was there putting down what turned out to be a phoney rebellion, he crossed the channel with Clarence and Jasper Tudor and a small army which grew rapidly in size as he marched toward London. Bishop Morton came with him and hurried tq London to prepare the way for Warwick's triumphal return.

'Warwick soon found himself facing problems he had not expected. The House of York was more popular in London and much of the country than the Lancastrians. He was able to take London, but his reception was not as enthusiastic as he had expected. He freed Henry VI from his imprisonment in the Tower and placed him back on the throne. Then he ran into real trouble.

'Edward had fled with some of his followers to Burgundy when Warwick invaded England. He came back to northern England a few months later and was soon able to recruit a new army. Had things gone as planned, Warwick should have been able to meet this challenge without difficulty. The Lancastrians had what appeared to be the superior army. But Somerset and Tudor, the two principal Lancastrian generals, withheld their support at the time when it was most needed. Then Clarence defected to his brother Edward on the eve of the Battle of Barnet. In the battle that followed, Warwick was killed and his army defeated.

'Queen Margaret crossed the channel with her party about the time the battle was fought. She chose to fight on; but her Lancastrian army was wiped out and its top officers slain, along with the Prince of Wales, at the Battle of

Tewkesbury. Henry VI died soon after Edward's restoration while Margaret was captured, imprisoned for a while in the Tower, and then returned to France.'

'What happened to Bishop Morton?'

'The defeat at Tewksbury brought him to the lowest moment of his life. Naturally, he lost all the benefits that had been restored after Warwick took London. He was terribly broken up over Edward's death. He had spent fifteen years educating the Prince and felt as if he had lost a son. More than that, his prospects for getting ahead at the time were near zero. But he still had an important friend at court in the person of Cardinal Bouchier.

'The Cardinal took care of him for a while and then advised him to petition the King for forgiveness and for a reversal of his attainder. It was the sensible thing for him to do because the Lancastrian party was totally routed. Fortunately, Edward IV had a forgiving nature. He accepted the bishop back at court and soon showed signs of trusting him.'

'Did his position improve after his return?'

'Oh yes. The Bishop started a steady rise to the top that took him to the Privy Council. He asked me to work as his assistant and I rose with him. The King gave him several important assignments and awarded him with the Archdeaconries of Winchester and Chester. He was named Bishop of Ely in 1479. His service was so trusted that it was he who comforted King Edward while he laid dying in 1483.'

'Did he have any trouble in supporting the House of York after all of those years he had worked for the House of Lancaster?'

'I would have to read his mind to know that. He has never discussed his feelings about that change in allegiance with me. I am sure he never lost his love for Prince Edward nor his respect for Queen Margaret. When it became obvious that their cause was dead, he recognised that there was no point in crying over spilt milk. What was done was done. He did what any sensible man would do. He accepted the proffered hand of Edward of York because that was his only hope if he was to use his skills and talents for England.'

'What did he do after King Edward died and Richard III became Lord Protector and King?'

'That is getting up to your time, my lad. Perhaps we can talk about that some other time. As for now, I must leave you and make my report to His Eminence.'

'Thank you, Father,' Thomas said as he prepared to leave.

'And thank you too, Thomas. It is hard to explain the pleasure an old person like me feels when a young man shows an interest in his memories of the past.'

Chapter Five

Father Gregory knocked on the heavy oak door and entered the dark panelled chamber that Bishop Morton fondly regarded as his favourite retreat. A brisk fire was burning in the fireplace and Morton, a stout, heavy-set man, was sitting before it on one of the room's two massive oak chairs. A small oil painting of a Biblical scene graced one wall, and a tapestry from Flanders filled the open space of another. At seventy-eight, Bishop Morton's white hair was getting thinner, but his ruddy cheeks, bright blue eyes, and engaging smile still spoke of vigour and inner strength.

'Come in, Greg,' his voice boomed. 'Sit here by the fire with me; but first pour yourself some wine. This last shipment from Burgundy is the best I have had for some time.'

Father Gregory poured his wine and took a seat on the other chair. For a few moments quiet prevailed as the two men sipped their wine. Then Gregory launched into a report on Chancery business. Morton listened attentively and raised only two minor questions.

When Gregory concluded his report, the Bishop dismissed it with his customary comment, 'Good work. It appears you have everything under control for another day.' He then added, 'How is our new class of interns working out?'

Morton was referring to an innovation he had introduced at the Chancery by which he employed a few promising young men on a short-shift basis to give them experience in governmental administration. All of the half dozen interns were students who were reading law at Lincoln's Inn. Unlike the average government clerk, they were expected to work for only four to six hours a day, and could stagger their work schedules to meet their study requirements.

The arrangement allowed Morton to appraise and test the abilities of a new crop of potential workers each year, while providing some of the brighter students at Lincoln's Inn with opportunities to supplement their meagre-living allowances. William Givens, Henry Abel, and Thomas More were members of the current group who had now been working at the Chancery for several weeks.

'They are working out better than I ever expected, Your Grace. As you know, I had reservations when you started this programme. I now admit I was wrong. It is encouraging the way things are going. Unlike our usual scribes and clerks, the young men we have working as interns seem to bubble over with enthusiasm. It takes a while for some of them to learn their jobs, but whatever we lose from their lack of experience we gain from the freshness of their attitudes and imagination.'

'Excellent. It is good to hear that the programme is working out as I hoped it would. How about the men in it? You have mentioned Thomas More's name a few times, and the lads who work with him. How are they doing?'

'Very well, especially Thomas More. The other two are trustworthy and reliable and their work is neat and accurate as long as they keep their minds on their business. But Thomas is the real star. He has shown more promise than any other new man we have ever had. He is a first-rate worker, knows how to organise his time and his work assignments, writes as well as he speaks, and always seems willing to take on additional responsibility.'

'That does not surprise me,' Morton observed. 'When I

had him in my household some years back, I figured he was a real comer. He was one of the most ingenious and clever lads I've had in my house. No one will forget that last Yuletide he was with us. We had the players in as usual to entertain us. Their lead actor started the performance with a prologue in which he outlined the plot of the play that was to follow. With no more than that to go on, young Thomas surprised everyone by slipping into their midst and assuming a considerable role not intended in the play. He made up his lines as he went along and forced the regular players to do the same, much to our pleasure. Talent like that calls for careful nurturing.'

'He excels at every task I put him to,' Gregory added. 'I have had him writing some of our reports because he can compose a better letter than I can. He is equally good working on the accounts. Somehow, he seldom needs supervision and hardly ever makes a mistake. He has a talent for knowing what needs to be done and then going ahead and doing it.

'There are some things about him that are almost uncanny. I've watched him at his work and noticed that he takes in whole paragraphs with not much more than a glance. He reads whole sentences while the rest of us are reading words. Unlike most of us, he gets by on very little sleep; and while the other interns beg for time off to work on their legal studies, he is making excellent progress with his studies while working almost a full schedule with us.'

'Would you like to keep him?'

'I certainly would, but that, of course, is not possible. Like the other interns, he will be leaving us in a few months. Anyway, he has far too much talent to spend his life working as a clerk. If we were to keep him, I'm sure you would soon be seeking a more responsible assignment for him.'

'There is no hard and fast rule that says he must leave at

the end of his intern year. We can make arrangements to keep him if he wants to stay with us. What we do about him depends a lot on what he wants. Has he indicated any plans he may have?'

'As you know, he has studied at the New Inn and is now reading law at Lincoln's Inn. Once he finishes his studies there, he will be accepted for the bar and probably start a legal practice in partnership with his father. But I do not think he has really decided for sure yet what he will do.

'Thomas is a very pious and religious person and talks of taking holy orders. With his speaking voice and keen mind, he should become a successful lawyer. If he becomes a priest, I would expect him to climb to the upper ranks of the clergy. With his talent though, you may want to find a place for him in government.'

'He is still quite young for a truly responsible post. I will keep my eye on him though. After some more seasoning, he may be just the man we need for some particular assignment.'

'That raises a question. Should I encourage him to take clerical orders?'

'Let's wait on that. If he expresses interest in being a priest, we should not discourage him; but he can serve in government these days just as well without a cassock. I have no enthusiasm for pushing him toward a career in the Church because if he has a pious nature we could easily lose him. I've seen too many bright young candidates for the priesthood retire to quiet lifetimes of poverty and prayers in some monastery when they had talents that could have better served us in more public callings. I have a feeling Thomas More might rise to a post in the Privy Council. God knows England needs men like that!'

Morton fidgeted as he looked at their now empty wine mugs and added, 'Is there anything else we should discuss while you are here?'

'One item, Your Eminence. I have had another letter from Brother Bernard. He requests transferral to our staff here at the Chancery.'

'Oh, your nephew,' the Lord Chancellor observed. 'He is able and deserving, but I think he should stay where he is for the time being. Don't dash his hopes. Both of us know he would like to work here, and I'm sure we will find the right niche for him. Tell him to keep in touch, but that it will be a while before we need him.'

'I will do that,' Gregory answered as he rose from his chair in preparation for leaving.

'Speaking of Bernard,' the Archbishop continued. 'We have many memories and secrets, you and I, that take us back a good many years. Don't be in a hurry to leave. Pour yourself some more wine and stay for a while. It is lonely here tonight, and I want nothing more than to talk to someone like you.

'It occurred to me this afternoon that there is no one in all England who is closer to me or who has my interests more at heart than you. You have served me well as my aide for more than twenty years, Greg. More than anyone else, you could ruin my career, or what is left of it, with a few unguarded comments about my past.'

'Any secrets we have are safe with me, John. You know I would never intentionally say anything that could discredit you. I am indebted to you for far too many favours to ever think of that.'

'I thank you for your loyalty, Greg, and also for the faithful support you have always given me, without ever once questioning my motives.'

'Supporting you was a pleasure; but I must admit I have sometimes wondered why you were doing what you did.'

'There is no good reason for you continuing to wonder, Greg. If you have questions that bother you, just go ahead and ask them.'

'I'm not questioning what you did. I am curious, though, about your relations with several people. I know you were close to Queen Margaret and the young Prince back when Henry VI was on the throne; but how did you feel about the Duke of York and his three sons?'

'Four sons actually. Edmund was killed in the surprise skirmish that Christmas time along with his father. As for how I felt about the Yorks, that calls for some sorting out of details. What you are really asking me is how a supporter of the red rose of Lancaster could end up in the camp of the white rose of York. Why did I switch sides from being Queen Margaret's advisor to become a functionary of Edward IV?

'I've never made a secret of the dislike I had for Richard of York. I realise that as Duke of York he had a claim to the crown that was superior to that of Henry VI. More than that, he was England's best military commander. He was a strong and vigorous leader while Henry was a weakling. Still, I resented him because he was a constant thorn in the side of King Henry and his Queen, both of whom I was sworn to support.

'If Henry had been a bold leader instead of a feeble, foggy-headed apology for a prince, who suffered from spells of insanity, the problem never would have arisen. Under the circumstances, Richard thought he ought to be king, but he lacked the resolve to take the throne when he had the chance. Parliament named him Lord Protector, not just once but three different times. It even designated him as Henry's heir. I hated him most particularly for that because he was running roughshod over the interests of Queen Margaret, and of Prince Edward whom I saw as the rightful heir to the throne.'

'Did you feel the same way about Richard's sons after the Duke was killed?'

'I suppose I did transfer my resentment of the father to

his sons. You will remember that I spent a long nine years with Queen Margaret and her party on the Continent working for Henry's restoration. My hopes for eventually seeing Edward on the throne were riding high after Warwick took London. Then they were dashed again with Edward of York's victories at Barnet and at Tewkesbury.

'When they captured me after their victory at Tewkesbury and I learned that Prince Edward had been killed, I was ready to give up my ambitions and become a simple friar in some abbey. Bouchier saved me from that. He told me I should ask the King for forgiveness. I did, and much to my surprise, he rescinded the attainder of my estates and asked me to join him at court, all of which seemed to prove that Edward IV was basically a good man at heart.'

'How did you rate Edward as a king?'

'I should be eternally grateful to him because he restored me to favour and gave me his trust. In plain fact though, he was an enigma. You probably remember that he was a tall, powerfully-built young man, not yet nineteen years of age when he became king, with a handsome face, golden curls, and already had a record as a proven warrior when he led his father's army to victory and seized the crown.

'He had almost everything going for him then, yet he did very little of note during the twenty-one years of his reign. He was a genial trusting ruler whom people found it hard not to like; but he had no talent for administration. He turned the business of ruling England over to his associates while he gave his wife's family, the Woodvilles, a free rein to plunder the Treasury.

'I had every reason to like Edward as a person. Yet I was far from pleased with what he did. As I said, Edward was a handsome, loveable man, and he was a womaniser of the first order. Women found him irresistible, and he showed no reluctance about excelling as a royal ram. He only had to wiggle his little finger at most of the ladies at court and they were ready to tumble into bed with him. In many respects they were his downfall. He had several mistresses, both before and after he was married.'

'Didn't his Queen object?

'She knew very little about his past activities when they first met. Elizabeth Woodville was a young widow at the time and one of the most beautiful women in England. Edward decided he wanted her; but unlike most of his other paramours, she refused to go to bed with him until he married her. He did not bother to tell her he was already secretly married to another of his conquests.,That secret was kept hidden until after his death.

'Queen Elizabeth already had two sons from her earlier marriage to Lord Grey. After her marriage to Edward, she gave the King two sons and four daughters. That was not enough for him though. He had an enormous appetite and kept on eating and drinking and whoring until the end of his days. At the time of his death, he was more a drunken heap of fat and blubber than a man, but he was still servicing three mistresses besides his wife.'

'Were George and Richard like their brother?'

'No, not at all. They were quite different. George was not as tall or as manly built as Edward, but he had golden curls, a fair complexion, and about twice as much ambition as his brother to be king. Poor George! There was a frustrated nobleman if I ever saw one!

'George was short on genuine ability, common sense, and good judgement, and he was greedy for power. He was handsome and likeable but never a man one could trust. He married Warwick's eldest daughter and with Warwick's backing schemed to overthrow his brother and seize the crown. To strengthen his claim, he even asserted in those last months before his death that his older brother and sisters were bastards. That charge, if anyone at court had accepted it, would have made him the logical claimant to the crown.

'George's conniving got him into trouble with the Woodvilles. His brothers were willing to put up with his antics, but the Woodvilles saw him as a threat to their interests. They insisted that a special board examine his case and the board condemned George to death for his treachery. Edward and his brother Richard resisted that decision but Parliament and the Woodvilles insisted that the sentence be carried out. Edward finally acquiesced, and George was executed, though I have never been sure how. It was said that his jailers drowned him in a butt of Malmsey wine. That made a good story but I doubt it happened that way. In any case, I cannot say I shed any tears when I heard of the deaths of either George or his father-in-law, the Earl of Warwick.'

'And what of Richard of Gloucester?'

'Hold on, Greg!' Bishop Morton cried as he eased himself up out of his chair. 'If we are going to talk about Richard III, it is going to take some time. I'm more than willing to tell you about him. As a matter of fact I should have been more open and frank a long time ago in telling you about my relationship with him. Before we get into that though, you must remember that I am an old man who sometimes has trouble holding his water. Right now, I must call for some time out while I empty my bladder.'

Chapter Six

Seated again in the two big chairs in Morton's study, the Lord Chancellor and his chief assistant leaned back against their cushions as they sipped wine from their refilled mugs.

'Let's see, where were we when we took our break?' Morton asked.

'I had just asked you about the feelings you had concerning Richard of Gloucester during Edward's reign,' Gregory replied.

'Oh yes, I remember now. The truth is, I detested Richard almost from the first time I saw him, and for no good reason. We had our differences, but when I try to analyse my feelings, I have to admit that my dislike, at least at the beginning, was based mostly on the fact that he carried his father's name. In many respects, Richard was the most capable of York's sons. He showed real ability as a military commander at an early age, and he, more than anyone else, was responsible for maintaining peace throughout the kingdom during the last half of Edward's reign.

'Unlike his brother George, Richard gave his full support to Edward, and the King in turn placed a lot of trust in him. Unlike the King, Richard had a keen interest in government and was a shrewd administrator. He also adhered to a higher set of moral standards. He disapproved of many things that went on at court, and much preferred the quieter and more modest life he lived at his estate in the North.'

'Your description makes him sound like an ideal leader.

He must have had some weaknesses.'

'He had weaknesses all right. He had a stiff-necked attitude regarding many things. He was openly critical of what he considered as licentious behaviour at court, when he could have advanced his cause and made more friends had he followed a less accusatory course. He wanted to scale down the rights and privileges of the clergy; and he favoured reforms that would have limited the rights of the nobility. He was also more trusting than a good leader should be. He just did not seem to recognise that several of the men he trusted and showered with honours were really rascals who would turn on him when it was to their advantage.'

'Did you have any differences with him before he became Lord Protector?'

'He visited the royal court only twice in the four years before Edward died, so I cannot say I had much contact with him. I doubt he had any reason to dislike me at the time and I recall only one instance in which we had a difference of opinion. That was when we negotiated that treaty with France.

'King Louis was anxious for us to endorse the treaty and brought along a bag of gold pieces which he apportioned amongst our negotiators. There were three or four bishops on our team, and I, along with the others, accepted the gold which we regarded as a token of appreciation for our willingness to co-operate. Richard refused to even touch his share of the coins. He said they were offered as a bribe which we should be ashamed to take. My fellow clerics saw nothing wrong with our acceptance of the gift, and resented the implication that Richard was adhering to a higher ethical standard than we were.'

'Whilst I am asking these questions, please tell me how you felt about the Woodvilles,' Gregory asked.

'What the Woodvilles did to Edward and to England

provides the best argument I have heard for seeking brides from across the channel for our kings. Elizabeth Woodville was a beautiful woman and a good person in her own right; but when Edward married her, he took on a family of bloodsuckers who made haste to attach themselves to the royal Treasury.

'Elizabeth had two sons from her first husband, as well as a mother and several brothers and sisters with her when she took her place in the royal court. Every one of them had an insatiable appetite for advancement. They were not willing to settle for a good living. They wanted prestigious marriages, and titles with estates and promises of perpetual incomes. Their openly displayed greed upset the nobility along with most of the right-thinking people in London. They even married the Queen's youngest brother, who was only eighteen, to the eighty-year-old Duchess of Norfolk in order to get their hands on her estate.'

'So you did not approve of the Queen's family?'

'I certainly did not, though naturally I had to be careful with what I said to or about them. Edward loved his wife and was not willing to hear any criticism of her or her family. I will say this though. Had it not been for their sorry record, I would have played a more strenuous role than I did in trying to put the young Prince Edward on the throne when Edward died. But none of the Woodvilles had shown any particular interest in me, so I did not go out of my way to promote their interests in the succession.'

'Did you offer your support to Richard?'

'In retrospect I admit that I probably should have; but it was a perilous time for me. Everyone on the royal Council was shocked when we learned that Edward had added a codicil to his will, stating that his brother Richard rather than the Queen should serve as Lord Protector.

'Queen Elizabeth insisted that Richard's designation was a mistake. The Woodvilles were in full control at court while Richard was far away in Yorkshire. When they proposed that no word be sent to Richard about his designation, and that we cut the term of his Protectorship short by bringing the young Prince of Wales to London for an early coronation, I went along with the rest of the Council in approving the plan. I thought it best that the matter of the succession be settled quickly.

'That strategy was foiled when Lord Hastings sent two messages to Richard. Richard marched south with an army which was more than doubled in size when the Duke of Buckingham joined forces with him. Fortunately for them, they were at Stony Stratford near Nottingham when Lord Rivers, the Queen's brother, came by with the army escort that was bringing the twelve-year-old Prince from Ludlow castle to London. Richard took control and marched on to London with the Prince and Buckingham.

'When Richard arrived in London, I found myself walking on eggshells. Elizabeth fled with her daughters and youngest son to Westminster Abbey where she claimed sanctuary. She still had a following at court, but her son the Marquis of Dorset, who had led her party, fled to France. Richard was soon in full control as Lord Protector. I had no particular desire to favour either side, and certainly wanted to avoid turning anyone against me, so I tried to stay neutral and keep my nose clean.'

'What about Lord Hastings?'

'William Hastings was Lord Chamberlain and had been King Edward's closest friend. When the King died, he sent two messages to Richard, who was living at Middleham Castle in northern England. The first message advised him of Edward's death and of his designation as Lord Protector. A later message alerted him to the Woodville plan for bringing his nephew from Ludlow Castle, where he was being educated, to London, for an early coronation.

'I was never close to Lord Hastings even though we

served together on Edward's Council. He was an ambitious man and I suspect he expected more recognition and more honours from Richard once he arrived as Lord Protector than he got. Like the rest of us, he was caught up in the uncertainties of the changing situation with the Woodvilles suddenly out of favour.

'Richard surprised all of us by putting trust in Buckingham and leaning on him for advice. Hastings, Lord Stanley, Archbishop Rotherham and I had all been members of the old royal Council. We could see that a new order was in the making, and none of us had a clear idea of how it would affect us.'

'As I remember, Lord Hastings was executed only a few weeks after Richard came to power. Was Hastings really guilty of treason?'

'I was there and should know; but the truth is I am not at all sure what happened in the Hastings affair. Buckingham disliked Hastings and may have used his spies to trap him or make a case against him. It is also possible Hastings felt he was being crowded out and that he saw an opportunity to further his position by conspiring with the Woodvilles to replace Richard. Then there was that complication involving Jane Shore.'

'There was some scandal about her, wasn't there?'

'Yes, she must have been quite a thriller. She was one of Edward's favourite mistresses in the months before he died. It was known at court that she was also sleeping with Dorset, the Queen's eldest son. Hastings had his eye on her too and arranged after Edward's death to take over with her where the King had left off. Whether Dorset's friends got her to encourage Hastings to conspire with the Woodvilles to put Richard aside, as some people claimed, is a charge I can neither prove nor disprove. All I am certain of is that it was known that Lord Hastings and I had talked with each other on various occasions. When charges were submitted to Richard that Hastings was conspiring with the Woodvilles to oust him, I found myself caught in the middle. Hastings was found guilty and executed a few days later. I was arraigned and committed to the Tower because Richard and Buckingham suspected I might have been involved. They had no case against me, but from that day on, I saw Richard more as my enemy than as a possible friend.'

'It was Henry Stafford, the Duke of Buckingham, who got you out of the Tower, wasn't it?'

'Yes, my relationship with Buckingham took an unusual twist. I had no particular liking for him when he was a young man growing up at court. He was a direct descendant of two of Edward III's sons, John of Gaunt and Thomas of Woodstock. That gave him a claim to the crown that was only a shade inferior to that of Edward IV and his brothers. The Queen arranged for his marriage to one of her younger sisters, but it was a match he despised because it was forced on him while he was a child.

'Buckingham showed some ability during Edward's last years. Most of us thought he was in the Woodville camp. Instead, he surprised us by offering military aid to bring Richard to London as Lord Protector. Shortly after that he established himself as Richard's principal ally in the contest against the Woodvilles. He used his talent as an eloquent and persuasive speaker to champion Richard's cause in Parliament, and also in swaying street crowds in his favour.

'From what I had seen of him at court and in the royal Council after Richard came to London, I thought of Buckingham as a vain and self-centred interloper who was pursuing his own agenda. I resented his rise to prominence because of the disrupting effect it had on our balance of power within the Council. After I was arrested and confined to the Tower though, my attitude softened, at least for a while.'

'Why was that?'

'First, I must tell you that several important events occurred in rapid succession after my arrest. Hastings was condemned and executed for treason. Bishop Stillington produced evidence that Edward had been married to Eleanor Talbot, the widow of Sir Thomas Butler, before he married Elizabeth. Parliament passed a law that declared his marriage to Elizabeth bigamous and barred their children from the succession. Then a crowd of Richard's supporters offered him the crown and demanded that he take it. He turned them down at first. After a display of reluctance though, he took it. Richard and his Queen, Anne, were crowned with great ceremony; and Buckingham was appointed Lord Constable.

'It was at about the time of Richard's coronation that Buckingham surprised me with a visit at the Tower. This meeting and the several visits that followed attracted no attention because as Lord Constable he had other duties at the Tower. He was riding high at the time. Richard had heaped honours on him that really went to his head. It was not long before I realised he was making amends to me and feeling me out to see what I could do for him if he could get me out of the Tower.'

'Did you see the two young princes while you were at the Tower?'

'No. We were housed in different parts of the Tower and I had no occasion to see them. I knew they were there though because my guards talked about them and their activities. Strange to say, Buckingham never mentioned them in any of his conversations there with me. He was preoccupied with his own ambitions. So far as I could see, he was mostly concerned with the possibility of becoming King himself.'

'Did he ask for your advice?'

'That is what it amounted to. I told him I was reluctant

to get involved, but that he could seize the crown if he made and carried out a careful plan to that end. To be honest with you, I felt more than a little ashamed of the role I was playing in putting grand ideas in his head. He was a lot like George of Clarence in that he had more ambition than genuine ability or common sense. I acted as I did because I felt no allegiance to Richard after he sent me to the Tower, and Buckingham was offering me a ticket to freedom.

'After his coronation, Richard released me into Buckingham's custody. Buckingham sent me under guard to a castle in Wales, ostensibly for safekeeping, but really to start planning a revolt that could topple the House of York from power. Then Richard left London with his Queen on a progress through the western and northern shires. A few weeks later Buckingham joined me in Wales.

'Buckingham was only one of several noblemen in southern England who were fomenting rebellions that year. Most of them wanted to release Prince Edward from the Tower and crown him as Edward V.

'Buckingham tried to solicit their support with various promises and then put out a report that Prince Edward and his brother had been murdered. I do not know whether his claim was true or not, but if he expected it to help his cause he made an error of judgement. Instead of coming out for him, most of the nobles he had hoped to attract to his banner shifted their support to Henry Tudor, the Duke of Richmond.'

'That must have come as a shock to him.'

'It was a shock, you can be sure. He was already too committed to make peace with Richard. I advised him to come out for Henry Tudor. He was disappointed with my advice, hesitated about accepting it, and vacillated back and forth as to what he should do. He told some noblemen from the western shires that he was supporting Tudor, but in reality, he was still holding to a grand illusion about his coming triumph when Richard's army caught him and put an end to his dream.

'I was with Buckingham at Weobley when the remnants of his army faded away. Poor Buckingham was caught and executed. I was fortunate and was able to escape. Friends hid me along the road to the channel. Once there, I crossed over to France and started making plans for Henry Tudor's escape from Duke Francis' palace in Brittany.'

'What was Henry doing in Brittany?'

'After Queen Margaret's army was routed at Tewkesbury, Henry Tudor was the last male descendant of John of Gaunt who had a credible claim to the crown. His father had died before he was born and his mother allowed him to grow up in the household of his uncle, the Earl of Pembroke. Edward IV wanted him to come to court where he would have been brought up as a prospective bridegroom for one of the King's daughters. Henry's uncle decided otherwise and sent him to Brittany to keep him out of Edward's hands.

'Duke Francis was kind to Henry, but never regarded him as a future king. I discovered after my escape to France that Richard wanted the Duke to send Henry back to England. I suspected his motives in this, so I sent word to Henry that he should flee to France while he still could.'

'I have no need to ask you about your support of Henry Tudor or about his victory over Richard at Bosworth Field. I am curious, though, as to why you decided to support him in the first place.'

'My decision to support Henry was not based on personal acquaintance. I am not sure I ever saw him while he was a child. Of course, I knew his father Edmund Tudor, who had been the Earl of Richmond, and his mother Mary Beaufort who married Lord Stafford and then Lord Stanley after Richmond's death. His father had royal blood and his mother was a descendant of John of Gaunt. With Henry VI and his son both dead, Henry Tudor was the House of Lancaster's chief claimant to the throne. Naturally, I was inclined to favour his cause, but I had no direct contact with him before Buckingham's rebellion.

'My support went to Henry by a process of elimination. I had burned my bridges with the Woodvilles, and with the House of York. I could not support Buckingham, so Henry Tudor was the only logical choice left. Joining up with him amounted to reviving my earlier support for Queen Margaret's son. Henry Tudor was tied to the House of Lancaster, and with him as my prince, I was home again.'

'King Henry was more than lucky to have you supporting him,' Gregory observed. 'Without your efforts, he would never have become King.'

'That may be true,' Morton chuckled. 'But don't ever express that sentiment to Henry. He is convinced in his own mind that it was God's will that he should seize, and hold the crown.'

Chapter Seven

Light from the early dawn was gradually dispelling the darkness that filled the small upper floor sleeping room in the Mores' house. Thomas More, the eldest son of the family, was sprawled out on his back on the narrow bed that almost filled the room. His heavy breathing signalled contented sleep. Rumpled covers on the bed told of a troubled night of fitful rolling and tossing. Now at the hour when he usually awakened, Thomas's slumbering mind and body seemed totally relaxed, caught up in a restful peaceful indolence.

A glimmer of a smile showed on Thomas's face as his deep slumber gave way to the fleeting fantasies of a dream. Without explanation, he saw himself in a darkened room with Will and Harry and three faceless women. He was undressing one of the girls – caressing her upper body, touching and kissing her breasts. A thrill of anticipation ran through his system. Both in his dream and there in his bed, the fantasy brought a pleasant stirring in his loins as his male member gorged with blood, stiffened, and rose like a tent pole in an erection that pushed up the bedding covering his naked body.

Friction from the contact of his swollen member against his sheet sent sparks of sensual pleasure through his body. The girl in the fantasy clung to him and guided his hands in a more extensive exploration of her mysteries. His body tingled as it anticipated a promise of pleasure yet unknown. She was so soft, so lovely, so inviting. Desire possessed him. He had to have her. She asked that he mount her and as he turned his body to do so, the dream exploded. He was suddenly awake. Conscious of the baseness of his fantasy, his mind filled with terror.

'Why, why?' he asked himself, 'does the Devil persist in tempting me this way? Morning after morning I awaken with a hard-on and nothing seems to prevent it.'

He flung back his bedcovers. His erect member stood fully to attention. It ached for contact with human flesh, for a caressing hand if not for a woman's body.

'What harm could there possibly be if I cuddled it with my hand, rubbed it, or just held it?' he pondered. Then with a painful grimace, he realised that this was another of Satan's tricks. The Devil was luring him again with promised joys of the flesh, while his real intent was only that of capturing his soul for an eternity in hell.

Thomas's mind turned back to the fantasy in his dream. It could be enjoyable, he thought. Surely I am old enough for such an experience. Why do I have to drag my heels while Will and Harry have no qualms about doing what I feel guilty even thinking about? Why must I fight during my every waking moment to keep my mind free of thoughts of forbidden sex? Why can't I walk down a street, sit in a tavern, or even read my court cases without feeling the stirring in my loins? Why does Satan send lurid thoughts through my mind every time I see a pretty girl or woman? And why must he torment me with these forebodings of damnation while other men seem undisturbed?

As he lay shivering in the morning chill, Thomas recalled the reason for his fears. He remembered a day some seven years earlier when he and another of Bishop Morton's boys were bathing before supper. He and Stephen had thought they were alone in the boys' washroom, and he had stood by while Stephen pulled back the foreskin on his penis and rubbed it, when Father Jason appeared out of nowhere, administered a quick slap to the buttocks of each boy, and ordered them to stop.

The lecture that followed was not something Thomas was inclined to forget. He could not remember all the details. Yet he clearly recalled that the good priest had insisted that boys who played with their bodies were defying the laws of God, that this sin could bring them a lifetime of grief with possible blindness or insanity, and that the Devil had a special spot in hell for anyone who persisted in this immoral practice.

Thomas and Stephen had told the other boys about Father Jason's stern admonition. Two of the older boys had hooted and one had even ventured the observation that their priestly guardian was full of hot air. Thomas, however, had taken Father Jason's words as gospel truth; as a fair warning of what would happen to him if he did not follow God's narrow path. Others could scoff at the good Father's warning, but Thomas knew he must be right. He knew it then; and the fact that Father Jason later became the prior of a sacred order of St Dominic was clear evidence that God had spoken through him.

As Thomas's thoughts turned to Father Jason and the two years he had spent living with several other boys in Bishop Morton's household, his phallus subsided to its normal size and he pulled the bed covers back over his shivering body. He knew he should get up as he usually did at dawn. Today though, he decided he would yield to comfort and stay huddled under his bedcovers for a while as he contemplated some of the issues he must deal with when he reported at the Lord Chancellor's quarters.

His thoughts then turned from his work to his family. His father was a successful barrister who had done well in his practice, considering his humble origins. His grandfather was a London baker who had married the daughter of a brewer. John More had often jested that he came from an ideal English family. With parents like his, one never needed to go in want for food or drink, because his father could always provide the bread while his mother could supply the beer.

Thomas remembered his grandfather as a jolly, rotund little man with flour on his smock, who baked the best bread in London and who always had a cookie or cake for little Tommy. It did not occur to him until years after his grandfather's death that being the son of a London tradesman, successful or unsuccessful, was not the best background for one who wanted to establish a successful legal practice.

John More had been married in 1474 to Agnes Granger, daughter of Thomas Granger, a prosperous London citizen. Their daughter Johanna was born the next year. Thomas, the oldest son, was born in 1478. Then came a sister who was born and died the next year; John who was two years younger than Thomas; a brother Edward who died as a child; and Elizabeth who was born in 1482.

As he thought about his family, he could not help but wonder about the different ways in which his parents and grandparents had treated him and his brother John. From the time he was a small boy, his father and his grandparents had drilled the idea into him that he was to go to school, get additional education at the university, read law, and eventually follow his father in the practice of law. Both he and John had been sent to St Anthony's school on Threadneedle Street where they learned to read, write, and do their numbers. Thomas had excelled there and attracted the attention of the clerics who taught his courses. John had been a more average sort of student who never caught the eyes of his instructors. Unlike Thomas, who had been a bookworm almost from the day he learned to read, John had shown a distinct preference for spending his spare time playing in the streets.

When he was twelve, Thomas was taken by the Principal of St Anthony's school on a special trip to Bishop Morton's house. He recalled his excitement when he learned of the impending visit. His father had already taken pains to tell him that Bishop Morton was the Archbishop of Canterbury, the highest churchman in all England, and that he also served as the King's Lord Chancellor. Equally important for Thomas was the fact that the good Bishop made it a practice each year to take a few boys of promising talent into his household where they could continue their education.

John More hoped Thomas would be accepted in this capacity. If he could be one of those selected, he would enjoy a wonderful educational opportunity. Besides his studies, he would learn etiquette and the art of getting along with others, and he would be able to observe and associate with some of the most important men of the kingdom.

Thomas and his Principal were interviewed by a member of the Bishop's household and then given a tour of the rooms where six to eight boys lived as part of Morton's household. Before the visit was over, Bishop Morton talked with him for several minutes and then asked him to read a long passage of Scripture out loud. Apparently, he came up to the Bishop's standards because his father was advised the following week that Thomas was invited to join the next group of boys who were to benefit from Morton's tutelage.

The practice of parents sending their sons to live in other households was not unusual. With the children of artisans, boys were ordinarily apprenticed to other artisans so that they might learn a trade. Among the nobility and gentry, sons were sent, often as pages, to other noble households to continue their education and learn things they presumably could not learn at home that would season them for later life. Admission to residence in Morton's household was a rare opportunity because the Bishop's staff prided itself on training young men to go on to Oxford and after that to professional careers.

The routine Thomas followed during the two years he spent in the Bishop's household appealed to him as entirely proper. Some of the boys complained about the strict discipline, the long hours spent in chapel, the emphasis given to studies, the prohibition on horseplay, and the monitoring of their every spare moment. But Thomas loved it and felt his experience there provided an ideal foundation for the two following years when he had gone on to study at Canterbury Hall in Oxford.

As Thomas thought of his own education, he wondered why his father had not placed his brother with some other family. The fact that no one had offered to take John in hand did not occur to him. John had continued at St Anthony's and then, far from going to the university, he had been apprenticed to a scribe and could soon expect to make his living as a clerk who would spend his life copying records for others. Thomas suddenly realised he had never discussed his brother's situation with either his father or with John himself. John had never complained to him about his treatment so it seemed probable that he had become a scribe rather than a prospective lawyer out of choice.

Thomas and John had argued and squabbled with each other as children. But there had never been a serious breach between them. They liked each other, and each felt considerable brotherly love for the other. If John envied him, he never showed it. But John's outlook on life was so different from his own. John was so ordinary. As a boy, he had always spent his spare time playing with other children, while Thomas preferred to share his time with the characters of the books he read. Nor had their inclinations changed as they grew older. Thomas continued his studious ways at Bishop Morton's and at Oxford while John devoted all the time he could spare to teenage sports.

Another distinct difference between the two brothers involved their attitudes concerning girls. Thomas had never shown much interest in the fair sex. Oh, he thought about them all right. Indeed he had thought far more about them than he cared to admit.

There was that girl Elizabeth who had caught his fancy when he was sixteen and just starting his studies at the New Inn. She was a pretty thing, the very embodiment of his idea of a beautiful young virgin. He has seen her among a group of girls and been smitten with a secret attraction to her. Yet his shyness with women had kept him from even speaking to her. He had never gotten up enough courage to ask her or any other girl to go to a party with him. Not that it made much difference to him. From his boyhood days on, he had always thought of women as being foolish things. They did not account to much in his thinking, and he had accordingly ruled out boy-and-girl games as frivolous pursuits that would only waste his time.

When it came to girls, John was not at all like him. He had displayed a definite liking for the opposite sex from puberty on. He enjoyed singing, talking, picnicking, and dancing with them. He had been wildly in love with two different girls when he was sixteen, and now at eighteen was keeping steady company with a girl he planned to marry as soon as he could find regular employment as a scribe.

Thomas had only a vague memory of his mother. She had died while he was at St Anthony's, and his father had remarried shortly after her death. He had an impersonal relationship with his stepmother. She was proud of his achievements but neither felt they really belonged to the other. Thomas supposed he had loved his mother but could not remember her ever spending much time with him. Probably with six children, four of them born in the four years following his birth, she had been far too busy to give him much individual attention and love.

As for his living sisters, Thomas hardly knew what to think. They were there and he loved them because they were family. Yet he seldom thought of them because women just did not rate very high in his vision of a man's world. Still, he remembered that Johanna had been kind and helpful to him while he was small. He had seen little of her while he was at Bishop Morton's place and at Oxford, and now she was married with a child of her own. As for his baby sister Elizabeth, she was cute and nice for a girl. He remembered her mostly because she had been the little pest who was always messing up his books and papers before he went into the Bishop's household. And now she was living in another household and looking forward to marriage within a few years.

Thomas's father was the person in the family to whom he felt most closely attached. John More had taken a personal interest in guiding his eldest son's upbringing from his days in swaddling clothes. John More was his friend, his strongest supporter. Father and son enjoyed each other's company, could speak each other's language, and could sit talking to each other for long stretches of time. Thomas knew that many of his ideas and values came from his father. Both were enthusiastic about their ties to Bishop Morton, and both were critical of Henry VII. Both had a studious streak, a love for learning. While John had been married twice and had two living daughters, both saw the society they lived in as being a man's world, in which women played only a supportive role. And both had a strong interest in legal matters which John carefully cultivated in his son in the hope that he would follow him into the practice of law.

Memories of the happy hours he had spent with his father filled Thomas's mind as he drifted back to sleep. For a while his mind was blank as his body replenished itself from a fountain of restful slumber. Then another dream started to take form. Out of fragments from his imagination a fantasy emerged in his subconscious thought. This time he was in a sultan's harem. He was dressed in a lavish robe and wore a billowing weightless turban. Several faceless damsels danced before him and gradually disrobed as the dance continued.

His eyes marvelled at their beauty. As he reached out to them, three came within touching distance. Their shapely arms stroked his body and his clothes disappeared as if by magic. He found the scent of their perfumed bodies intoxicating. It filled his being with a surge of desire. A carnal appetite took command of his body. His loins reacted as they always did. His heart pumped a flood of blood into his flabby member causing it to distend and then swell to rigid erection. All three women beckoned to him to take their bodies, but as he tried to decide with which one to start, his fantasy was shattered again as he suddenly awoke. With the rational thinking that comes with full consciousness, he was both ashamed and angry.

'Damn, damn!' he swore to himself. 'No,' he caught himself, 'I cannot swear like that even in my thoughts. But why must the Devil persist in torturing me this way?' A glimmer of a memory from earlier years flashed through his thoughts. 'No! No, please don't make me think of that. I won't remember it. You may claim my soul. But I'll fight you. I must fight off this temptation!'

With a burst of determination, Thomas sprang from his bed and dashed cold water from his bedside pitcher on to his naked splendour. The chill of the water and the cool air restored his body to its normal state. As Thomas dressed, he wondered if he could cheat Satan of his seductive tricks by getting up earlier in the morning.

'There is more truth than I thought in the saying that an

idle mind is the Devil's workshop. My only defence against him is to get up early and fill my mind with thoughts of other things!'

Chapter Eight

'We will not try to buy their love!' the King snorted as he glared across his desk at Richard Foxe, the Bishop of Winchester. Like Henry, Bishop Foxe was a man of average build with a thin angular face and a sallow complexion. Unlike him, he had a rich baritone voice and a fawning manner that spoke of ambition and desire to please his superiors.

'Nor should you,' Foxe replied. 'Your subjects should cherish and love you for your own sake, not because of what you can give or do for them. They should know that according to God's law, you have been endowed and entrusted as owner and custodian of all the land and wealth of the realm, and that it is only by your good will that they enjoy any rights to use or possess any of it.'

'You mean the taxes they pay are just another form of rent for the use of property that is really ours?'

'That is right, Your Majesty.'

'Then we have no legal or moral duty to lower taxes, nor to spend money just for the sake of spending.'

Cardinal Morton entered the King's chamber just in time to hear Foxe say, 'That is true, My Lord. The property is yours by divine right.'

Morton had no clue at first as to the topic under discussion, but soon sensed that Henry was again concerned about his popularity and that Foxe had come out four-square for the feudal concept of royal prerogatives. If Foxe had ever heard of the Magna Carta, he had conveniently forgotten it.

After Foxe excused himself and left, the King said, 'We like Bishop Foxe. He has good ideas. Do you think he is worthy of serving on our Privy Council?'

Morton stroked his chin as he quickly thought of an appropriate answer. Here was Henry, he thought, probably the wealthiest man in Europe, yet dressed in dark sombre apparel that matched his demeanour. Most princes in his position would be attired in military gear, or in rich velvets adorned with masculine jewellery. But not Henry. With his miserly, frugal nature, he was delighted with the idea that he might own everything in England and have no responsibility to provide more than a minimum of service for his subjects.

'Bishop Foxe on the Council?' he said. 'He is a capable man so far as I know and probably could serve satisfactorily. My chief concern is that his colleagues say he is a toady.'

'How do you mean, a toady?'

'He has a reputation for courting the favour of his superiors.'

'We see no harm in that.'

'By itself, it is not harmful. But advice can be flawed if it comes from one who is said to be willing to sell his own mother if it will get him a promotion.'

'Well, we like him.'

'The decision is yours, Your Majesty.'

'Who else should we consider for the Council?'

'Should you want someone from the Church, I could recommend Bishop Warham.'

'Warham is a good man, but he is young and we want someone with more experience.'

'You could fill the position with a lord of noble blood such as young Buckingham or the Earl of Suffolk.'

'Buckingham may be loyal, but he is both stubborn and stupid. Suffolk has been loyal, but no grandson of Richard of York will ever serve in my Privy Council.'

'The nobility would be pleased if you picked someone like Lord Stanley or Lord Percy.'

'We do not trust Stanley. He is shifty like his father and like his uncle whom we had executed. The same goes for barons such as Percy of Northumberland and Baron Clinton.'

'Then we are back to the Church.'

'We are surprised that you have not mentioned your Father Gregory.'

'Would you take away my most valued assistant? Gregory is a gem as an administrator and he knows the ins and outs of the royal government; but he is not the man you need. He has one major fault. He has no ambition for power. He is a follower who has no desire to lead. No, Foxe is probably your best bet.'

'Before you came in, the Bishop was talking about our popularity with the people. Do you think we are more popular now than we were five or ten years ago?'

Bishop Morton shuffled through some papers on the table before answering. Privately, he was thinking, He is concerned about his popularity again. Has any king in recent times felt as insecure as this one? He knows what no one dares to tell him, that he is the most despised king England has had in the last half century. Henry VI, poor simpleton that he was, had thousands of subjects who loved him. Edward IV was widely acclaimed because he looked and acted like a king. Richard III also enjoyed wide popular support throughout most of the realm. But Henry VII has the support of the nobility only because they have no other choice. The Church tolerates him. The people of London cheer for him when they are told they must. Aside from his family, no one really loves him. Most of his subjects hate him because they see him as a mean skinflint. Yet they support him because he stands for law and order.

'You are more popular than you were, Your Majesty,' Morton responded. 'To tell the truth though, my agents tell me they hear little talk about you.'

'Well then, what do they hear?'

'Most of the talk they hear is about business conditions and the succession.'

'Succession! Is anyone suggesting that the crown will not be passed on to another Tudor?'

'Not that, sire. Their concern is with Arthur's health. It has been bandied about that he is a sickly lad.'

'That is a tender issue. No father ever wants to admit it, but the truth is Arthur has never been as robust as we would like. His delicate health worries me, I mean us. His brother Harry is twice as big and much more active than Arthur was at his age.'

'We thank God you have a stout second son standing at the palace door.'

'We will have none of that! It is Arthur who is Prince of Wales. He is my anointed successor and neither you nor anyone else at court should forget it.'

'I mean no challenge to him, sire. What I was thinking was that it is good that you have two fine sons who have better claims to the succession than any son of a Plantagenet.'

'The Plantagenets be damned! Their line produced kings for England for three hundred years; but their time has run out. It is the Tudors who rule now.'

'Yes, but Your Majesty has significant Plantagenet blood from your mother's side, and your sons have even more.'

'True. Yet you know as well as we that those few Plantagenets who are still around secretly snicker about the legitimacy of our ancestors. We say our royal Tudor blood is as good, even better than theirs.'

'No one would dare deny that in public, My Lord.'

'No, and for a good reason. We've given everyone who

has a claim to royal blood a clear choice. They must either support the Tudors, or lose their heads!'

'None of them are going to cause any trouble.'

'We'll keep our eye on them just the same. Meanwhile, you said you had heard that people were unhappy about the economy. What are they complaining about?'

'It's mostly about taxes. There is nothing unusual about that. People always complain about taxes regardless of whether they pay a great deal or virtually nothing.'

'Is that all?'

'Oh, there are also complaints about your system of fines.'

'So they do not appreciate Morton's fork. Well, we do! They can forget about us asking for Parliament's approval. We would never get it, so we will not bother to ask. Fair, or unfair, we like the fork, because it brings in money to fill the Treasury.'

'That is a feature they complain most about. From their comments, one could think that people are more concerned about your not spending the funds you collect than about how you collect them.'

'They want us to spend our revenues at a faster rate? Why? There is no harm in having savings on hand. Savings spell security. Money gives us power. We have no cause to splurge it on frivolous balls and banquets; nor do we want to run a royal circus as they do in France. We are a frugal monarch. That is a trait we picked up in Brittany where frugality is a virtue. Do you think any of these complaints can lead to trouble, Counsellor?'

'I see no evidence that anyone is taking them that seriously.'

'If that is so, we can sit easy on the throne.'

Morton's thoughts wandered again as he heard the phrase 'sit easy on the throne'. Yes, Henry was able to sit easy on the throne because of his complete disregard for what his subjects thought of him. In his view, he ruled by divine right and with divine approval. Never once had he acknowledged his debt to Morton for putting him on the throne. True, he had made Morton his Lord Chancellor and secured a cardinal's cap for him, but these honours could as easily have gone to a less qualified man. What the Bishop really wanted was some frank acknowledgement of gratitude for his faithful service and advice.

Does he keep me near him only to use me? Morton asked himself. I wonder how different my life might have been had I sent word to Richard about Buckingham's perfidy when I was in the Tower. I would probably be serving here as Richard's Lord Chancellor. Henry could be dead, or living somewhere as the Earl of Richmond. I would be serving a popular monarch and would be looked up to, not cursed, by the people of London and of England. But enough of 'what if'; I made my choice and there is no turning back. I may not love or even like my King but I must make the best of my situation.

'God give you comfort of that!' Morton effused as he gave his full attention back to the King. 'On that matter of your popularity, I've been giving serious thought to things we might do to remedy the present situation.'

'What suggestions might you have?'

'Whether one is popular or not usually involves an element of comparison. There is no need to change your behaviour or your policies if we can get people to focus on how much better off the realm is with you than it would be with others who could be wearing the crown.'

'You mean we should play up the fact that we have brought peace to England after years of war?'

'That and the fact that you are a good and virtuous monarch who is infinitely better for England than your predecessor.'

'How do we do that?'

'We should start with the question of what happened thirteen years ago to the two princes in the Tower. We must put an end to the idle speculation that has been gnawing away at your reputation these many years.'

'Whoa there! What do you mean gnawing away at our reputation?' Henry demanded.

Morton hesitated. Had he set a trap for himself? For months he had been assuring the King that all was well, that he need not concern himself with possible opposition or complaints. Now in an unguarded comment he had let the cat out of the bag. What should he say now? Should he hedge around the issue or tell the truth?

Henry did not wait for a reply. Instead, he bellowed, 'Give us a straight answer, my Lord Archbishop. Are you saying someone suspects us of being involved in their murder?'

'No one says anything like that in public, sire. Everyone is careful what they say in alehouses and other places where they might be overheard. My men have made examples of enough gossips with loose tongues to keep anyone with any sense from making slanderous remarks in public. We hear rumours though, rumours we cannot run down, of loose talk in private conversations.'

'Get to it, man – what are they saying about us?'

'To put it bluntly, My Lord, there are more than a few of your subjects who argue that you killed the two princes and then married their sister to cement your claim to the crown.'

'That is a lie, as you well know!' Henry snarled. 'I have never killed anyone.'

'I spoke inaccurately, Your Majesty. No one says you killed them yourself. They whisper that you had it done.'

'And what do they say of your role in the matter?'

'No one has accused me to my face of anything. I am sure though that a good number of your subjects suspect I had a hand in what was done.'

'Then these rumours have your hands as bloody as ours. That means you have as much reason as we have for ending this idle speculation. The big question is, what can we do to put an end to it?'

'The best thing we can do is something I should have suggested when you married the Princess Elizabeth. Instead of ignoring the issue, we should have announced that the two princes were dead and supplied the public with a believable explanation of how and why they were killed. We can do that now. First though, we must decide on whom we will place the blame for their murder. Richard is a logical possibility. Enough of his associates are now dead that we can safely saddle him with the blame without being crossed by any denials.'

'A brilliant idea. We should have pointed our finger at him as the murderer a dozen years ago. Do you think people will believe us if we do it now? We can say that we erred in not proclaiming the death of the two princes and ordering prayers for their souls when we first came to power. That was when we should have charged Richard with their murder. If we do it now after all these years, won't our delayed action be misinterpreted? Won't people see it as a cover-up?'

'That is a risk we must take, My Lord. There will be doubters whatever we do. The point is that we now have an opportunity to shift the suspicions people have of you on to Richard. Most of your subjects will accept your explanation if we can supply them with a plausible story. That is what we must do.'

Turning to his counsellor, Henry implored, 'Morton, you are in this just as deeply as we are, and you know perfectly well we can not stop people from talking simply by telling them that Richard did it. Isn't there something more convincing we can do that will cleanse this blot on our reign?'

'There is no simple solution to our problem, sire. We do not have the option of going back and remaking past decisions. There are several things we can do though that can weight people's judgement in our favour.'

'What do you have in mind?'

'We could start by identifying the villain who killed the two princes for Richard and get a confession from him.'

'Excellent. Do you have any likely suspects in mind?'

'Not right now. I'll give that option some thought. It certainly is a course we should not overlook. It could do more than any one thing to bring these speculations to a halt.'

'You talked of other things we could do?'

'Yes. We should take more action to clean up the circumstantial evidence and nudge it to further implicate Richard in the double murder of the princes.'

'That's a good idea, but what action?'

'I am referring to our official records here at court and the records kept by the shires and the churches. For some time now, I have had men checking them to see what they say about Richard and his reign. I have followed your lead from the first year of your reign when you had Parliament rescind that obnoxious law, Titulus Regius, had every copy of it destroyed, and ordered your subjects to forget that it ever existed. With that action, you were able to rewrite history. I have used the same technique to have several towns and shires delete favourable comments about Richard from their records.'

'If the news of that gets around, it could do our cause more harm than good.'

'That is a risk we can be more than willing to take. The truth is, erasing a sentence here or a paragraph there has not stirred up much notice. We have fined a few officials who were slow to follow our suggestions, but their complaints have had more to do with the fines than anything else. What we do in sanitising the records will have little effect on what people say now. It can have a significant effect though on what future chroniclers think and write. If they find complaints about Richard in the records and no statements of praise, they will see him as a real monster.'

'Splendid. How much more checking do you need?'

'There are still several church and shire records we have not examined. I can send out some inspectors to finish the task. That part is easy. We have a bigger problem in dealing with private records.'

'Private records? They cannot be very important.'

'They can be more important than many people think. Actually, there are two types of private records that can cause trouble. With oral records, we can not completely control what people think or what they tell others. Your policies have done much to control possible damage. People have been warned not to talk about Richard and his reign. You have also either eliminated or neutralised most of Richard's close associates. The others who knew him have died, or will be passing on within a few years.

'Written records pose a more enduring threat. We have rid England of the most obvious ones. My informants are keeping a sharp lookout for other examples. Unfortunately though, there are some private records I cannot very well touch.'

'What do you mean, you cannot touch?'

'England has some scholars, mostly priests, who have a bad habit of writing down their observations. Their manuscripts can be filed away in places where no one will see them until years hence. Fortunately, most of their writings go to clerical and university libraries. There are several manuscripts at Oxford, for example, that contain comments and passages we cannot delete without causing a scandal that will do your reign more harm than good.'

'There must be some way we can act to rid ourselves of any writings that could cause trouble.'

'There is, Your Majesty, and this brings up an option you should consider. My efforts thus far have been directed mostly at removing favourable references to Richard. As a long term policy, we should go further and generate accounts that condemn him and his reign, and point to you as England's saviour. I have already taken some first steps along this line. The trouble is that it is well known that I have been the source of the information reported. That is not good for us because my critics have already put it about that any information that comes from me must be tainted.'

'You have not told me this. Who have you been talking to and why?'

'I have given information to several people from the Continent, including that Italian fellow, Dominic Mancini, who I thought might write letters that would help your cause. I have also supplied information about various details of events in Richard's reign to some priests at Croyland, who have talked of writing an account of that period.'

'And you are suggesting that we do more talking to scribes who might write about our reign?'

'We should go farther than that, Your Majesty. We need a long term strategy to shape what writers of chronicles will tell future generations about us. We want them to see you as a great king who saved England from Richard and his henchmen. We must register our own version of what happened. If we do not plant the seed, the story we want told will never sprout and emerge as the recorded truth.'

'How shall we proceed with the planting of this crop?' asked the King.

'First, you should bring a learned scholar here from Rome or from France and commission him to write an unbiased history of your reign. While he is here, you could give him authority to requisition books and manuscripts from all the libraries and collections in England.'

'You would have him look at those accounts you were criticising a few moments ago?'

'When I said "unbiased history", I meant that it would be presented to the public as unbiased. Of course, it would be understood from the beginning that the history he writes will be favourable to you. Writing the history would give the author an excuse for having the manuscripts we want to censor. He could insist that they be brought to him here in London, or wherever he does his writing. Once he has them, I would expect him either to revise or destroy those that do not mesh with our version of what happened. He should have instructions to erase short references that are critical of you, and either lose or forget to return those books and manuscripts that are written in a way that could be damaging.'

'Good, but how will he know what manuscripts to requisition from the libraries?'

'If he is a competent researcher, he will find some by himself. I can also help by providing a list of manuscripts that I think should be revised or destroyed.'

'Can you recommend a scholar at Rome we could induce to come to England to write the history?'

'It may take some time, sire, to line up the proper man. I will make some inquiries. Letters to Rome move slowly so it may take some months before we get an answer. There is no need to hurry though. The history we have in mind is for future generations, not for us. You can take care of your present critics. What we are really looking for is someone who can cause the people who live in England a hundred years from now to look back on you with pride.'

'And not remember Henry VII and his Lord Chancellor as the men who murdered the princes in the Tower!' Henry added with an impish smile of satisfaction.

'Especially not that!' Morton agreed. 'Since we are talking about a history of your reign, it is probably just as well that we wait a few years before engaging a scholar. That way, he will have a longer reign to write about.'

'Morton, you are a deliciously devious devil for thinking up this plan. You really should be sent to the Tower; but we like your proposal. It looks like the answer to our dilemma. Still we have one concern. If we commission the history ourselves, won't readers consider it a biased account that is weighted in our favour?'

'They probably will. That is why we must supplement the history with one or more accounts written by men who will be regarded as completely independent and unbiased.'

'Are you suggesting that someone who has no ties to the court will come out of the woods and pen a chronicle that is favourable to us? It is good you are a cardinal because that may call for a miracle!'

'Miracle or no miracle, it is what we need. Our problem is how to get someone to write the account we want without realising that we are putting the idea in his head.'

'Do you know anyone who is a good writer and who has a promising future ahead of him who might do this for us?'

'Hmm... When you put the question that way, it is just possible that I have the man who fits our bill.'

'Who is he? No, don't answer that! If he is to write an independent account, it is best we never learn his name. That way he will get no conscious preferment from us. That should lessen the prospect that people will regard his work as biased.'

'That is a good precaution. I can tell you though that he is a brilliant and trustworthy young man of good family, whose talents could make him Lord Chancellor some day, or perhaps an archbishop if he chooses to take holy orders. With his outlook on life, he could even become a pope, or perhaps a saint.'

'How old is this young genius? If he is no more than a

boy, we may be taking a big chance by counting on him.

'He is much more than a boy, sire. If one divides the stages of a man's life into four seasons, the period when he grows to manhood, the years when he establishes himself, those productive years when he is established, and the older years when he lives on his laurels, I would say he is in his second season. He is mature beyond his years and has already displayed the rare abilities that will carry him through a productive career.'

'A comer in his second season. That can be a great time of life.'

'It can indeed, Your Majesty. It can be a time of trouble and tribulation, but also a time most of us look back on with fond memories.'

'Might it be a time of trouble for our young saint?'

'Yes, even for the likes of him. It is a time for important decisions, decisions that can make or break a man.'

'As it made us a king,' Henry mused. 'Yes, we like the idea. A saint in his second season to serve our cause. God is sending us a saint to cleanse our dirty linen. A saint, whose name I shall not know, in his second season. Saint —'s second season. I like that.'

Chapter Nine

Morton had seldom felt as alive or as proud of himself as he did when he left the palace that day.

He had always been a man of action, and congratulated himself on his accomplishments when he got the King or anyone else to accept his recommendations. What he had done today was particularly pleasing. Henry had accepted and endorsed his plan for rewriting the history of Richard's reign. Congratulations were in order, if they ever were, for his proposed strategy.

He marvelled at his success. Henry was no fool. He was usually cautious and had a calculating complex that usually caused him to postpone judgement on new proposals until he had time to weigh the arguments for and against them in his mind. He could be obstinate and was often a hard man to please. Today though, he had seemed anxious to pursue Morton's proposal for sanitising the records and planting new evidence that would put the blame on Richard for the death of the two princes.

From his boyhood on, Morton had clearly recognised the barriers that would keep him from becoming a conquering warrior or a king. But he had been quick to sense that the son of a commoner like him might rise to the top through proper use of his wits. He had succeeded in achieving his ambitions where most others had failed. His early hope of rising to a position of influence and power as Prince Edward's mentor had collapsed with Edward's death. His machinations at the court of Edward IV brought advancement but his hopes were again dashed by the chaotic twists of fate that brought Edward's younger brother to the throne. His conniving with the Duke of Buckingham had freed him from the Tower but brought him near disaster. And then he had turned to Henry Tudor.

He had not been one of Henry's early supporters. He could name several noblemen who came out for Henry long before he did, and he knew he had not turned to him because he was a great warrior or leader. A half smile came to his face as a fleeting memory passed through his mind of the account one of Henry's bodyguards at Bosworth Field had told of Henry cowering safely behind the shields of his guards as Richard led that fateful charge against him and hurled out his chivalrous challenge for hand-to-hand combat with the princeling who would claim his crown. Lord Stanley had saved Henry's life that day and won the crown for him when he betrayed his King by sending his personal army in to ward off Richard's charge.

No, Henry was not a military hero; and he had not been attracted to him by any other qualities he might have had as a leader. He had chosen to support him because Henry was the last remaining prince of Lancastrian blood who seemed capable of claiming the crown.

Bishop Morton had served his new King well. He had played a crucial role in bringing Buckingham's supporters into Henry's camp. He had supplied vital information to Henry while he was a virtual prisoner at the court of Duke Francis of Brittany. He had engineered Henry's escape from Brittany to France and his later invasion of England.

He had counselled Henry after his accession to the throne. As Lord Chancellor, he had devised the revenue collection device, popularly known as Morton's fork, which had bypassed Parliament and was helping to fill the King's coffers. Yes, Morton was the real power behind the throne. He was the strategist and planner who had made things happen for Henry. He had devised the move to concentrate more power in the King's hands. It was his cunning guidance that was giving the Tudors an increasingly firm hold on the throne.

Morton was an old man with a ponderous figure and a left leg that dragged slightly when he walked. Today though, there was a spring in his stride. He was walking on air. He had sold the King on the idea of having Thomas write an account of the fall of Richard III. The idea had come to him like a flash while he was talking to the King. God had certainly favoured him at that moment. It was a brilliant stratagem and Thomas was well qualified to carry it out. Thomas More would write an account that would rewrite history forever and would for all time shape what future generations would think of him and Henry VII.

New projects, new ventures that could affect the course of what people think and do, had always excited and challenged the Bishop. He had no reason to be unhappy with the smooth routine of his life as a cardinal and Lord Chancellor; but here was a new project, an important bit of secret intrigue that would test his wits and provide a refreshing outlet for his imagination and ingenuity.

Morton had no fear of failure as he walked back to his quarters. He was already relishing the joy and satisfaction of having accomplished another political coup. Young Thomas would undertake the new assignment and he had no doubts as to More's ability to supply the desired account. Of course, they would not publish it right away. Mediocre or excellent, the chronicle would soon be there to fill a void in the historical records; and best of all, it would appear as the work of an unbiased scholar.

A sudden realisation jolted him to reality, as he thought, If the chronicle is to appear as unbiased and not be associated with me, how am I to get Thomas to do the necessary writing? Even if he should come up with the idea of writing it, how and where will he get the factual details we want included in his account? Putting ideas into the King's head is a simple matter. Henry is inclined to adopt any good suggestion he hears as a product of his own thought. But Thomas has a keen mind and is not easily fooled. If I ask him to write the history, he will quickly see that I have an ulterior motive. The same will be true if one of my associates asks him. It will be necessary to somehow spark his interest, and make him think it is his own idea to come to me for the information I want him to use.

The Archbishop returned to his study in the Chancery where he poured himself some wine, sat down in one of his big chairs, and tried to think of a workable answer to his problem. But as hard as he tried, no ideas came to his mind. The exhilaration he had felt earlier had seemingly drained dry his normal flow of inspiration. The harder he tried to concentrate on the issue, the more he felt he was facing a blank wall. Why couldn't he think straight? He was tired and knew he should rest. But this was not a matter he could put aside for a day or a week of reflection. He needed to work out a strategy now.

After what seemed like hours spent wrestling with his own mind, Morton concluded that what he really needed was the counsel of someone else. Their advice might not be what he wanted, but the mere act of talking to someone might clear his mind and redirect his thinking along productive channels. Who could he talk to? Father Gregory was his long-time confidant and was easily available. But much as he liked and trusted Greg, he had always been careful to hide some aspects of his activities from him. It was important that Gregory hold him in high regard. The plan he had in mind was not something he wanted Greg to know about.

After some reflection, he realised there was no one except the King whom he could take into his confidence. He had one option though. He could talk to Greg about some other matter. That might free his mind for concentration on this puzzle. So it was that he pulled the cord that rang a bell in Father Gregory's quarters.

Gregory rushed to Morton's study and on entering asked if something was wrong.

The Bishop assured him he was all right. 'I should apologise,' he said, 'for calling you this way. I ring the bell so seldom you might easily have thought I was suffering from some spell. The truth is, I just need to talk to someone for a while.'

Morton poured Gregory some wine and then proceeded to tell him that the King wanted them to step up their programme for checking official records throughout the country. 'He wants us to delete any and all favourable references to Richard III and his short reign. He also wants a list of those manuscripts held in Duke Humphrey's library and any other libraries that we know contain laudatory observations or comments concerning Richard, or that are critical of Henry Tudor.'

'Examining all those records calls for considerable work,' Gregory observed. 'We have already done a lot of checking here and there, but I doubt we have inspected even half of the records that may contain references to our former King. How much time has King Henry given us?'

'There is no specific timetable. To do the job right, we need to send one or two men to the field to examine shire and church records and do the necessary erasing and expurgation.'

'That will call for adding people to our staff, Your Eminence. Might I suggest that we ask Brother Bernard to serve as one of the inspectors?'

'Brother Bernard? Yes, he has the qualifications we need and we have almost promised him a calling on our staff. As I recall, he wants to work here at the Chancery. If he is willing to start by spending a few months making inspections out in the shires, we can make room for him here later.'

With this item of business covered, Morton asked a few questions about matters pending at the Chancery. Gregory gave him a progress report and added, 'I asked Thomas More to prepare a report on that Southampton affair. It is amazing how he pulled all those messy details together into a logical account. That lad is a genius when it comes to analysing issues and writing up his findings.'

'So you consider him a good writer?'

'He is one of the best we've seen,' Greg replied.

The Archbishop let this response pass without comment. After a few more minutes of general conversation, Gregory sensed some impatience on Morton's part to be alone. He excused himself, and Morton sank back in his chair and turned his thinking again to the question of how he might get Thomas to write the desired history.

This time his mind was responsive to his will. Several possible scenarios occurred to him as he thought about ways to get Thomas to see the project as his own idea. Could he get one of Thomas's associates, an instructor at Lincoln's Inn for example, to suggest the need for the history? No, that approach could be traced to him and could misfire if Thomas sought the information he needed in the wrong places.

Might it be practical to work on Thomas through his father or another member of his family? No, that would not work. Greg had said that Thomas had some interest in taking holy orders. Could he get a priest or friar to direct Thomas's thinking? No, that too might be risky. Close association with a cleric could capture his life for God and leave Morton with no one to write the necessary chronicle.

The evening passed rapidly as Morton considered one possible strategy after another and rejected each one for its deficiencies. His candles were burning low when he finally concluded to himself, This is going to be a bigger and much slower process than I had at first expected. To do this right, I must issue a paper trail. I will ask Thomas to come to read to me on a regular basis and plant some comments in his reading materials that will hopefully stir his curiosity.

With luck he will take the bait and turn to me with questions asking for information and maybe even volunteer an interest in writing the report. Before going further though, I must write my own account of what happened so I can keep the details of my story consistent. Other details can be added later if necessary. With a man as sharp as Thomas More it is essential that I don't foul things up by having contradictions in the story I tell him.

Father Gregory was asked the next day to arrange for Thomas to spend one or two hours a day with Morton on those days when he had uncommitted time. Thomas was to work as his reader.

'My eyes are not as strong as they used to be,' Morton explained. 'A good reader with a pleasant speaking voice such as Thomas has can do much to take a burden off my mind.'

'I would gladly do the reading for you, Your Grace,' Gregory said, but Morton assured him that he already had enough work to do.

'And besides, Thomas has a good voice and is an excellent reader as I recall. Anyway the experience will do him good if he is to become a practising barrister.'

Thomas started his new assignment the next day. His hours with the Archbishop continued at various times as Morton's schedule permitted. With each additional visit, Thomas felt closer to the old gentleman and more free to raise questions with him about his experiences and his attitudes.

Morton started his readings with a pamphlet that had

come from Rome. On the days that followed, Thomas read letters and manuscripts from an ever changing pile of documents that cluttered Morton's desk. With each hour in Morton's presence, Thomas was more captivated by his charm and wit. Any doubts he might have had about the great man's honesty and integrity were dispelled. He became Morton's whole-hearted servant, his intellectual slave.

Ten days passed before he read a letter from a foreign visitor who observed that far too little had been reported about Richard III and his reign, and who recorded his wish that someone in England would write a historical account of the reign so that he and others might have a better picture of what had happened.

A week later, he read a passage in a manuscript destined for the library Oxford that described Richard as an ugly, malformed schemer who had the most despicable record of all England's kings. The comment bothered him, so he asked the Archbishop, 'Could this be true? People do not talk much about King Richard but the little I have heard has always been respectful.'

'Alas, I would prefer not to go into any details now; but the comment does contain a germ of truth.'

The parade of damaging references to Richard continued, sometimes one or two a week, a few weeks none at all. By the early months of 1499, Bishop Morton was beginning to feel impatient. A week later Thomas read a letter supposedly written by Bishop Whitmore, recently deceased, who had been an administrative aide to Thomas Rotherham, the late Archbishop of York, who had served as Lord Chancellor when Richard became Lord Protector.

Bishop Whitmore complained about the confused and incomplete nature of the historical accounts he had seen of Richard's reign. He added, 'I have considered taking on the task of preparing a truthful account even though I am only partly familiar with the details of what took place. I would still undertake this work were my hands not so feeble and my days numbered. Forsooth, the account that's needed should come from Bishop Morton. He more than anyone knows what happened. Unfortunately, he is far too busy for such a chore.'

'I'll say "Amen" to that!' Morton observed when Thomas read the last comment.

'It is too bad that you don't have time for it,' Thomas responded. 'Perhaps you could tell some of us what you know and we could draft the report for you.'

'Thank you for your offer, Thomas. I seriously doubt though that many people in England would take a report prepared by or for me very seriously. My association with Henry Tudor makes anything I say or write about Richard suspect.'

'I do not agree,' Thomas persisted. 'You are the most honourable source of information on this matter in all England. You owe it to the country to report what you saw and what you know.'

'No,' Morton replied. 'I cannot take on this responsibility and at my age it would be foolish for me even to consider doing so.'

'Would you permit me to do it then?' Thomas asked.

'Thomas, you are a good man. You have an abundance of ability and I am sure you can do a credible job. However, I doubt that you realise what you would be getting yourself into.'

'With your permission and blessing I would like to do it, if you could spare the time to tell me what happened.'

Morton clenched his fist and gritted his teeth as he strained not to show the thrill of triumph that surged through him. He felt like a cat who had finally caught a bird that had flown around him for weeks just out of his covetous reach. Of course, he would give Thomas the requested permission, but he must not appear too anxious. He solemnly stroked his chin, gazed at his young companion, and said, 'Let me think about it for a day or two. Maybe we can work something out.'

When Thomas came in to read for him the next morning, he extended his usual cheery greeting and said, 'I've been thinking of your proposal, Thomas, and have decided to give you my permission to write the history of Richard III. I'll also give you my full co-operation if you will agree to a few simple conditions.'

'What are the conditions?'

'First, you must agree to serve as sole author of your account. No credit should be given to me. I do not want your reputation to suffer because of your association with me. As an added requirement, I would stipulate that while you might prepare your chronicle during the next few months or years, you will not seek its publication until after King Henry and I have passed on. This condition is necessary to protect the names and reputations of some people who are still living.'

Chapter Ten

The crowd of onlookers who filled the commons had been restless and at times rowdy. But the audience became more attentive and more apprehensive as the play approached its predictable climax. For almost two hours, actors had depicted a scene of conflict and turmoil as the forces of evil had contended with those of righteousness to capture the souls of the town's residents.

Merbo, a small, spidery, dark-visaged man attired in black, had led Satan's forces and come perilously close to triumph. Now in the closing moments of the morality pageant, his doom was sealed. The Archangel Michael stood with a host of singing angels on a raised platform on the left as a tall blond warrior and a band of followers clad in white forced Merbo and his demons to retreat into the yawning jaws that represented the gates of the underworld.

'Get thee back to hell!' the blond champion of the Christian force bellowed, in what was supposed to be the final statement in London's annual pageant. At this moment, almost as if on cue, the storm which had been threatening throughout the performance broke forth. Like a sign from heaven, a bolt of lightning crossed the sky behind the temporary stage. It was followed by a rumbling roar of thunder, a rise in wind velocity, and a downpour of rain that soaked everyone on the crowded field.

Most of the people in the crowd covered themselves as best they could. The hero of the play, sensing an opportunity to add to his role, dropped to his knees, stretched his arms upward toward the heavens, and shouted, 'We thank thee God for this sign of thy approval and thy eternal grace!'

Thomas More stood spellbound throughout the final scene. To him, the sign from heaven was no accident of weather. It was proof of divine intervention. As he and his brother John left the open field where the pageant had been staged, he could not restrain his praise for the glorious performance.

John was less impressed. 'Most of it was pretty boring,' he complained. 'They kept saying things over and over. I liked it better last year when they had some humour in it and when the jugglers performed.'

Thomas was taken back by John's appraisal. He chose not to argue with him. He knew from long experience that they had honest differences of opinion. For years they had responded differently on matters of this nature. John was as a good and devout a Christian as he was. He went to mass and confession and accepted all of the Catholic doctrines, but John was seldom moved by the spirit of occasions such as this. Sermons and moments of grandeur such as the final scene of the pageant, which thrilled Thomas and touched to the inner core of his being, had no visible effect on John.

Thomas was often troubled by what he regarded as a basic conflict between the popular concept of enjoying a happy fun-filled life and being a good Christian. Not so with John. John saw no reason why he should not criticise a tedious play, a boring sermon, or Church practices that brought him discomfort. With Thomas it was different. Any practice or doctrine that was sanctioned by the Church was sacrosanct. He could accept the fact that others took less rigorous positions than his own; but as for him, it was necessary that he obey – the salvation of his soul was at stake.

The night that followed was a long and disturbing one

for Thomas. He had difficulty in getting to sleep and was restless during those periods when he did doze off. A haunting dream followed him through the night. A host of evil demons headed by Merbo, the vile monster from the pageant, pursued him persistently. Time after time, he awakened just as Merbo was ready to seize him, and every time he broke into a cold sweat as he fought off the haunting sensation of the dream and tried desperately to clear his mind and get back to sleep.

There was no doubt in his mind that this vile creature had been sent by Satan to pursue him, to capture his soul. Somehow the blond warrior and the Archangel Michael never came to his rescue. Merbo became a more foreboding and more sinister character as the night went on. He was stooped and ugly, his long grasping arms had claws where fingers should be, and horns sprouted and grew on his head.

Thomas was more than happy to get up when the hour of dawn approached. He was tired and unrefreshed, and memories of his recurring nightmare filled him with chill and repression. The only good thing about the night was that for the first time in weeks he woke up without that stirring in his loins. He dressed, attended to his morning chores, and then read a while to steady his nerves before walking to the Chancery.

Away from his father's house, he saw that there was little in the outside environment to commend the day. London was experiencing another of its more dismal days. The skies were dark and foreboding. The morning fog smelled strongly of smoke. Nor did he find anything to cheer him at the Chancery. The day was so dark he had to work by the light of a candle, a candle that sputtered and glowed with uneven light. Even his work, which he usually greeted with enthusiasm, seemed tedious as he spent the day copying dull and pointless reports.

It was a happy interruption for Thomas when Bishop Morton finally called for him late in the afternoon to come to his study. Here at last, he might find something more cheerful, more edifying to read or discuss. He was disappointed at first though, when the Chancellor asked that he read an epistle he had recently received from Rome.

It was a discourse concerning the nature of man. All mankind is condemned by original sin. Everyone is inclined to accept temptations of the flesh. Salvation can be attained only if one follows a narrow winding path to glory, a path frequented by forces of evil that lurk around every bend with temptations that only those with pure hearts and strong wills can withstand. It is not enough to reject temptations known to be evil, one must also not be deluded by impostors who are not what they seem to be.

Once Thomas finished the reading, Bishop Morton said, 'I think this is a good time to tell you about Richard's character. The good brother writes that we should eschew those people who pretend they are something they are not. In my whole life, I have never known anyone who fitted that description more than Richard III. He was a scoundrel and villain at heart. He compounded his wretchedness by pretending to be humble and fair, when his real purpose was to gain power and wealth.'

'Did you know him personally?' Thomas asked.

'I probably knew him as well as anyone did,' Morton replied. 'He spent little time at court during the ten years I served his brother, Edward IV. I had ample opportunity though to take his measure on those few occasions when he was there. From early on I had as much reason to love him as any prince of royal blood. Yet unlike some others at court, I recognised early that he could be a threat to England's welfare.'

'Why did he stay away from his brother's court?'

'Edward entrusted him with command of his army. I

must admit that he was a successful and enterprising general. Though not much more than a boy, he commanded the right wing of Edward's army that turned Warwick's flank at the great battle of Barnet. Also, unlike many commanders, he was a foolhardy warrior who fought with his men in the forefront of every battle. After Edward took the throne, he put down several uprisings that could have disrupted what peace we had. Between uprisings, he could have been popular living here in London, but he chose to isolate himself at one of his castles in Yorkshire.'

'But why? Why did he avoid people?'

'Richard was not a handsome man. To be truthful, he had a repulsive appearance. His three older brothers were all tall and good-looking with blue eyes, fair complexions, and golden curls. Richard was almost the opposite. He was short with black hair and a swarthy countenance. He was gruff and wore a perpetual scowl on his face. More than that, he was deformed by nature. He walked with a limp; he had a withered left arm; his back was hunched and twisted; and he carried one of his shoulders much higher than the other as though his left arm and shoulder were pulled down by some hanging weight.

'From his outward appearance, Richard was a human monster. He can not be blamed for all of that. I have learned from reliable sources that he was born that way. At the time of his birth, his body was turned and refused to leave his mother's womb. A surgeon had to use a knife to open her womb. Even then he came into this world feet first much as did the emperor Nero. His body was covered with black hair and he already had teeth.

'The attendants at his birth saw that Lady Cicely had given birth to a monster, not a normal baby boy. It is reported as truth that some of them argued that his body should have been exposed to the elements and allowed to die as it would have been in ancient Greece. It was a kindly vicar who was there to baptise him that insisted he be allowed to live.'

'Was he still that hideous, that despicable, when he became a man?' Thomas asked.

'He was sickly and a weakling as a child. But his family indulged him and allowed him to have a normal boyhood. Richard was bright – much smarter than his brother George who became Duke of Clarence. He recognised early in life that most people would find his appearance repulsive and that he could not rise to power on the basis of his looks. To make up for his deficiency, he developed a carefully planned strategy to make people see him as something other than what he was.

He told his brother Edward he was his staunchest supporter and that he would do everything in his power to protect and defend the claim of Edward's son to the crown, when his real intention was to take the throne for himself. He pretended to be meek and humble and to oppose bribery, when really he was using these false virtues to advance his ambition of acquiring wealth and power for himself.'

'Tell me more about the way in which he pretended to condemn things he really supported?'

'Yes, indeed I will,' Morton responded. 'He condemned the gaiety of Edward's royal court as being overly frivolous, while he was secretly enjoying what it had to offer. He criticised the arrogance and greed of the Woodvilles, but did nothing while Edward was alive to stop it. Then there was that time when he made a cheap bid for public favour when Edward was negotiating a treaty with France by accusing the bishops who were advising the King of accepting bribes from King Louis.

'There were other examples too. He pretended to be pleading for the life of his brother George while he was secretly urging the king to have him executed. He tried to blacken the reputation of Queen Elizabeth by accusing her of using sorcery to wither his left arm. He acted as if he was a saint administering God's laws when he ordered Jane Shore to march half naked like a common whore through the streets of London.'

'Jane Shore? Who was she?'

'She was one of Edward's favourite mistresses. At the time of his death, she was cheating on him by sleeping with the Queen's eldest son, Dorset, who was the King's stepson. Lord Hastings, who had been Edward's best friend, also had his eye on her and claimed her as his mistress after Edward died. She was involved with Hastings and the Woodvilles in a conspiracy that led to Hastings's execution. Richard condemned her to walk through the streets of London clad only in her petticoat. Wise men have told me though that she was punished not for her part in the conspiracy but rather because Richard wanted her for himself and she resisted his advances.'

'Was Edward sexually depraved too?'

'There was no question about it. It was common knowledge at court that the King was a moral debauchee. He was not yet nineteen when he became King, but already had several mistresses and some bastards. From then on, no man at court who had a pretty wife or daughter felt sure of protecting their virtue when Edward was around. The list of his conquests was legion. Early in his reign he promised marriage to Elizabeth Lucy to get her into bed with him and then abandoned her. He made the same offer to Elizabeth Woodville but she insisted on a wedding ceremony before witnesses before she yielded to his carnal appetite.'

'Did Mistress Lucy make any trouble for him?'

'She made a child for him, but she voiced no claim against the King himself. After Edward's death, Lady Cicely, Richard's mother, charged that Edward had promised himself in marriage to Elizabeth Lucy. If true, that promise would have made his later children illegitimate. That was a very serious accusation. The matter was referred to a Bishop's court. Mistress Lucy was still at court and she swore that no such promise was ever given. That should have ended the matter; but Richard used the charge to persuade Parliament to question the legitimacy of the children Edward had with Elizabeth Woodville.'

'That was an evil and unbrotherly thing to do.'

'Most of us thought that way. It was a convenient charge for him though because it fitted in with his strategy for setting his two nephews aside and claiming the crown for himself. The thing about his plan that puzzles me most, is why Lady Cicely was willing to question the legitimacy of her own grandchildren.'

'Was Richard as morally decadent as his brother?'

'They were cut from the same cloth. He had the same sexual cravings as Edward but he did a better job than Edward in hiding them from public view. He lived a wild licentious life and had a son born to one of his women in his youth. That did not stop him when he became of marriageable age from casting a covetous eye on Anne, the youngest daughter of the Earl of Warwick. His brother George opposed the match because he was married to her sister Isabel and wanted the Warwick estates for himself.

'What did Richard do? He thumbed his nose at our customary conventions. When George hid her away in one of his castles to protect her, he sought her out, kidnapped her, raped her, and forced her into marriage. After he was King and she had given him a son, he abandoned her.

'Poor Anne, she was a delicate child and he used her only to satisfy his lust. She was in London that first Christmas after their coronation. He ignored her at the court festivities while he fixed his lecherous eye on the Princess Elizabeth, who was his niece and is now our Queen. Already, he was planning to get rid of Anne so that he might marry his niece. Oh, he denied ever considering the possibility of an incestuous marriage; but it was easy to see that he was protesting the very act he was planning. Poor Anne died of a broken heart a few months after that. It is for truth reported that he had her poisoned to get rid of her.'

'What happened to their son?' Thomas inquired.

'Are you asking about Richard and Anne's son, little Prince Edward?'

'Another Edward!' Thomas interjected. 'That makes three of them. Henry VI, Edward IV, and Richard III, three kings in a row had eldest sons named Edward and every one of them died before they could be crowned.'

'Don't limit your count to just those three. Edward III eldest son, the one we call the Black Prince, was also named Edward, as was his eldest son who died in infancy thus opening the way for his brother to become Richard II. Edward has not been a lucky name to give a first born prince during this century. Our present King wanted to name his first son Edward too, but I advised against it.'

'Back about King Richard. He must have been a real monster to have treated his wife that way.'

'Monster indeed,' Morton agreed. 'And what I've told you is only part of it. He was a cold-blooded murderer too. I have on credible information learned that it was Richard who ordered that Prince Edward, the Prince of Wales, be killed after he was captured at the Battle of Tewkesbury. After murdering the prince, he hastened to London and had himself let into the Tower where Henry VI was imprisoned, and strangled that poor old man.'

'How horrible,' Thomas shuddered at the thought.

'I must tell you more of his hypocrisy and false humility. Near the end of Edward's reign, he made two charges that no man of high moral virtue would ever make. Not only did he claim that his brother Edward had married Elizabeth

Lucy to get her into bed, which meant that his children by Elizabeth Woodville were bastards and thus not eligible to succeed to the crown. On another occasion he also charged that his mother had committed adultery, that all of his older brothers and sisters were illegitimate, and that he was the only true son of Richard, the old Duke of York.'

'What a terrible charge for any child to make against his mother.'

'Yes, Richard was a vile creature. His actions were despicable enough, but it was his false humility, hypocritical morality, and untrustworthy nature that made him the worst of kings.'

'How can a just God have allowed it?' Thomas asked.

'That is not a question I can answer,' Morton replied in a solemn tone. 'We mortals do what God wills. What we do here is part of a divine plan, only a small part of which any of us can see. All I can tell you is that God's plan, strange as it was, was at work in Richard. It may well be that He was using Richard's despicable behaviour as an example of what we should eschew.'

Thomas left the Archbishop's study with a troubled mind. He knew he faced an unpleasant task in preparing notes for his private files that would record the details Morton had told him. What troubled him most though was an uneasy feeling that he had made a mistake when he committed himself to prepare a chronicle of Richard's reign. It was not that he doubted his ability to write the history. He just was not happy with the subject matter. Richard had been a vile creature and his reign was a disaster. He would be much happier writing about a more loveable and praiseworthy monarch.

As he stepped out into the night, he felt the chill and continuing damp smog of the day. He walked to his father's house in St Giles Cripplegate parish by a longer and more twisted route than he usually followed. Walking down a strange alley through a district outside the city walls, he was surprised to encounter a man with a hunched back who was wrapped in a dark cloak and wore a hood that covered all but the shadow of a face.

The figure asked some unintelligible question, then reached out to touch him, and suddenly vented a string of filthy curses when Thomas dodged to avoid him. Was the dark figure dangerous or merely a harmless drunk? A vision of Merbo sneaking through the dark streets to snare his soul filled his mind. His normal logical thinking gave way to panic. Thomas More, a budding barrister and assistant to the Archbishop, thought only of escape from this apparition of evil as he ran all the remaining distance to his father's house.

Chapter Eleven

John More was sitting in the family kitchen munching on a roll and drinking his morning ale when Thomas asked, 'Was Richard III a popular king?'

The question surprised him because he could not remember when his son had last asked a question of that nature. After a moment of reflection, he answered, 'Yes, I would say so, as popular at least as any king we have had in my lifetime. Every king I remember has been more popular at some times than at others. We Londoners were pretty satisfied with Richard when he first took power, because he took action to put an end to the shenanigans the Woodvilles kept pulling. His short reign was over though before we had much chance to turn against him.'

'Was there any particular reason why the people liked him?'

'He was liked as much as anything because he was King Edward's brother and York's policies were popular here. Richard was also well received because he was a great warrior and was known to favour some reforms that would have helped the merchants and the common people.'

'Was there some reason why we backed York rather than Lancaster?'

'Not everyone did. Out in the country, people almost always support whoever their baron or earl supports. It is different here in London where we have no liege lords to tell us what to think. We go our own way, and with as many citizens as London has, we often divide our support between contending parties.

'The House of York had the support of most of the people here for a long time because the old Duke of York and his sons favoured good trade relations with the Dutch and Flemish ports and the merchants of Burgundy, while the Lancastrians were forever doing things that disrupted trade. Most of the common people went along with the merchants, because the Duke's policies seemed to provide us with more work and better incomes. The princes of the House of York were also popular because they looked like kings and had glamorous reputations as warriors. There was something about them when they rode through the streets that made you feel proud you were an Englishman.

'Henry VI, by contrast, was a poor excuse for a King. He looked more like a friar in last year's robe than a prince, and he let his Queen and her advisors run roughshod over our best interests. Queen Margaret was particularly disliked because she managed to lose most of the large estates the royal family held in France without getting anything for England in return.'

'Did Richard do anything to increase trade?'

'To tell the truth, he did little that affected trade one way or the other. He continued with his brother's policies. He might have done more had he been King longer. As things worked out, he wasn't King long enough for most of us to get a real feeling as to his worth. His coronation was a really grand affair and all London rejoiced. After that we saw little of him, because he spent most of his time on progresses throughout the kingdom.'

'What about you? Did you approve of him?'

'My feeling for King Richard was carried over from the respect your grandfather and I had for Edward IV. It was during his reign and with the approval of his government that I was able to rise from being a baker's son to become a successful lawyer. The single thing I liked most about

Richard was the concern he showed for revising our judicial code. In his short reign, he decreed some long-needed reforms. He probably would have done more had he had more time.'

'What sort of character was he? Did you ever see him?'

'I never met him and have no personal knowledge of his character. Most of what I heard about him while he was alive was good. One hears more and more critical comments and downright vicious accusations now he is dead and not able to defend himself. So far as seeing him goes, I probably saw him a half-dozen times and then always on horseback and at a distance.

'He looked like any average English rider. He had a plain face, no beard, and dark hair. I recall nothing distinctive about him other than that he was content to appear in public in simple clothes when he was not wearing his light armour. Except for when he came to London with Prince Edward, he was almost always accompanied by several other horsemen who were dressed very much as he was. When I saw them, I was often at a loss to know which one was Richard.'

'Did you ever have any reason to question your favourable opinion of him?'

'It is odd you should ask that question. There was one time when I wondered what his objectives were. While King Edward was alive we had a neighbour who worked for Richard, who was the Duke of Gloucester then. One night a man from the palace came to his house with a report that the King had died.

'John Potter was shocked by the news and said, "By my faith, friend, will my master the Duke now be King?"

'At the time, I thought the Duke might be party to some conspiracy. On second thought though I realised that John spoke without thinking. There was nothing going on that I heard of that in any way suggested a conspiracy. When

Richard came to London a few weeks later, he had young Prince Edward riding at his side and he was treating him with all the respect due a king.

'I tried to keep an open mind about the succession later when the prince was set aside and Parliament opened the way for Richard to become King. I had to admit that England had no need for another boy king, especially if he was to be guided by the Woodvilles. Yet, my sympathies were with Prince Edward because I was a father who felt strongly that a man should be succeeded whenever possible by his son.'

'Do you have any other memories about Richard?'

'You have me feeling as if I were a witness in a court case, son. I enjoy talking to you like this; but is there some reason for these questions?'

'Yes and no,' Thomas answered. 'Bishop Morton said some things about King Richard yesterday, and I wondered if you had some first-hand impressions of him.'

'Bishop Morton talked about Richard! If you want to know anything about Richard III, the Archbishop is your most reliable source. He knew the King while he was still Duke of Gloucester, and later when he was Lord Protector. I doubt there is anyone now living who knew Richard better.'

This endorsement of Morton's qualifications checked with the comment from Bishop Whitmore he had read in Morton's study a few weeks back. It was all the confirmation Thomas needed to realise his good fortune in being able to sit at the edge of history as he talked to Morton. Nothing his father said in any way contradicted the Bishop's assessment of Richard's character. Quite the opposite, it illustrated Richard's duplicity and his remarkable ability to delude others about the true nature of his character.

During the weeks that followed, as winter waned and

spring burst forth, Thomas spent many hours closeted with the Bishop. Morton enjoyed having Thomas read to him and when the occasion seemed appropriate would take time out to spin more of his account of Richard's wrongdoings. He was careful not to tell Thomas too much in any one session. He wanted him to digest the meat from his story slowly and have ample time to prepare notes on each segment of the larger picture before he saw it in full view.

Thus it was that having once described Richard's character, he went on to present a picture of conditions at Edward IV's court. Edward had started as a jovial, good-natured King who wanted to please his subjects and do right. The Church had been victimised by unjust criticism and Edward acted to protect the rights of the clergy. Aside from that he showed little interest in and virtually no talent for administration.

Fortunately, he had been able to lean heavily on a group of competent clerical advisors that included Rotherham, who was Archbishop of York and Lord Chancellor; Russell, the Bishop of London and Lord Keeper of the Privy Seal; and John Morton, the Bishop of Ely. Less fortunately, Edward also accepted advice and gave a free hand to the Woodvilles, all of them members of the Queen's family and all of them intent on lining their purses while they enjoyed wealth and power.

As the twenty-one years of Edward's reign passed, he devoted more and more of his time to the pursuit of pleasure. He was a womaniser to the end; he ate and drank far more than any normal man should until he became a mass of blubber and died when he was only forty. Richard was paying one of his rare visits to the court when Edward died. He fawned over his dying brother and professed his love for the King's family. It was not until after the two brothers talked together in private that Edward called in his executors and made some final changes to his will.

Much to the dismay of the Queen's family and his advisors on the Council, the codicil to Edward's will designated Richard as Lord Protector to rule during the minority of Prince Edward. Everyone had assumed that the Queen would be named as regent to serve during her son's minority. The Woodvilles were furious and argued that Richard's designation was a mistake not truly intended by the late King.

Richard stood by with a smirk on his face as he watched their confusion. Oddly enough, he did nothing to take over as Lord Protector. Instead, he stood aside while the royal Council issued an order for bringing Edward from Ludlow castle, the fortress in western England where he was being educated, to London where he could be promptly crowned as King.

Richard realised that an early coronation would put an end to his Protectorship. He had no intention of allowing that to happen. Already he was scheming to seize the crown and to do so he knew he must have Prince Edward under his control. He let Thomas Grey, the Marquis of Dorset, who was the Queen's son, take charge of the transitional arrangements. 4th May, a date only three weeks away, was set for the coronation, and word was sent to Lord Rivers, the Queen's brother, to bring the Prince to London by that date. The only stipulation Richard made was that Lord Rivers should limit the size of the party accompanying the Prince to no more than two thousand men.

Richard and the Duke of Buckingham then slipped out of London and gathered two armies which met at Northampton where they intercepted Rivers and Prince Edward who were on their way to London. When they met there, they treated the Prince's party with respect. But after supping with them, Richard sent Edward to his quarters and had Lord Rivers, Sir Richard Grey, who was the Queen's second son by her first marriage, and some of their associates arrested, charged with treason, and executed without trial. From there Richard marched on with the young Prince to London.

When Queen Elizabeth heard of Richard's success, and of the murder of her brother and her son, she gathered all the goods she could from the palace and fled with the young Duke of York, Prince Edward's brother, and his sisters to Westminster Abbey where she asked for asylum. Meanwhile, Dorset and the others among the Woodvilles seized as much as they could from the Treasury and fled from London.

Richard arrived in the capital as Lord Protector of the realm. Those who saw him could easily have thought that nothing had happened. He acted as though everything was running smoothly when the situation could not have been more hectic. With the Woodvilles gone, the Treasury was empty and no one seemed to be in control. Richard could have looked to the bishops in the royal Council for sound advice. Instead, he upset the earlier balance by leaning heavily on Buckingham for advice.

That was a misguided decision. Buckingham was not Richard's true friend. The honours that were heaped on him only went to his head. Far from showing his gratitude with faithful service, that vain and ambitious Duke soon saw his new found favour as a path to personal power.

Requests were sent to the Queen to surrender Prince Edward's younger brother so they could be lodged together at the Tower. The Queen refused to give him up because she feared Richard's motives and knew that Prince Edward would be safe only as long as his brother enjoyed the sanctuary of the Church.

Parliament was called into session to establish several laws favoured by Richard. About this time, the old charge that King Edward had married Elizabeth Lucy before getting her with child was revived. The King's brother

George, the Duke of Clarence, had used it earlier in an effort to gain the crown. It had been laughed at during Edward's lifetime and it was laughable now. This time though, a vicar preached a sermon in London in which he accused Edward of bigamy. Buckingham used his eloquence to rehash this argument at several public gatherings and thereby discredited the assumption that Prince Edward was Edward IV's legitimate heir.

Matters came to a head in early June. The Queen finally gave in to Richard's demand for the release of the Duke of York.

'I well recall,' Morton said, 'Elizabeth's tearful farewell to her son. He was a stout handsome lad, and brave. Elizabeth's heart was breaking because she knew full well she might never see him again.

'I was there against my will. I protested against the pressure the Lord Protector put on her and on the priests at the Abbey, because he was openly violating our accepted right of sanctuary. Yet while everyone in the Queen's party was sad and tearful, and a band of workmen were busy boxing up the Queen's clothing and furniture for her return to the palace, Richard stood watching the pathetic scene with no more concern than if he had been watching someone rowing on the Thames. He even turned to me and said, "I hear you have some excellent strawberries at your house, My Lord. Have some picked so we may taste them too."

'That,' Morton continued, 'was the last time I saw the young Prince. Nothing else Richard had done so revolted me as the carefree attitude he showed in violating the holy law of sanctuary.'

Morton went on to explain that the atmosphere at court was tense because there was talk of conspiracies against Richard. There was a fear that bordered on hysteria among his supporters that the Queen might somehow gain the upper hand and take control of the government. Spies were set to watch the activities of several people at court.

At a royal Council meeting on 7th June, Buckingham accused Lord Hastings of conspiring with the Woodvilles to overthrow the Lord Protector. A heated argument ensued in which several councillors lost their tempers and some drew their swords. Without even listening to Hastings's plea for an opportunity to explain his actions, Richard declared the Lord Chamberlain guilty of treason and ordered his summary execution.

'I do not know for sure whether Hastings did anything that was wrong,' said Morton. 'He had been Richard's friend and benefactor. It is true he felt Richard did not give him as much credit as he deserved, and that he resented Buckingham's swift rise to power. He may have talked to Elizabeth and to Dorset but I doubt he actually conspired against the Protector. It was argued that Jane Shore carried secret messages to Hastings from the Woodvilles. That charge was nonsense. The only way in which she was involved was that Richard coveted her just as his brother had. When she rejected him in favour of Hastings, poor Hastings's fate was sealed.'

'What happened to you after the flare-up in the Council meeting?' Thomas asked.

'That meeting ended my direct association with Richard,' Morton replied. 'I was guilty by association in his eyes, and I was promptly arrested and lodged in the Tower, where I spent the next two months until Buckingham took me to Wales.'

Morton explained that after his incarceration, questions were raised as to whether the plans for Prince Edward's coronation should be cancelled. Some of Richard's advisors saw an opportunity to ingratiate themselves with him by arguing that England needed a strong king and could not afford to be ruled by another boy king. The friends of Buckingham and Richard then pressured Parliament to declare Edward's children illegitimate.

A crowd of Richard's most ardent supporters gathered outside the palace and demanded that Richard take the crown. That was precisely what he had planned for all along; but he did not want to appear too anxious. At first he had disavowed interest in the crown. That was a display of false humility to disarm those who saw him as plotting to make himself king. But now Buckingham took the lead in getting the crowd to clamour for Richard's accession and Richard finally agreed after feigned reluctance to being crowned.

Morton was still imprisoned in the Tower at the time of Richard's coronation which he was told was a lavish affair. By mid-August, Richard was King and had consolidated his power in London. He then left London with a small party of courtiers to make a progress through the northern and western shires.

The Duke of Buckingham, whose numerous titles included that of Lord Constable, was left in charge in London. He visited Morton several times where he was imprisoned at the Tower. With each successive visit, Morton saw him in better light.

Their conversations touched on several matters including the nature of Buckingham's claim by right of birth to the throne. He was a direct descendant on both his father's and his mother's sides from Edward III and had a claim that was very nearly as good as Richard's. Then much to Morton's surprise, he found himself released from the Tower and sent with an armed guard to one of Buckingham's castles in Wales.

Morton concluded, 'I had no idea what was going on in the Duke's head. It turned out that he thought I could help him organise a successful rebellion against Richard, a rebellion that would put him on the throne. From the time he first broached this ambition to me, I warned against it.

By then I knew my fealty to Richard had ended. I advised Buckingham to give his support to Henry Tudor who had a stronger claim than his to the crown. He talked of doing so; but up until the day his feeble army melted away, I think he felt I could work a miracle that would make him King of England.'

Chapter Twelve

As Thomas's reading sessions with Bishop Morton continued through the winter months, through the forty days of Lent, till after the glorious festival of Easter, the Archbishop came to look forward with eager anticipation to the time he spent with his young intern. Thomas, meanwhile, saw the Bishop more and more as a pillar of strength and integrity.

Their sessions came at a time of the Bishop's choosing and usually lasted for an hour or more. Then they would talk, often about Morton's memories which ranged much further than the comments about Richard III which he carefully slipped into their dialogue when the occasion seemed appropriate. Much of their time was also spent in discussions of philosophical issues, and of the ins and outs of King Henry's administrative policies.

Thomas found that Morton was an excellent teacher, particularly on topics involving government. He knew how to get things done; how to play contending interests against each other; how to diffuse opposition to his policies; and how to wheedle his way among the great lords and barons at court. Thomas soon discerned that Morton had only a limited interest in philosophy. He was a rigidly conservative champion of the Church who opposed almost everything suggested by the word reform, and who stoutly defended the perquisites of the clergy.

As for Bishop Morton, he found he was becoming increasingly fond of and also dependent on his young assistant. Thomas's enthusiasm, his questions, and his wit had an invigorating impact on the old man. His visits were like a tonic that rolled back the older man's years and made him feel younger and more vibrant. He soon decided that precedent or no precedent, Thomas must be asked to stay on for a second year of internship.

Morton also gave serious thought to what he might do to further Thomas's career. Yet what could he do without overplaying his hand? With anyone else, he could have recommended him to the King or taken other steps to find him a profitable post. He could not do this with Thomas though, because he had to be kept free from royal influence if he was to write what would appear to be an unbiased chronicle of Richard's reign.

An opportunity for broadening Thomas's horizons came in the early summer when William Blount, Lord Mountjoy, who had been studying in Paris, returned to England and brought one of his teachers, a scholar who went by the single name of Erasmus, with him. Erasmus was a Dutch writer and cleric whose brilliance was already renowned in northern Europe.

Though only thirty, Erasmus was the author of several essays and poems. He had also written a book called *Antibarbari* which had not yet been published, but manuscript copies were in circulation. Thomas had read parts of it to the Archbishop.

Lord Mountjoy was staying in London for a few days before taking Erasmus to his country estate. Morton invited Mountjoy and his guest to dine with him and Father Gregory and Thomas. Much as the Bishop hoped, Erasmus and Thomas took an almost instant liking to each other. They conversed in Latin because Erasmus knew very little English. Throughout the evening Erasmus charmed them with the sparkling brilliance of his observations. But Thomas too surprised both himself and his colleagues with the pithiness and wit of his comments. As the party was breaking up, Morton asked Mountjoy about his plans, and finding that his lordship needed to remain in London for another week, volunteered Thomas's services to Erasmus as a companion.

Erasmus's first week in London saw the birth and flowering of a lifelong friendship between him and Thomas More. Thomas recognised that here was an inquiring mind that was not content to accept the intellectual world as it was. Not since he had left Oxford had he been able to discuss serious philosophical issues with such an astute authority. He was full of questions he wanted to ask, and here was a knowledgeable friend who invited his inquiries and who seemed almost eager to supply reasonable answers.

Thomas inquired about the underlying theme Erasmus had explored in the discussion between the four characters in his *Antibarberi*. 'What is the true nature of learning?' he asked. 'Does it consist in memorising sermons and long lists of words, or should one study geography, history and literature? Can true learning be found in study of the classical writings of Greece and Rome? Might the study of writers such as Plato and Aristotle have a corrupting effect on our Christian faith as some clerics have charged?'

Erasmus was delighted with the tenor of these questions. Thomas was surprised though when he responded, 'Don't judge me by what I wrote in that book. It has been five or six years since I wrote it. Back then I was still fighting to break away from the grip of my monastery. I see now that I was defending the monastic system at the very time I was questioning it. If I were writing the book today, I would give greater emphasis to the need for studying classical literature. The time has come when people like us must face the issues squarely. What we accept as education has been corrupted by the influence of centuries of scholastic nonsense. We must take humanism as our goal, and work for the reform of our educational system.'

'I am not sure I understand the full meaning of what you are saying,' Thomas protested. 'What, for example, do you mean when you speak of scholastic nonsense?'

'My concern is with some of the issues the scholastics spend time arguing about. Some priests at the College du Montaigu in Paris have seriously debated the question of whether God is more apt to listen to a twenty-minute prayer than to four five-minute ones. Some have speculated on how many angels can stand on the point of a needle. They even had a rousing discussion about whether angels fly in a horizontal upright stance or must assume a vertical position in flight as birds do. It would have made more practical sense for them to ask whether angels and other supernatural beings have any need for wings for flying when it is possible that they might move about like rays of sunlight.

'Many scholastics look at the Scriptures as a cumulative effort, as something that can profit from continuing additions. I see no fault in new interpretations if they make sense and are based on sound thinking. The emphasis given to allegorical interpretations in many sermons though, is not only nonsense but often wrong.

'Take that passage in the Old Testament that tells of the Queen of Sheba's visit to King Solomon. She brought him presents of gold, gems and frankincense. Many a sermon has been preached that tells us that the gold stood for true belief, the gems for holy virtue, and the other gifts for other things. Allegories such as that make a simple story of some historical event stand for something of doctrinal significance. No one reminds us that we should read the words for what they say. One ruler in ancient times brought gifts on a visit to another. We have no reason for believing that the gifts had any mystical significance. What Sheba really wanted was a military alliance, a possible trade agreement; or maybe she simply wanted a first-hand look at a king who could keep forty wives happy.'

'Are you familiar with Father William Grocyn's study of the supposed writings of Dionysius of Areopagus?' Thomas asked. He was referring to a study of *The Celestial Hierarchy*, a book long accepted as Scripture attributed to Dionysius, an Athenian who was the first Bishop of Athens after his conversion by the apostle Paul. The book prescribed a rigid stratification of classes both in the clergy and in the secular world, and endorsed the resulting class structures as something sanctified by divine plan. Grocyn's research had shown that the book was written more than three hundred years after Dionysius's time and thus could not be regarded as Scripture.

'Yes, I know of his work and hope to meet him while I am in England. What he has done provides an excellent example of the good that comes from humanistic studies. Dionysius's book has been accepted for generations as gospel, and used by churchmen and the nobility to justify their claim that it is God's will that some people hold rank and are rich while others are doomed to a mean existence, and that therefore nothing should be done to correct this iniquitous situation. Grocyn's research shows that this line of reasoning has no spiritual substance because its basis never was part of the true Scripture.'

'Some priests complain that humanism is anti-Catholic. Are you arguing for what they condemn?'

'There is no conflict between the humanism of which I speak, and the Church. For me humanism means focusing our attention on the classical roots of knowledge. We must accept the Bible, but not blind ourselves to the value of writings of the great thinkers of Greece and Rome. Humanism calls for recognising the value of all types of great literature, and encouraging enquiries that will help us understand who we are and why we act as we do.'

Erasmus's ideas found a ready disciple in Thomas More.

They reminded him of some lectures he had heard while he was a student at Oxford. William Grocyn had argued that there was a need for the Church to get back to the original sources of its teachings. John Colet too had impressed him with the historic-humanistic tone of his lectures, and with his charge that clerics should place more emphasis on what the Bible actually says and less on the allegorical illusions many churchmen associated with Biblical quotations.

When Thomas told Erasmus of his memories of Oxford, he was delighted to learn that Erasmus would be going there later in the year and would have an opportunity to meet Colet. When Erasmus revealed that like Colet, he had an interest in church reform Thomas was ready to defend the Church, until Erasmus assured him that his reforms would leave the central core of the Church and its doctrines intact. 'I am not challenging the authority of the Pope or the Scriptures,' he insisted. 'My objective calls for getting the Church back to what it stood for in earlier days. The doctrines and sermons preached by the scholastics are overloaded with conjecture as to what selected words and phrases mean.

'We must go back to the original words preached by the Apostles and read them for their simple meanings. We need to chuck out unnecessary frills, get our priesthood to rededicate itself to the true nature of its calling, and rid the Church of its dependence on ideas and illusions that have done more to cause controversy and rancorous debates than to advance the word of God.'

The two friends did not spend all of their time in philosophical and theological discussions. Thomas took pleasure in showing Erasmus both the beauties and some of the seamier aspects of the city. They took long walks in the nearby countryside. One afternoon they went to the grounds of Eltham Palace on London's outskirts.

While walking through the beautiful grounds of the Palace, they encountered three of the royal children. Prince Arthur was not there but Princess Margaret, now a pretty lass of ten, Prince Henry, a sturdy lad of eight, and little Princess Mary were. Prince Henry approached them and Thomas introduced himself and the visiting scholar. Being prepared for the occasion, Thomas presented Henry with a commendatory poem. The young Prince invited them to sup with the royal party, and during the course of the meal sent word to Erasmus that he expected to receive a product of his pen. Erasmus was taken aback, but promised to write a poem for him, which they delivered two days later on a second visit to the Palace.

Erasmus and Thomas shared some of their innermost thoughts with each other. Thomas felt no hesitation in asking Erasmus why he had a single name.

In response, Erasmus chuckled and said, 'That may be a temporary situation. Some day, if my reputation warrants it, I will add another name, but it will be something special like Erasmus Grandioso.'

'Now you are putting me off,' Thomas protested. 'There must be some simple explanation for your having only one name.'

'There is, and the reason is very simple,' Erasmus replied. 'I am what you English call a bastard. My father was a village priest, and had an illegitimate liaison with my mother. He lived openly with her, and with my brother, sister and me in the village rectory. Their relationship brought me much abuse in the village as I was growing up, so I resolved never to take his surname as my own.'

Thomas caught himself before he could show his initial reaction of shock and revulsion. He accepted the legitimacy, and indeed, the necessity of sex within marriage. Sex between men and women who were not their wives was sinful and an act to be deplored; but for a priest to have sex with a married woman or a woman unmarried was intolerable. Few sins were worse in his eyes than for a priest to lust after a woman and disregard his vows by having a sexual relationship with her. To do this and live openly with the woman could only be worse. He most certainly did not condone the priest's behaviour; but he quickly decided that in Erasmus's case he would overlook it. After all, it was the father not the son who had sinned.

Erasmus went on to tell him that he had been sent to a school operated by the Brethern of Common Life. He was miserable there both because of the frequently administered beatings, and because of the strict discipline which permitted no play and required the senseless memorisation of long passages from textbooks for no apparent purpose.

He was pressured into joining a monastery at Steyn when he was eighteen, took his vows the next year, and almost immediately began to repent his decision. He enjoyed the opportunities for study at the monastery, but found his surroundings, and the company of the other monks stifling.

Throughout most of the six years he spent at the monastery, he pined for an opportunity to leave and go to a place where he could study and teach. But unhappy though he was, his years there did allow him to acquire a broad knowledge of the writings of the Christian scholastics and introduced him to the study of the classics. It also saw the beginnings of his writing career, for he wrote two books and started a third.

After six boring years of monastic life, Erasmus was given leave to serve as Secretary to the Bishop of Cambray, who was planning a trip to Rome where he hoped to become a cardinal. The trip was delayed and then cancelled. Two years later he was able to extend his leave so that he might study at the College du Montaigu, a part of the Sorbonne in Paris, for a doctoral degree in theology.

Erasmus studied in Paris during the next four years. He lived in poverty, taking just enough courses in theology to justify continued payment of the small stipend that came with his leave from his monastery. Most of his time was spent on further exploration of his interest in the historical basis for the Church's teachings. Near the end of the four years, he abandoned his study of theology, hired himself out as a tutor, and looked for patrons such as Lord Mountjoy who could finance his ongoing pursuit of humanistic studies.

Erasmus displayed an avid interest in learning all he could about Thomas, his family life, his ambitions, his experiences at Oxford, and his work at the Chancery. Thomas was quite willing to open up the pages of his life for examination. Of course, he said nothing about his sexual fantasies and obsessions. That was too private a topic to discuss with anyone. But unlike him, Erasmus seemed eager to talk about sex.

He shocked Thomas early in their discussions by asking Thomas to introduce him to his mistress. When Thomas denied that he either had or wanted a mistress, Erasmus showed surprise.

'You Englishmen cannot be that different from your cousins in France!' he insisted. 'I would wager that well over half of the men in your class and position, both married and unmarried, have a mistress on the side. I just do not believe you when you say you do not.'

Erasmus quickly dismissed Thomas's claim that he abstained from sexual activity for moral and religious reasons. He insisted that any young man with Thomas's charm must have a long record of sexual conquests. He assumed that Thomas was not a virgin and pushed aside his denials of sexual activity as a display of modesty. When Thomas admitted that his brother John had had love affairs, Erasmus jumped to the conclusion that this was a veiled revelation of Thomas's own experience.

When Thomas mentioned that his favourite saints were Augustine and Aquinas, Erasmus said, 'Ah, the Plato and Aristotle of Christian thought! Did you know that some have argued that their thoughts and writings are so much alike that the soul of one must have passed into the other? Perhaps that soul has now passed into you, Thomas More.'

Erasmus showed little interest in law or in Thomas's prospects for becoming a lawyer. And when Thomas spoke of his piety and his alternate possibility of taking holy orders, Erasmus hooted and sternly advised, 'Forget that idea. Don't be a fool like I was. Let someone who has been there tell you the truth. With your talent you could never enjoy life in a monastery where everyone lives by the law of silence; nor would you like it any better in a talking order where nine out of ten of your brothers would be ignorant slobs. Your life would be wasted in a monastery. You can do far more to help reform the Church and promote real learning by avoiding that trap.'

When Thomas protested that he was a pious believer who looked with favour on asceticism and who wanted to turn away from the sins of the world in the interest of his own salvation, Erasmus exploded, 'You, an ascetic? What nonsense! That makes no more sense than taking owls to Athens or wine to Bordeaux. You have a mind, man; and you can think. God wants you to use your intelligence for a worthy purpose. He loves you. He does not want you to torture yourself in his name. All that fasting and flagellation will do nothing for you other than give you a weak stomach and a sore back. Join a monastery and you will regret your poverty, the stifling silence, and those endless prayers. You can do far more for the salvation of your soul by staying in the world of the living and doing something positive to correct the ills of the world.'

Changing the tenor of his remarks, he asked, 'What does

your father think of your plan to take holy orders? What does he want you to do?'

'He wants me to be accepted at the bar, and then to marry and have children.'

'Then do as he advises. You cannot marry and be a good priest too.'

Chapter Thirteen

Erasmus was like a blind man who had suddenly gained his sight. He was curious about everything. He asked endless questions about Thomas's work, what he did, what he thought. Without ever intending to do so, Thomas told him of the sessions he was having with Cardinal Morton, and about their long conversations concerning the reigns of Edward IV and Richard III.

Erasmus wanted to know more. What was the basis of Henry's claim to the throne? What caused the conflict between the Houses of Lancaster and York? Thomas told him what he could, but had to admit that he had no answers to many of the questions.

In the midst of one of their discussions, Erasmus protested, 'I find these scraps of information about your recent history most confusing. Put it in perspective for me. How did all this squabbling and feuding start?'

Thomas shook his head. 'To be honest with you,' he replied, 'I do not really know. No one teaches history in our schools, and I doubt I have ever heard a logical account of what happened.'

'Then we ought to seek out someone who can provide one for us,' Erasmus insisted. 'Do you know anyone who can give us the facts?'

'We could go to Bishop Morton, but he is a busy man and I should not disturb him. Let me ask my father if he can help us.'

John More was pleasantly surprised when Thomas asked

that evening for assistance. 'I know of no records or chronicles you can go to for that information,' he said. 'Glimmerings of the information you want are reported in various official papers, but I know of no attempt having been made to pull them together. Our recent kings have been too busy fighting to worry about having someone report on their activities. Some priests have probably kept records, but I have no idea who.'

But as they were having breakfast the next morning, John said, 'I think I have a possible answer to the question you asked me last evening. Several months ago, I had occasion to meet and talk with Sir Francis Musgrave who served for many years as a Justice on the King's Bench. He is in his mid-eighties now, but had a sharp mind and a healthy memory when I last spoke with him. I think he would enjoy talking to you. If we can set up an appointment with him, I would like to come along.'

Two days later, Sir Francis gave every appearance of being delighted when John More, his son Thomas and Erasmus knocked at his door. He insisted on serving wine to his guests and, discovering the purpose of their visit, he beamed.

'You gentlemen do me honour. Not many people visit me; and hardly anyone ever asks me questions about the past. That is my favourite subject, but no one seems to be interested in history. It is a pity, because our past mistakes often repeat themselves.'

'Our friend Erasmus has stirred our interest in the cause of the wars between the Houses of Lancaster and York,' John told him. 'We have come to you, because you more than anyone we know can give us a clear explanation of what happened.'

'That is a tall order, but I will try not to disappoint you,' Sir Francis replied. 'It is a topic I could spend a day or a week discussing. I'll try to be brief and to the point, as I always insisted that the lawyers who practised in my court should be.

'The cause of those wars goes back to Edward III,' he continued. 'We usually honour men who have several sons. But that can be a source of trouble with kings. A good king should have one healthy son with a possible second one who can fill in if need be. Edward had seven sons. Five of them lived to maturity, and that was four more than England needed.

'His first son was Edward, the Black Prince. He was a great warrior who had the makings of a good king. Unfortunately, he and his eldest son both died while his father was still living. At Edward's death, the crown went to the Black Prince's second son, Richard II, who made a mess of things as boy kings usually do.

'King Edward's second and sixth sons, both of them named William, died young. His third son, Lionel, was made Duke of Clarence. I've been told that he was an able leader, but he too died before his father. He was important for our account, because his daughter Philippa married Edmund Mortimer, the Earl of March, who was one of the most powerful barons in the realm. Their son Roger was the presumed heir of Richard II until he was killed at some battle in Ireland. He had two children, Edmund and Anne Mortimer, of whom I will have more to say in a moment.

'His fourth son was John of Gaunt, who became the Duke of Lancaster. Let me talk first though about his fifth son, Edmund of Langley, the Duke of York.

'Langley was a good military commander. He married a daughter of the King of Castile and had two sons: Edmund, the second Duke of York, who died at Agincourt without issue; and Richard, the Earl of Cambridge.

'Richard was important for us because he married Anne Mortimer, the granddaughter of his cousin Philippa. He was executed a few years later for being implicated in a plot to put Anne's brother, Edmund, on the throne. Richard of Cambridge and Anne had one son, Richard, who succeeded to his uncle's title as the third Duke of York. Upon the death of his uncle Edmund Mortimer he also acquired a premier claim, under our rules of succession, to the throne. Going a step further, Richard of York married Cicely Neville whose mother Joan Beaufort was a daughter of John of Gaunt. Their children thus could boast of three direct lines of descent from Edward III.

'That explains the rise of the House of York,' John agreed. 'What of the House of Lancaster?'

'For that, we must go back to John of Gaunt. He was the most powerful and most hated nobleman in the realm during Richard II's reign. People say he wanted to be king, but he always held back when he had opportunities to seize power. His son Henry of Bolingbroke, who became Henry IV, acted with less restraint when he wrested the crown from King Richard.

'Henry IV was John of Gaunt's son by his first wife. John was married second to a daughter of the King of Castile. His true love though was his mistress, Katherine Swynford. He had four children by her, all of them royal bastards because he did not marry her until years after they were born.'

'Does that mean they had no rights of succession with respect to the crown?' Erasmus asked.

'That is what most people thought. Henry IV liked his half-brothers and made one of them, John Beaufort, the Earl of Somerset. Somerset became one of the most powerful noblemen in the country, and was followed by his two sons: John, who became the first Duke of Somerset; and Edmund, who succeeded him as the second Duke of Somerset.

'Henry IV's son Henry V became our great warrior King when he defeated the French at Agincourt and went on to conquer much of France. Henry married Princess Katherine of France. Their son Henry VI was born only a few months before Henry died. England got another boy king, along with the usual mess of royal kin and powerful barons trying to run the country in his name.

'Two important developments related to your question came with the death of Henry V. Queen Katherine left court some months after his death, and lived with Owen Tudor who had been a dance instructor at court. They had two bastard sons; Jasper Tudor who became the Earl of Pembroke; and Edmund Tudor who became the Earl of Richmond.

'Worse than that, Henry VI turned out to be more a muddleheaded priest than a real ruler. He neither looked nor acted much like a king. Henry's wife, Queen Margaret, took control and ran the country into the ground with the aid of a few unsuitable advisors. Richard of York became disenchanted with what was going on; and for years thereafter, we had a running civil war with the forces of Richard of York and Queen Margaret fighting for supremacy.'

'Did the right side win?' Erasmus asked.

'How one answers that would depend on who you talk to. Margaret and Henry had a loyal following among the gentry. As far as the people of London were concerned, Richard of York was our hero and Margaret was nothing more than a headstrong bitch who was willing to sell the whole kingdom for her own purposes. As fortune had it, Henry had no mind for his job. He suffered from blackouts and spells of insanity. His advisors should have insisted that he step aside. Margaret wouldn't hear of it. She fought like a tigress to keep the crown for him and her son. In the process she and the two Dukes of Somerset frittered away almost everything England had left in France.'

'Was that the time when York's followers started to wear

the white rose as their emblem while those of the house of Lancaster turned to wearing to the red rose?' Erasmus asked.

'Yes, partisans on both sides took to wearing red or white roses as a symbol of support for their cause.'

'Did their war have a name?' Erasmus wanted to know.

'Some people called it Queen Margaret's war,' Sir Francis replied. 'Had it not been for her dogged determination to keep the throne, the feuding could have stopped years earlier.'

'One could imagine that people might call it the war of the roses,' Erasmus opined.

'Maybe they will sometime in the future when they get far enough away from the war to start romanticising it. For now, the King discourages discussion of recent events; and those who remember the feuding consider it a blot on our history.'

'I know about Richard of York and his sons and how Edward IV and Richard III claimed the crown,' Thomas interjected. 'But how do our present King and the late Duke of Buckingham fit into the picture?'

'Let me comment on Buckingham first,' Sir Francis responded. 'Thomas of Woodstock was the youngest of Edward III's sons. He became Duke of Gloucester and was a powerful nobleman in his day. He had one son who did not survive him, and his only daughter married the Earl of Stafford. Their son, Humphrey Stafford became the first Duke of Buckingham. His son, another Humphrey Stafford, married Margaret Beaufort, a daughter of the second Duke of Somerset. Their son Henry became the second Duke of Buckingham after his grandfather's death. With two lines of descent from Edward III, Henry had a claim to the crown that was junior only to those of his cousins Edward IV and Richard III.'

'And now Henry Tudor?' Thomas pressed.

'One does not talk about our present monarch's ancestry in public, so I must trust you to keep my comments on that matter private,' said Sir Francis. 'Margaret Beaufort, the daughter of the first Duke of Somerset and a granddaughter of John Beaufort, the bastard son of John of Gaunt, married Edmund Tudor, the Earl of Richmond, who was the bastard son of Queen Katherine and Owen Tudor. They had one son, Henry Tudor, who is now Henry VII and who, except for his own sons and two or three others is the only surviving male descendant of John of Gaunt.

'There you have it, my young friends,' Sir Francis concluded as he proceeded to pour more wine into the cups of his three visitors. 'Do you have any questions?'

'I have one,' Thomas ventured. 'If Edward III had seven sons, and his sons and grandsons also had children, shouldn't there be more than three or four legitimate claimants to the crown by the time we get to the fifth generation?'

'Good question,' Sir Francis answered. 'Of course, there were more sons and daughters in each generation than I have mentioned. I have noted only those who affected the succession. There are several people now living both in England and on the Continent who can trace their ancestry back to Edward III through their mothers or grandmothers. Apart from those I have mentioned though, all the direct male lines have died out. The royal line did a poor job in reproducing itself. Henry IV, for example, had five sons, four of whom grew to manhood. Yet he had only one legitimate grandson, and only one great-grandson. All of Edward's sons died in their beds. It was a different story with their grandsons. What with the ones who died without issue, and those who died in childhood, who chose careers with the Church, or were executed or were killed in battles, there are few men left.'

'How long did the war in which the grandsons were

killing their own cousins last?' Erasmus asked.

'Sixteen years. The Lancastrians and the Yorkists both had strong followings. Control of the kingdom see-sawed back and forth between them from the time when York challenged Margaret's authority at the first battle of St Albans in 1455, until Warwick was killed during a great battle fought in a dense fog at Barnet in 1471 and Edward's final victory over the remnants of Margaret's army at Tewkesbury a few weeks later.'

'How many battles were there?' Thomas asked.

'There were more than a dozen major battles, plus several skirmishes and the besieging of many castles. Of all of them, I would rate St Albans and Barnet along with Wakefield and Towton as the most decisive so far as their effects were concerned. The war really started with St Albans, and Margaret's hopes were doomed after Barnet. Wakefield was important because York had been riding high as Lord Protector until the Lancastrians ambushed and killed him and his party there during a Christmas truce in 1460. Edward got his revenge the next year at Towton when he won the victory that stripped Henry and Margaret of their crowns. That battle was fought in a raging blizzard and will probably go down in history as the biggest and bloodiest battle ever fought on English soil. Of the one hundred thousand men who fought in the two armies, around forty thousand were killed.'

John More sensed a lull in the questioning, and concluded their visit by thanking Sir Francis for his help. 'We are indebted to you and do not want to tax you further today. If it is all right with you though, I would like to come by another day to visit you.'

Later that day, Erasmus and Thomas talked of their writing ambitions. Poverty had kept Erasmus from doing much writing in Paris.

'In those days I could not afford the pens and paper I

would have needed for writing,' he told his friend. 'I am living better now. Once I settle down, I will write again. Indeed, I will not be able to help myself. I am a born scribbler who has a driving passion for putting ideas on paper.'

Erasmus explained that he expected to write more essays and books. 'I have one big project in mind. I want to prepare a version of the New Testament as it was originally written. Of course, I will not be writing the gospels. I want to put together the books of the New Testament as they were first written, in Greek, and present them without the trappings that translators and well-meaning but often misguided scholars have tacked on to them. Before I can do that though, I must improve my ability to read and write in Greek.'

'And you really intend to do all that in Greek?' Thomas exclaimed. 'That will be a monumental work. You must tell Colet about it when you get to Oxford, and tell Grocyn too if you chance to meet him. I envy you your knowledge of Greek. I would really like to read Plato in the original.'

Erasmus then indicated that he also had ideas that could provide the grist for another book. He had been collecting an array of anecdotes about the misconduct and unseemly behaviour of priests, lawyers, merchants, and other leading citizens that could provide interesting reading.

Thomas questioned the propriety of publishing anything that might poke fun at priests. Erasmus cut off his objection with a blanket denial that his book would in any way be critical of the Church. If his expose of the nefarious activities of some priests proved scandalous enough, it could even serve a worthy purpose by causing the Church to cleanse itself.

'It is all right to cleanse the Church,' Thomas agreed, 'but please stop short of trying to wash it away, not that any book is going to shake the solid foundation of our Holy

Church.'

'You need have no fears about that,' Erasmus answered. 'But let's change the subject. I have told you about my writing plans; now let's hear about yours.'

'But I am not a writer like you,' Thomas objected.

'Nonsense,' Erasmus insisted. 'I know in my heart that you can become one of our best writers. All you have to do is start. You have written reports for your Chancery, and I am sure Bishop Morton would not have you writing them if someone else on his staff could do a better job. As soon as you finish your work at the Chancery, you should start writing essays on topics that interest you.'

'I would not know where to start,' Thomas protested.

'You can make a good start by translating some piece that is written in Latin into English. You could also make a name for yourself by going back to Sir Francis Musgrave for more details, and then write a chronicle of your recent English history.'

'That would be a bigger undertaking than I am ready to take on,' Thomas confessed. 'But there are two other topics I might sometime write about. Our late King, Richard III was one of the most debauched and villainous men who ever ruled. God willing, I would like to write a history of his reign. I also have thought of writing a book with a very different theme. It would be about an ideal society in which the most admirable Christian virtues prevail, and people enjoy peace and plenty.'

'A capital combination, Thomas! What a perfect pair of contrasting themes. With one book, you can examine the nature of tyranny and provide a moral lesson on what kings and nations should avoid. The second book can show us the world that could be ours.'

Chapter Fourteen

The small cubicle to which the Prior took him was poorly lit and almost devoid of ventilation. It contained a narrow cot, a bench and table, and little else save for a candle stub and a crudely carved crucifix which hung on an otherwise bare wall. Brother Bernard was tired and utterly disgusted. Three months had passed since he had left London on his inspection of clerical and town records in the shires of northern England. He had visited dozens of abbeys, cathedrals, villages and cities. The reception he received was almost always the same. He would stop at some abbey, be granted the charity of the house, be assigned to a room or bed, eat and pray with the members of the order, and carry on his irksome inspections.

As a Grey Friar of the Franciscan order, he had long been pledged to a life of poverty and service, but the poverty he had endured these last three months galled him. It was not that he objected to being poor. He had lived in poverty all of his life. The irritant that eroded the compassion he ordinarily felt for others sprang from his feeling that he was being discriminated against by his fellow clerics in the various orders he went to in his quest for bread and a bed. Few indeed were the occasions when he had enjoyed sleeping accommodation at all comparable to that which he had been accustomed. More important was the irritating conviction that he had not had a good full meal since he had left London.

Bernard was a big man: taller than most, big boned, and

the possessor of a sizeable paunch. He loved good food and readily admitted that his capacity for relishing a tasty meal was his leading vice. But if this be a sin, he had surely lived the life of an emaciated saint these last three months. He had not tasted a good meal since supping with his uncle, Father Gregory, on his last evening in London.

Brother Bernard had more education than the average friar. He was studious by nature, liked to read such manuscripts as were available to him, and had enjoyed success in his calling as a teaching friar. He was a Grey Friar mostly because he had lived as a boy and youth with the Franciscan brothers who cared for him after his mother's death.

He had been content for many years with his life as a simple friar. As he approached middle age, however, he had felt a need to do something different. His uncle enjoyed an active life working with the Archbishop at the Chancery, and the possibility of working there appealed to him as an option that would enable him to make better use of his talents and at the same time allow him to live a more enjoyable life.

He had no illusions about living a soft life when the invitation finally came for him to join the Lord Chancellor's staff. Both Father Gregory and Cardinal Morton had taken pains to explain that his work would not be easy, and that his first assignment called for several months of travel about England inspecting clerical and town records.

He had also been advised that he must hold down his travel costs where possible by staying with local monastic orders. The King's Treasury had no intention of paying for a bed and meals at local inns if its representatives could live at no cost at some abbey or monastery. The rub, Bernard soon discovered, was that most abbots and priors were well aware of the King's niggardliness. Most of them could and would provide good rooms and food for travellers and visitors of quality who paid for the service, whilst they provided spartan fare only for poor friars.

Though he did not enjoy his living conditions nor the fact that he was continually moving from one village to another, Bernard had few complaints about his inspection work. Churchmen and town scribes were always willing to show their records to him. He usually read only the entries recorded between the last years of Edward IV's reign to the early years of Henry VII.

In village after village he found no mention whatever of Richard or of any other king. He had not expected to find much, because he knew he was working on the residual group of churches and towns that had not already been checked.

Most of the few references he found were commendatory. A town would thank the King for sending food at a time of grain shortage; express gratitude for a pension granted to a wounded warrior or his widow; praise him for correcting some legal injustice. He found requests for royal favours but nowhere complaints about the King or his ministers. Surprisingly enough, he encountered no objections beyond raised eyebrows when he suggested that commendatory comments be erased or torn out. After fourteen years of Henry's rule, no local scribe wanted to make an issue of protecting a comment concerning a half-forgotten monarch.

The next town along Bernard's travel route was one of those listed as already inspected. More out of curiosity than anything else, the friar decided to stop there and see what changes, if any, had been made to the shire records. No questions were asked when he asked to see the records. He had little trouble in identifying a passage that had been scratched out so that the original writing was illegible.

When he asked about it, the old man who served as custodian said, 'That passage referred to our acknowledgement of the benevolence of King Richard in sponsoring a town festival. Bishop Morton did not like it. We resisted his suggestion that we erase it at first. He fined us fifty pounds and threatened to double the fine every month thereafter if we did not remove it. Scratching it out was our only practical alternative.'

'Did that experience change the attitude of the people here about King Richard?'

'Not at all. Richard was always popular here. We remember him as a King who really cared for his subjects.'

'Did it affect your attitude regarding Henry VII?'

'Of course – we did not like being told what we could put in our records. But what could we do? We decided it was best just to follow orders and keep our mouths shut.'

This exchange marked the beginning of a change in Bernard's feelings about Richard III. To be sure, he knew what his responsibility was to his employers at the Chancery; but his sense of justice caused him to question the fairness of his charge. In his eyes, the order to remove all commendatory references to Richard from the records was an unjustified attempt to rewrite history. Richard had been a popular leader in these northern shires, and he was not happy with the role he was expected to play in discrediting this popular perception.

As he worked his way farther north during the following weeks, Bernard found numerous indications of Richard's popularity. A young priest at one abbey showed him a record in which almost half a page had been erased and not written over. When he remarked on this, the priest showed him a letter signed by Archbishop Morton which ordered the abbey to expunge the passage from its records. The cleric did not remember the incident because it had happened before he joined the order. He recalled an older priest's account of Richard spending a night at the abbey, when he had contributed handsomely to its charitable funds, and sent his guards out to capture two highwaymen who had been vandalising the abbey's property and stealing its livestock.'

Stops at other towns and abbeys provided similar examples of erasures of accounts that had spoken favourably of Richard. With few exceptions, however, he found that most of the records were cared for by a new generation of custodians who showed little concern about the deletions.

Bernard's quest for enlightening details climaxed during the fifth month of his inspections when he visited the small village of Leighbury. There was little that was unusual about Leighbury except that it was not on Morton's list of already inspected towns. No official records were kept in the village, but it did have an abbey which was presided over by an elderly prior who had a penchant for keeping records.

After he identified himself and explained the purpose of his visit, Prior Joseph sorted through several volumes of notes and produced an account that predated by a few months the period that Bernard usually examined. He found a reference to Richard that was far longer than a few sentences or paragraphs. Prior Joseph had devoted five pages to describing a major event in the village's history, in which Richard came to the town's rescue just in time to save it from imminent rapine and destruction.

During one of the Scottish wars some twenty years earlier, a renegade band of Scottish warriors had invaded the shire. Villages only a few miles away were plundered and burned, their women raped and their men mutilated and killed. The outlaw band was approaching Leighbury for what promised to be an easy sacking, when Richard bore down on them with a troop of border guards. The Scots were totally defeated, their leaders captured and hanged in a quick action that left the village unscathed. In grateful recognition, the people of the village offered their thanks to Richard, renewed their pledge of fealty to him, and declared a three-day holiday to celebrate their deliverance from harm.

Bernard felt apologetic as he explained the King's order to expunge this comment from the abbey's records. When Father Joseph protested, he explained that, while he agreed that the order was not just, it was his duty to recommend that the Prior delete it from the abbey's records.

He went on to explain, 'As far as I know, the order applies only to official records. I would not want to be quoted on this but it is my opinion that it can be cut out and kept as your private record. Our good sovereign may not like it, and his agents could very well punish me for telling you this, but there is nothing in the King's orders that makes the keeping of private records illegal.'

When they had reached an apparent agreement on expunging the account, Bernard asked the Prior if he had ever met Richard.

'Yes, I had that honour,' he was told. 'That was one of the proudest days of my life. Richard was the Duke of Gloucester then. He came into the village after the battle with the Scots. I can see him still as he and his men rode up to the abbey. He was riding a huge black horse and was dressed in his light field armour. He stopped here to wash the blood and soil from his hands; and at our invitation supped and spent the night with us. He ate at this very table we have been using to examine these records.'

Prior Joseph went on to recount some of his memories of Richard and then said, 'If you want to learn more about him, you really should talk to Miles Fenton. He was the Duke's squire until he was wounded at Tewkesbury. He lives with his wife here in Leighbury.'

An hour later Bernard found Miles Fenton and his wife at their cottage in the village. Miles was a big man with a strong muscular frame. About fifty, he was already wrinkled and grey. From his quick appraisal of the cottage, Bernard could see that the Fentons had lived a hard and not overly prosperous life. The reason for this became apparent when he noted that Richard's one-time squire had only a dangling stump where his right hand and arm should be.

Miles responded with a hearty 'hallo' to Bernard's greeting, and seemed delighted when the inspector told him of his interest in Richard of Gloucester.

'I knew him well,' Miles told him, 'and never have I known a better man.'

At Bernard's request, Miles then spilled out the story of their association. Richard had been only nine when his brother was crowned as Edward IV. Until that time, he lived mostly with his mother on one of the family's estates in Yorkshire. He had been a skinny and sickly child, not nearly as robust as his three older brothers. When Edward became King, he arranged for Richard and his brother George to go to the Earl of Warwick's castle at Middleham where they were to be educated along with several other young noblemen. With them went Miles, who was eleven, and his brother James, who was Richard's age, who were sons of one of the old Duke of York's retainers. They had been boyhood playmates of George and Richard, and were sent with them to Middleham to be prepared for careers of service.

George stayed at Middleham for only a short period while Miles and his brother stayed on with Richard at the castle for three years. Like the young noblemen, they got up at dawn, went to mass every morning, breakfasted on meat, bread and beer, and then went to class. The young noblemen were taught Latin and French, mathematics, penmanship, law, music, etiquette, and all aspects of English culture by a priest and a learned clerk. Their retainers also attended classes but had a less rigorous curriculum that gave more emphasis to the rules of service. Both groups spent their afternoon hours learning the arts of war: self defence, horseback riding, use of armour, and fighting with swords, daggers, and battle axes.

The retainers at the castle who supervised their training saw little reason to designate periods for simple play. But the boys invented their own games, competed with each other, and in many cases cemented strong bonds of friendship that were to last their lifetimes. As growing lads who were approaching and entering puberty, they also experienced growth both in size and strength.

Richard joined his class as a sickly spindly youth. By sheer determination and exercise, he became one of the healthiest and strongest members of his group. He soon showed himself to be a leader, both because of his shrewd judgement and because of the daring agility he displayed as a fighter who could hold his own against boys who were taller, heavier, and older than him.

Miles watched his young lord grow in strength, skill and ability. King Edward kept himself informed of Richard's progress and appointed him commissioner for several northern shires when he was only twelve to assemble an army and lead it to join Edward's army in England's midlands. Miles begged Richard to take him along as his squire on that occasion. Richard agreed and the two lads established an intimate relationship that continued for a full seven years until Miles lost his forearm at the Battle of Tewkesbury.

Richard and Miles returned to Middleham after their first taste of military service but left a few months later. During the six years that followed, Miles accompanied Richard on his infrequent trips to the court in London; lived with him on various York family estates; and fought side by side with him in putting down several uprisings. He was with Richard and Edward when they fled to Holland after Warwick took London in 1470; came back with them a few months later, and was with Richard when he commanded flanks of the King's army in its great victories at Barnet and Tewkesbury.

'How did you rate Richard as a person?' Bernard asked. 'Was he easy to get along with, or proud and haughty?'

'Richard and I were together in York and I came to love and respect him at Middleham. He could have been a pampered weakling all his life, but he was determined to rise to the top on his own merits and worked like a demon to do it. He and his brother George were as different as night and day. George was haughty and always expected the rest of us, both noblemen and retainers, to defer and yield to him because he was the Duke of Clarence and the King's brother. Richard was completely different. He treated James and me as if we were his brothers or cousins. He commanded our respect because he was a worthy person, not because he had a title.'

'Did he show respect for the other men who worked under him?'

'Maybe my view is biased because of our friendship, but I think he would have gone out of his way to help anyone for whom he felt responsibility. I was wounded in our last big charge at Tewkesbury. Once it looked as though victory was ours, Richard had his brother George send out men to round up the stragglers of Somerset's defeated army while he took me to his best surgeon to bind up my stump before I might have bled to death. He was there with the surgeon comforting me when George's men came back with their report that Prince Edward had been killed while resisting capture. Richard was really upset over that, because he had ordered that the Prince be taken and held as a prisoner.'

'I have heard that Richard was hard and cruel. That does not match your description at all.'

'He could be tough when tough decisions were needed, but he was never what I would call cruel. When we were in battle, he was always an aggressive leader who never willingly yielded an advantage to the enemy, and who neither gave nor expected quarter. Once the fighting was over, he was willing to forgive. We would round up the soldiers of a defeated army and treat them as prisoners. It never was his practice to slaughter them as some commanders do. He was strict on discipline and did not hesitate to punish men for breaking the rules, but his concern for justice kept him from punishing men if there was any question as to their guilt.'

'You make him sound like one of Jehovah's angels. Was he really that good a person?'

'He was a good man but no angel. He had a tender streak in him when it came to family and close friends. His men respected him because he was fair and insisted on good discipline. They also loved him because he was a strong leader who never asked us to do things he would not do himself. He was a shrewd commander who knew how to win. Yet he never hesitated when it came to leading us into battle and setting an example by fighting like a bewitched demon in the thick of every skirmish.

'I admired and loved him because he had high standards and would fight like a wild beast for what he thought was right. Yet as a companion he was as ordinary a person as one could find. We were just teenagers when we started fighting together. We had our jokes and horseplay. We even sowed our wild oats together. The Richard I knew then was far from perfect; but he was the best friend I ever had.'

'How did he get along with his brothers?'

'He loved and was loyal to Edward, and the King trusted him and gave him several honours which he well deserved. He had a lot of family love for George too; but George was cut from a different cloth than his brothers.'

'Tell me more about George.'

'George was three years older than Richard. He was tall, handsome and had blond curly hair like King Edward. He could be charming when he wanted, but he was self-centred and arrogant. His biggest problem was that he had more ambition than brains. He seemed to think it was he, not his brother Edward, who should be king.

'George joined up with Warwick in his opposition to Edward, married Warwick's eldest daughter, and fled with them to France. He came back as Warwick's co-commander when Warwick invaded England with the Lancastrian army that marched on London. King Edward was caught off guard, and Richard and I escaped with him to Holland. We were back a few weeks later with Edward when he raised the army that crushed Warwick at Barnet. George defected to Edward just before the battle and begged for Edward's forgiveness.

'George should have known better by then, but his name was trouble. His wife died early and he had two of her servants executed on a false charge that they had poisoned her. When he didn't get everything his own way at court, he conspired with some disgruntled noblemen in two or three unsuccessful uprisings; then he shocked everyone with a claim that his brothers were bastards and that he was the sole legitimate son of Richard of York. That charge was the last straw. The Woodvilles and almost everyone except his two brothers were fed up with his deceitful behaviour. He was arrested and convicted of treason. Richard begged for his life, but Parliament insisted on his execution.'

Bernard felt he had exhausted Miles's supply of information, and was preparing to leave when Miles's wife said, 'You have asked Miles about his memories of King Richard. Now let me tell you about mine.'

Bernard was taken back for a moment. He had had limited experience in talking with women, and thought of Richard as a person who lived in a man's world. Yet Prior Joseph had said that she knew Richard, so he quickly decided he should listen.

'I was a maid servant at Middleham when the young Duke Richard was there,' she explained. 'That is where Miles met me. Naturally, I had nothing to do with the classes the boys took. The Earl and Countess of Warwick had two daughters, Isabel and Anne, whom I served. The girls were younger than us, but the Countess let them play and dance with the young noblemen especially when she had parties at which they practised their court manners and etiquette.

'George met Isabel at Middleham and later married her. Richard was four years older than Anne. They played together as children at first, but I remember her telling me when she was only eight that she was going to marry Richard when they were older. They were still just friends when Richard and Miles went off with that army together; but they really liked each other. Richard was back at Middleham several times after that and they saw each other both there and at court. I think there was an understanding between them before Warwick took her off to France.

'Warwick was determined to marry his daughters to royalty, and arranged for Isabel to marry George. Then when he got to France, he betrothed Anne, who was only thirteen, to the Prince of Wales. Anne fought against that decision; but Warwick went ahead with his plan and was arranging for a royal wedding to take place when Anne came over from France with Queen Margaret, when he was killed at the Battle of Barnet.

'I was with Anne when she came from France. She was upset when she heard of her father's death; but she was more relieved than saddened when she got the news of Prince Edward's death at Tewkesbury a few weeks later.

'After Tewkesbury, Richard got Edward's permission to marry Anne. George, who was now head of the Warwick family, refused to give his consent. He had no intention of sharing the Warwick estates with his younger brother. He even had Anne carried away to one of his remote castles to hide her from Richard. I helped smuggle a message to Richard. He was only nineteen and could have waited a while before marrying. But when he heard of her plight, he hurried to her aid. He slipped past the guards George had watching her and was able to steal away from the castle with her, and they were married before his brother could stop them.'

'Then he did not kidnap her as some people claim?'

'Not at all. It was a carefully planned elopement. George fumed about it and was indignant and rude. But it was too late for him to stop the marriage.'

'Was their marriage a happy one?'

'Richard and Anne loved each other until the day she died. He was a loving and devoted husband. I should know because I was her maid servant. She had a beautiful son, little Prince Edward. Too bad for all of us, both she and the little Prince got the lung disease and both of them died just a few months after Richard became King.'

'Did he remarry?'

'No, and he showed no interest in doing so even though some of his advisors suggested that he should. He and Anne were a perfect couple, and he never seemed to get over her death.'

'And what happened to you and Miles and James?' Bernard asked.

'Richard and Anne settled at Middleton after their marriage. He had Miles supervise his stables there after he lost his hand. I came back here with them, and Miles and I were married. As for James, he took over Miles's spot as Richard's squire after Tewkesbury. He died fighting at Richard's side during that last fatal charge at Bosworth Field. After that, our lives took a turn for the worse and we found we had to turn to a new way of earning our living.'

Chapter Fifteen

Bishop Morton was a builder. Several stately structures stood in London as monuments to his foresight, and to the ability he had shown in wheedling money from the King to pay for their construction. Sheen Palace on the Thames had been one of his most notable achievements. When that imposing structure was gutted by fire in December 1497, Morton had quickly arranged to have Richmond Palace designed as a larger, more lavish, and more sumptuous replacement.

Construction was proceeding on the new Palace, and on two other new buildings in 1499. One of the walls at the Tower of London also was being rebuilt. Much to Morton's annoyance, progress on these projects came to a temporary standstill during the summer months. London was suffering, as it did every few years, from the ravages of a plague.

Hundreds of people were afflicted with the sudden onset of a fever that forced them to their beds and often claimed their lives within a matter of hours. Dead bodies were laid out every day in the crooked streets of the poorer sections of the city for public collection and burial. Hysteria gripped much of the city. The royal family removed itself to one of Henry's outlying castles. Most of the nobility and the wealthier townsfolk followed this example as they too moved to safer rural locales. Fear for their health and their lives also kept many skilled workmen from reporting for their usual employment.

Morton wished he too could be with the royal court away from the poisonous air of London. But there was work here that had to be done. The administration of Henry's government could not be brought to a standstill simply because of widespread sickness. There were too many decisions that could not be postponed until the return of cooler weather brought more healthful living conditions.

As Lord Chancellor, Morton insisted that his building projects retain a high priority among the public and private activities that continued unimpeded by the plague. When his foremen complained that workers were dying or staying at home, he ordered them to recruit more workers from among London's seemingly inexhaustible supply of poor men who were eager to find work so that they might buy food for their families.

Even with this help, most of Morton's projects could no more than limp along without their normal contingents of workers. These delays irritated the Bishop. Time after time he spoke of the need for meeting his construction deadlines, and most particularly of the absolute necessity of completing the remodelling of the Tower before the royal family returned from their stay in the country.

The Lord Chancellor also had concerns of a more personal nature. He had fervently hoped he, his household, and his staff could remain free of the plague. Unfortunately, two of his clerks had already been stricken and Henry Abel, that brash young intern who boasted of manly pursuits and an iron stomach, had succumbed to the fever.

Thomas More, the Bishop thought. I must do something to save him. I have far too much invested in him to risk losing him to the plague. I must avoid making his case look conspicuous; but for the good of England he must go to the country until it is safe for him to be working here.

As Morton thought about Thomas and the need to safeguard him from the plague, he recalled the session they had had two days earlier. They had discussed the deaths of the two young princes. He had been almost eloquent as he told his listener of their confinement in a rude chamber at the Tower. Richard had been travelling north on his progress when the calculations of his evil mind told him that he could enjoy no peace from the conspiracies of the Woodvilles as long as the boys remained alive. He was perched on a plank relieving his bowels when he made his fateful decision. Almost to himself, he cried out, 'Who can I get to do this deed for me?'

One of his pages heard him and volunteered, 'My cousin is your man, Your Grace. He would do anything for you to gain favour in your sight.'

That very day Richard called this henchman to his presence and dispatched him along with two confederates to ride to London. Once there, they rode to the Tower, showed their pass to gain entrance, and proceeded to the chamber where young Edward and his brother Richard were sleeping.

Thomas had caught him off guard at that point when he interrupted the narration to ask for the name of the King's henchman. That was a question he should have anticipated.

He thought he handled the situation with adroit skill when he replied, 'Sorry, Thomas, I have his name on the tip of my tongue but it has slipped for the moment from my memory. One of the men who went with him was called Forrest, or was it Green? and the other man was called…' He stopped to think and then said, 'I will remember their names shortly and give them to you.'

That was a detail he should have settled weeks ago. Thomas would need the names for his history, and then there was that recommendation he had promised to provide for the King. The need to attend to another irksome detail occurred to him later in that same session.

After he had described the villainous work of the three men in smothering the two princes and hiding their naked bodies under a staircase, Thomas had asked, 'Were the bodies found there? If not, how does anyone know they were really murdered and their bodies hidden there?'

'There was no need at the time for anyone to conduct a search because no one announced or admitted that the princes were missing. Richard's party acted in complete secrecy and maintained an evil conspiracy of silence even within the Tower. I was a forced resident of the Tower at the time; and prisoners of status like me usually heard enough gossip from the guards to learn just about everything that was going on. But we heard not one word about the princes or their disappearance. It was not until some weeks later when I was staying at Buckingham's castle in Wales that I learned that the two princes had been murdered. Even then I was not sure they were dead.'

'But they *were* murdered, weren't they?'

'Oh yes, I am sure of that now. There was no sign of them either at the Tower or anywhere else when Henry came to power.'

Bishop Morton was satisfied with the rambling account about Richard III he had provided during these reading sessions with his young assistant. Thomas now had all the basic facts he wanted him to have. Of course, they should discuss some details at greater length. Some parts of the tale he had concocted could profit from fine tuning. Perhaps he could implicate Richard twice in the murder by charging that he had once before asked one of his lieutenants to kill the boys but had been rebuffed when that lord refused to commit so atrocious a crime. But details like that could wait. The important thing now was that Thomas must have a chance for using the ammunition Morton had provided in the preparation of the chronicle on Richard III.

With this much of his plan accomplished, Morton knew

that Thomas would be leaving his service at the end of his internship, and hoped he would at some later date write the necessary history. As he thought of the situation, he decided he did not want Thomas to leave. He had come to depend upon his service as a reader, and wanted him to continue both because he found himself looking forward to their conversations and because Thomas's reading had taken a burden off his failing eyesight.

Thomas must be asked to stay on for a second year of internship, and immediate steps must be taken to safeguard him from the plague. He sent for Father Gregory and asked if there was not some assignment in Oxford to which Thomas More could be detailed for several weeks. Gregory assured him he could find things for Thomas to do in Oxford, but questioned whether Thomas would be willing to absent himself from his legal studies. Morton waved away that obstacle with the observation that the readings at Lincoln's Inn had been suspended for the duration of the plague.

Before the week was out, Thomas was on his way back to Oxford. After five years in London, his return to the university seemed to him like a visit to heaven. There were old haunts to revisit, tutors whose acquaintance he wanted to renew, and England's finest library for him to use. Here he could spend time discussing philosophy, not law, and he could associate with some of England's foremost scholars. He also had some hope of finding Erasmus there, but that pundit was tarrying at Lord Mountjoy's estate before travelling to Oxford.

As Thomas settled down, he could not help but compare his current status with that of the Thomas More who had reported at Canterbury College as a fifteen-year-old student. He had been a poor lad with little financial support from home. Like many students, he had subsisted only a step or two above begging. Now he had both his still meagre allowance from Lincoln's Inn, and his stipend for work at the Chancery. Compared with his earlier visit, he was living in luxury. More than that, he could pick and choose the books and manuscripts he read and the lectures he attended.

Oxford was not like London where so much of the talk one heard was about commerce and trade. Most of the classes at the university were taught by clerics, and the students lived in a religious environment that appealed to him more than the brash materialism that surrounded him in London. He almost wished he had stayed on at Oxford, as he certainly would have had he aspired to a career in the Church. But he had chosen law, and those who chose to read law always went on to one of the inns of court in London.

He found he had arrived at the university just in time to hear a series of William Grocyn's lectures on the nature and acceptability of religious doctrine. Like Erasmus, Grocyn argued for simplification of the Church's message, for taking its basic tenets and doctrines back to their origins. He questioned the notion that the wisdom of the Church was cumulative, that it could profit from new additions and endless revisions.

Thomas was troubled at first by Grocyn's assertion that several religious writings besides Dionysius's *The Celestial Hierarchy* could be forgeries not written by the authors to whom they were attributed. He had questions like those he had raised earlier with Erasmus about the impact this charge could have on the scriptural foundations of the Church. But once he considered Father Grocyn's evidence, he was quick to accept his view that careful effort should be exerted to evaluate both the accuracy and the authenticity of the body of scriptures and commentaries that were accepted as Church doctrine.

Thomas enjoyed his discussions with others concerning

the nature of man, the role of the Church, and the sanctity of its doctrines and sacraments. He found himself questioning whether or not he had missed his calling. Perhaps he should have taken holy orders, become a philosopher, freed himself for a lifetime of studying, preaching and writing, rather than turning to a legal career. He could really have enjoyed life as a scholar, a teacher and writer. Then it occurred to him that there was no reason why a lawyer could not enjoy a good life and still give lectures and write.

Thomas's sphere of acquaintance at Oxford was by no means limited to clerics and tutors. He associated with different kinds of people, some of them businessmen, some scholars, and some visitors like himself who had used this return to the university as an excuse for absenting themselves from plague-ridden London. One of the men who impressed him most among this latter group was Thomas Howard, son of the Earl of Surrey. Howard was five years older than Thomas and was staying with his wife at a lodge on the outskirts of Oxford.

Howard had less scholastic inclination than Thomas, but had a keen interest in government and was impressed by the fact that More worked with Lord Chancellor Morton at the Chancery. What was at first a casual acquaintance ripened into a lasting friendship, as each took the measure of the other and recognised a colleague who might some day become one of England's leaders.

In one of their conversations, Thomas raised a question about the relationship of the fortunes of the Howard family to Richard III. 'It is no secret,' Howard told him, 'that my father's father owed his elevation to Duke of Norfolk to Edward IV. He was killed as he led one wing of Richard's army at Bosworth Field. All of our estates were attained after Henry's victory. My father was imprisoned for three years before the King forgave him, restored our estates, and made him Earl of Surrey.'

'Did he put any conditions on your father's restoration?'

'My father had to swear fealty to the crown, of course; and being a military man, he was soon busy protecting the King's interests. He commanded an army that put down an uprising in Yorkshire when I was sixteen. I begged him to let me fight with him, but he bundled me off to Oxford while he went and won enough glory to quash all questions about our loyalty to King Henry.'

'Do you have any memories of Richard III?'

'Not really. I saw him a few times at court; but I was only a boy, and children were not particularly welcome at court functions.'

'Do you remember what he looked like or how he acted?'

'No, he was just another man in my eyes. I have one vague memory of him talking to my father once and patting me on the shoulder. He said he had a son about my age who would need a playmate like me when he came to London. I probably would have remembered more if my father had talked to me about him as I was growing up, but he never did.'

Thomas saw no point in pushing his inquiry further. It was obvious Thomas Howard remembered nothing that supported Bishop Morton's assessment of Richard III. But nothing he said disproved what the Bishop had said either.

Back in London, the Lord Chancellor was again lounging in his favourite chair while sipping his goblet of wine. The first chill of autumn made the flames in his fireplace a welcome sight. Cooler weather had arrived, and already the plague was beginning to dissipate. Thomas More would be back soon to read to him again. His eyes really were not as good as they had once been, and he missed hearing Thomas's resonant voice. And he missed more than just Thomas's reading; he missed Thomas, his questions and enthusiasm. Had he only had a family like most other men, someone like Thomas could have been his grandson.

He stretched his arm out for no special reason and in doing so bumped his still half full goblet. It crashed to the floor. Morton looked at the mess and lamented, 'And so goes my lost manhood.' With sudden resolve, he stood up and moved to his other chair. As he sank into its cushions his thinking turned back to Thomas.

'Yes,' he said aloud, 'I will be happy to have you back because I covet your company. We have more details we need to discuss. Now as to the name of Richard's henchman, the man who murdered the princes. Was it Sir Robert Brackenbury? He was Constable of the Tower and could have been involved. No, he was a good Catholic who would never have participated in a murder plot. Besides, he died at Bosworth while fighting for Richard. Could it have been John Howard who was Duke of Norfolk or his son Thomas? They were both leaders in York's camp, but the Duke was south of London with the army when the boys were killed. Besides, he was killed at Bosworth too. As for Thomas who is now the Earl of Surrey, he is too close to Henry VII to touch. How about Sir James Tyrell? He was one of Richard's trusted lieutenants, and he was away in Calais when the battle was fought at Bosworth. Now there is a likely prospect.'

Chapter Sixteen

With the coming of autumn Thomas returned to London. Erasmus left Lord Mountjoy's estate at about the same time to go to Oxford, and the two friends did not have the good fortune of meeting. Looking back on his summer's experience, Thomas knew he had thoroughly enjoyed his stay in the university town, but also had to admit that he was happy to be back in the hustle of London.

He had enjoyed the quiet and subdued environment of Oxford just as he welcomed an occasional walk through green fields away from London's maze of twisted narrow streets and lanes that often were nothing more than stinking bogs in the winter. Yet he cherished an affection for London, where dozens of bakers, cooks, confectioners, butchers, fishmongers, and fowlers supplied the vitals for gluttony and joined with others in giving the city its pulse of life.

Thomas came back to the Chancery refreshed and eager to settle back into his old routine. He soon found that while most of his duties were unchanged, he now had more to do. His relationship with the Archbishop continued as before, and he was still Morton's eyes when it came to reading long letters and manuscripts. In addition, Father Gregory charged him with the supervision of the new class of interns.

In his close contact with the Lord Chancellor, Thomas quickly noted that Morton looked tired and worn. It was obvious that the burden he had carried during the summer months had taken its toll. He was still Henry's closest advisor, but he had lost much of his drive and he was now asking aides to do many things that he himself had done before.

It was only occasionally now that the Bishop displayed his characteristic zip and cheer. On one of those occasions, he beamed with satisfaction as he told Gregory and Thomas that Perkin Warbeck had been sent to the gallows for trying to corrupt his jailers, and that Edward Plantagenet, the retarded Earl of Warwick, had been beheaded for his complicity in Warbeck's plot.

'That news surprises me,' Gregory remarked. 'I thought the King was using Warbeck as an example of the mercy he can show to law breakers.'

'Henry showed mercy when Warbeck was captured two years ago, and again after he made his public confession last year that his so-called claim to the throne had been a hoax. He was condemned because he did not have sense enough to quit tampering with the King's justice.'

'I am also surprised about Warwick,' Gregory added. 'I had heard that he was incompetent.'

'Competent or not, he talked to Warbeck, and he was condemned on the basis of the evidence,' Morton said putting further discussion of the topic to rest.

Erasmus stopped for a while in London in December, on his way back to the Continent. In many respects he was quite changed from the poet and philosopher who had come from Paris earlier in the year. He was now fired up more than ever with a passion for learning Greek. Colet had convinced him that mastering the language was the next necessary step in his education. Thomas arranged for him to meet Grocyn, who was now in London, and the three of them spent an exciting half day in a lively discussion of their common interests in humanistic studies.

One unexpected complication spoiled Erasmus's farewell as he left England. Henry VII had revived an old law which forbade the export of currency when travellers left England. Thomas was sure it did not apply to scholars like Erasmus, and that Erasmus's twenty pounds would be safe if he first converted them into Dutch guilders. The advice was not good. Poor Erasmus was allowed to depart in peace, but eighteen of his twenty pounds stayed to pad out King Henry's coffers.

The winter that followed Erasmus's departure was a cheerless season. London had even more dark dank days with fog and occasional sleet than usual. Sickness seemed to abound. Thomas stayed healthy enough, but many desks at the Chancery were empty as their occupants found themselves bedridden with fevers and aching heads and joints. Bishop Morton was one of the less fortunate ones. He became seriously ill in February. Thomas joined Father Gregory in trying to nurse him back to health. Their efforts met with only partial success, as Morton was confined to his bed for days at a time by his bouts with ague.

Thomas went frequently to Morton's chambers to read correspondence and reports to him. The old Chancellor loved his young attendant, and his feelings were reciprocated. The two would talk for a while after every reading session, but their conversations no longer concerned Richard's reign. Morton wanted to discuss cheerful topics and Thomas obliged.

On the two occasions when Thomas asked about Richard, the Bishop said, 'Not now. Some day when I am more up to it perhaps, but not today.'

The Archbishop was taken to an estate in Kent during the late summer, and it was there that he died in September. Father Gregory was shaking with grief when he conveyed the news to Thomas. Both men broke into tears.

Bishop Morton's last words had been, 'Tell Thomas not to forget.'

Somehow the message unnerved him. He felt devastated. He had lost a bosom friend; the good Bishop had become his confidant, his advisor, his chief benefactor. With him gone he knew he was committed to write the history of King Richard, but he no longer wanted to work at the Chancery.

King Henry also felt a loss with the passing of his Lord Chancellor. The counsellor who had so carefully engineered his rise to power and who had served as his right arm by giving sound advice on how to run his kingdom was gone. He pondered for days as to whom he should now turn to for advice. With no obvious successor in mind, he decided to leave the post vacant. He would govern with the counsel of Bishop Richard Foxe, who was now Keeper of the Privy Seal, and his other ministers, until he felt the need to name a Lord Chancellor.

King Henry insisted that Father Gregory remain on at the Chancery where he continued to function as deputy chief administrator of governmental operations. Gregory asked Thomas to continue with his internship. He saw a productive and profitable future ahead if Thomas would remain in the King's service. Thomas, however, had other plans. He wanted to help Gregory, but his studies at Lincoln's Inn were almost completed and he thought it best that he give full attention to his legal studies.

Immersing himself in the law became Thomas's primary interest. He soon found though that he had sufficient spare time to start learning Greek. Within a few months, he was called to the Bar and was ready to start his legal practice. And he had also learned enough Greek to start reading books and manuscripts written in the language of ancient Athens.

Thomas was still living in his father's house. One evening when he was supping with his father and his stepmother, Alice, his father surprised him with the observation, 'You are getting your feet wet by beginning to practise law and you will soon have sufficient income to have a house of your own. I think it is time for you to start looking for a wife. Your brother has been married for almost a year now. You should consider following his example.'

This gentle reminder that his family expected him to marry caught Thomas completely by surprise.

'But where am I to find a wife?' he protested. 'There were no women at Lincoln's Inn, none at the Chancery, and there are none except for witnesses and plaintiffs in the law courts.'

'If you are seeking a possible wife, you should try looking where the women are. Your brother never had any trouble finding them. He liked girls more than you ever have. In the old days, I would have found a bride for you. Nowadays though, most men prefer to find their own.'

'I know a girl who would make a perfect wife for you,' his stepmother offered.

'Don't bother!' Thomas snapped.

Two evenings later, the Mores had a guest at dinner. Alice More had invited her young cousin Isabel Swanton to visit and eat with them. Isabel was twenty – she was just the right height, and had blonde hair and a comely face and figure. Thomas had reservations on meeting her. He did not appreciate his stepmother's attempt to play the role of matchmaker. Yet he soon admitted to himself that she was lovely and spirited.

He enjoyed talking to her, but was disappointed by the limited range of her interests and knowledge. She knew her letters, but seldom read anything. She could talk at length about clothes, or neighbourhood and family gossip, and all sorts of frivolous matters. But she was either dumb or disinterested when questions were raised about church doctrines, King Henry's policies, or the law.

Thomas saw Isabel home after supper. As he walked home afterward, he admitted that she was charming in a way. To be sure, she lacked many of the qualifications he wanted in a wife, but he liked her and wanted to see her again. He had only just met her, he was definitely not in love, and had no reason to think of her as his. Yet as he let his thoughts rove freely, he suddenly found his thinking engulfed by another of those teasing sexual fantasies that always prompted a stirring in his loins. This time Isabel was the companion in his fantasy.

Suddenly jolted to reality, he was disgusted with himself for what he had been thinking, 'Why?' he demanded, 'why must I forever have to fight off this obsession with sex?' Only by deliberately concentrating on the details of a legal action he was handling was he able to clear his mind and reduce the swelling in his crotch.

Thomas saw Isabel on frequent occasions during the next few weeks. He took her to mass. They picnicked along the Thames, went to parties, and took long walks in London and its countryside. He was feeling more relaxed and more under control in her presence, but the mere thought of her often triggered visions of sexual exploits that he fought desperately to suppress. He knew from her response that she welcomed his attention and was expecting more from him than just friendly conversation.

Thomas held back, however. He was uncertain as to what he should do. In his mind he was still conducting a lively debate about her. She was pretty; she was empty headed. He enjoyed her company and liked talking to her; her conversation had shown few marks of intelligence and was usually boring. She was full of spirit; she had no interest in doing anything to improve her mind. He enjoyed it when she praised him and patted his hand or cheek; she and the devil were obviously setting a trap for him.

Isabel was growing restless. She wondered if she should be more aggressive. She wanted action or at least some sign that Thomas would declare his affection for her. She liked him. He was an eligible bachelor with a promising future. He was witty, sensitive, always a gentleman. A girl could not hope for a better catch. But he was a cold pickle and not the least bit exciting.

When she complained to her cousin about Thomas's reticence in showing signs of awakening passion, Alice counselled her to be patient.

'Thomas doesn't know his own mind yet. You two make a perfect couple. I am sure he will come around. Don't be misled by his slow progress. Still waters runs deep. Once he thinks things through, he will want you, and he will be a steady man for you, not one of those lover boys with a roving eye who will cast you aside for another woman.'

Isabel listened and wondered. Thomas did surprise her with a gentle kiss on their next meeting and he showed some pleasure in cuddling her in his arms. Still, his responses to her overtures were disappointing.

He touches me as if I were a piece of fine pottery, she told herself. I want him, all of him, and I do not want to be treated like some holy relic that is to be seen but not caressed.

Two days later, Thomas and Isabel returned to the More residence to find both John and Alice gone for the afternoon. Thomas kissed her gently on her cheek and squeezed her hand as they entered the house. Once inside, he sat down and started to read a legal brief while she excused herself and went into Alice's bedroom. She returned a few moments later wearing nothing more than a thin robe. Thomas was shocked. He knew he should be revolted by this provocative behaviour; but he allowed his curiosity to dictate his response. He was dumbfounded when she stripped off his shirt and dropped her robe to reveal the nakedness of her upper body. A surge of excitement engulfed him, as he watched with his eyes wide open as she tossed her robe on to a vacant chair.

Hers was the first unclothed body of a grown woman he had ever seen. He was enchanted with what he saw. Her body was far more lovely than he had imagined. It was perfection. She was the image of desire. The revulsion he had started to feel faded into nothingness. Instead, he felt suddenly elated as his physical being and his male member responded in anticipation of an unexpected exciting new adventure.

Isabel pushed him back on to a chair, sat on his lap, and ignored the expanding bulge in his trousers as she grabbed his hands and insisted, 'Touch me here, and here. Now here!'

Thomas obliged and felt a thrilling sensation as his bare chest touched her naked body.

Isabel revelled in her conquest. 'Put your lips here,' she instructed, and then giggled when he did as he was told.

'Let's go to the bedroom,' she whispered in his ear. 'It is time and I want you so.'

Thomas was in a daze. This was a dream, another of his fantasies. It could not be real. He stood up to do her bidding and suddenly came to his full senses. 'No,' he protested. 'No, no! That is forbidden. We are not married.'

'It is all right, my darling, we will be soon,' Isabel pleaded.

'No! God has commanded that a man must know a woman only for procreation, and then only his wife. We are not married, and cannot do this.'

'Please Thomas… my body is yours and is ready for you.'

'No, never. Do you want us both to go to hell? I have sinned enough just by looking at your naked body.' He grabbed his shirt and put it on in preparation for leaving.

Isabel broke into tears and shouted, 'You old killjoy! I thought you were a real man...'

'I am a thinking man,' was his response. 'Eve tempted Adam with her apple of knowledge. Adam yielded and did what he knew he should not do, and they were forced to leave the Garden of Eden. You have offered me that same apple, Isabel, but I am strong enough to resist the temptation. I will not do this to you when I know that the salvation of our souls is at stake.'

'Strong, my eye! You are nothing but a cold unfeeling pickle. Go away with your priestly piety! Go join your monastery. That is where you belong and that is all you are good for. I don't want you. I want a real man.'

Thomas left the house in a foul mood. His mind was troubled, his temper frayed, and he had difficulty organising his thoughts. His walk took him through some of the seamier streets of London but he was oblivious to the squalor around him. He tried to analyse Isabel's attempt to seduce him. At first nothing seemed to make much sense. It was obvious, of course, that he had been right. He had followed the only righteous course he could choose.

The more he thought about the episode though, the more a counter line of reasoning squeezed its way into his thinking. Perhaps Isabel did have a valid reason for rebuking him. She did have a beautiful body. He had to admit he had enjoyed embracing her, holding her bare body next to his, fondling and kissing her bosom, and touching her tummy, and down there. Had he committed a different sin by rejecting her?

As his thoughts turned in this direction, his body went its own independent way and he began to sense the onset of an erection. Whether it was this, the half smile on his face, or something else, he did not know, but he suddenly sensed that he was not alone. A total stranger, a woman of the streets, was walking at his side. She seemed attractive and vivacious, though she was really only a pock-marked girl of sixteen or seventeen.

She brushed against him, smiled, and said, 'Would you like to have some fun, honey?'

He stared at her in disbelief. With his unsettled mood, he was half inclined to say 'yes'; but at that moment his mind focused on his predicament. Satan was using foul trickery again to gain control of his body and his soul. Without a word, he bolted from the scene and quickly directed his steps towards home. As he hurried along the winding streets, he asked himself again and again, How can a poor soul like me walk a righteous path when Lucifer is so determined to control my thoughts as well as my loins?

Isabel was gone when Thomas got back to his father's house. Alice More met him at the door and asked, 'Did you and Isabel have a spat? What happened between you anyway?'

'Why do you ask?'

'I know there was some trouble, probably no more than a lovers' quarrel. She was crying when I came home, and when she left she said she never wanted to see you again.'

Thomas had another sleepless night. The old fantasies of naked women came back time after time to haunt him and rob him of the sleep he needed. This time though, their figures were not faceless. Everyone of them looked like Isabel. Their sensuous bodies all had the smooth gentle curves of her inviting figure. They were neither hesitant nor reluctant to touch him, strip his clothes from his body, caress him, and pull his arms around them.

He fought against this recurring fantasy until the first glimmering of dawn brought light into his room. He then arose in disgust and resorted to the cold water treatment he usually used to subdue his turgid arousal. As he dressed, he concluded that his affair with Isabel could not end at this point. He had to see her again.

Perhaps as a warning, his thoughts turned to a fable he had heard about a sick fox and a lion. The lion found the fox lying in a narrow cave and tried to comfort him, saying, 'Let me lick your back my friend. My tongue has healing powers and can bring you back to health.'

'Your tongue,' replied the fox, 'may indeed be able to cure me of my ills, but my concern is that your tongue has bad neighbours.'

Thomas thought of the moral of the fable and realised that he could be playing with fire. Isabel's companionship could bring him comfort but her passion could be his undoing. Perhaps it would be best for everyone if he could avoid a possibly painful entanglement. Yet he wanted to take a chance. Surely he had enough self control and presence of mind to avoid trouble.

He had an early breakfast and then walked to her house. She was not up yet. He waited while she dressed and was mildly disappointed when she finally appeared and greeted him without enthusiasm. He did not apologise for his actions. He saw no reason for that. Instead, he told her he was sorry about their disagreement and asked that they forget yesterday and start over.

Isabel was slow to answer and then spoke with calm defiance, 'No Tom, it is definitely over between us. Like a fool, I offered you my body and you rejected it. I will never forgive you for that. I know now there is no future for us together. I want a man who wants to have fun. You are too strait-laced, and too holy for me.'

Chapter Seventeen

John More had suggested that Thomas find a wife and establish his own household. Was he merely jesting or was this a veiled request that he move from the house he had always considered home? Thomas was reasonably certain his father was not trying to push him out. But he also realised that his parents had earned a right to privacy and that the time had come for him to leave the parental nest.

A wife; a companion he could face life with, that was the rub. He was ready to admit that he had rather enjoyed his brief courtship of Isabel. Her refusal to see him any more singed his pride. It had left a void he must somehow fill. Yes, it was time for him to get a wife, but how should he proceed? He had spent little time talking to women outside his family while growing up, and he felt decidedly uneasy about his need to meet and talk to them now. Had he just had the foresight to have gained more experience in talking to women earlier, he would now be in a better position to make a sound decision in selecting a wife. It could have been far easier for him if his father had shouldered the burden by arranging his marriage to a client's daughter.

As he mulled over the question of how he should proceed in his quest for a wife, Thomas found it easier to push the issue aside than to come to a decision. Perhaps he would be spurred to action if he saw the right young lady. For now though, there were no prospects in sight which particularly appealed to him. It was easier and more logical, as he saw it, for him to devote his attention during his daylight hours to his two major passions: promoting his legal practice and improving his ability to read and write in Greek. After dark, he gave most of his attention to reading books and manuscripts he borrowed from libraries and friends.

Who, he asked himself one day, would my father have picked as my bride if the decision had been left to him? He realised his case was not at all like that of a royal prince. Dynastic considerations did not dictate an alliance with some other family. His father probably would have favoured marriage to a prospective heiress of a sizeable estate, but he knew of no possible brides with that qualification. Most likely, John More would have picked the daughter of some family friend.

As Thomas's mind explored this possibility, he thought of Joyce Leigh. She was about seventeen, the daughter of a close family friend who worshipped with the Mores at the church of St Stephen Walbrook. Joyce was a pretty girl, quiet, shy, sedate, and obviously very pious. Her brother Edward had already taken his vows for the Church. With these qualifications, Thomas felt she could very well be the girl for him.

Thomas carefully arranged to greet her the next time they were at mass together. He walked home with her. He visited with her several times and took more than one long walk with her along the Thames. She was an appreciative listener when he talked about religion and other serious matters. From her questions and brief comments he concluded that she had wit and an active mind. He felt a growing affection and respect for her. She was timid and not at all as aggressive, as Isabel had been. This pleased him as he was not ready to pursue a whirlwind courtship. For now, at least, he preferred to go slow and let her gradually become better acquainted with him. Later, if all went well, he might decide to push his case.

The illusion of a leisurely courtship Thomas had built in his thoughts came to a sudden and unexpected end when the Leigh family announced that their pious daughter had chosen to become a bride of Christ. She was forsaking the world and taking the veil as one of the Poor Clares in a convent of the Minories outside the walls of London. Thomas was startled by the news but also pleased.

Partly to console himself, he turned to an enterprise that had lain dormant in his mind since his last meeting with Erasmus. Erasmus had told him that he should start a writing career by translating some worthy publication from Latin into English.

As he considered his possibilities, Thomas thought of a recently published volume of the papers of Giovanni Pico. Pico, the Earl of Mirandula, was an Italian scholar and humanist who had died a decade earlier at the early age of thirty-one. He was a devout layman who had earned wide respect as a student of Biblical literature. In the last months of his life, he gave most of his property away and indicated an intention of becoming a Dominican friar and spending his remaining years living in poverty as an itinerant preacher.

Contrary to the wishes of some Church authorities, Pico had pushed an ambitious plan for bringing together a group of theologians with divergent points of view from different countries with the hope that they could iron out their differences and agree on a common doctrine. As a humanist, he also wrote tracts which some critics considered heretical. Among these was his essay 'On Human Destiny', which asserted that man occupies a central place in the universe and is a free agent who can determine his own behaviour.

Thomas felt himself fully in accord with Pico's writings. Translation of his works into English appealed to him as a worthwhile project which he could pursue with enthusiasm. His translation of *The Life of Picus* was soon completed. Once it was published, a special copy went as a New Year's gift to Joyce Leigh at her convent.

Despite the concentrated emphasis he gave to his law practice, to learning Greek, and to pursuing his humanist studies, Thomas was still haunted by his inability to escape from the persistent misery and torment he suffered from his sexual fantasies. By diligent effort he could keep his mind relatively clear of such thoughts while he was awake. At night, they were never far away and always seemed ready to rise like a hydra-headed monster to strike at him and take control of his subconscious mind. Try as he might he had yet to find an acceptable way to keep them from filling his head with erotic dreams at the hour of waking.

His affliction tore at the core of his well being. In his misery, he feared that his soul might already be lost and that he could gain its redemption only by superhuman effort. There must be some relief from this scourge, he told himself. Masturbation is a sin I cannot accept. Fornication is an even greater sin. Even within marriage, I am not sure I will be able or willing to limit my cravings to acts for procreation only. If stating my vows for the priesthood could save me from this torment, I would gladly do so. But that can be a deception. With a depravity such as mine, I could never be a good priest. And a priest who ignores and disobeys his vows is the worst sinner of all.

He concluded that marriage was the only workable solution for him. When he considered the problem of finding a suitable wife, however, he felt himself caught in a paralysing bind. He just was not ready to commit himself. He wondered if it would help if he confessed this shortcoming to a priest in some other part of the city. Desirable as it appeared, he held back from this option because the advice and admonitions he had received the few times he had mentioned his erotic fantasies in his confessions had always fallen short of providing answers he could make use of.

Perhaps frank recognition of his fears could save him. One thing for certain, the haunting torment that plagued him was wrecking his happiness and disrupting his peace of mind. Tired though he often was, he dreaded the prospect of going to sleep because he knew that with sleep his guard would be down and Satan would be there to prey upon his mind with evil thoughts.

It was after yet another restless night when an erotic fantasy had filled his thoughts, and he awakened to see that his erection had raised his blanket like a midget's tent that he recalled that forbidden memory he had tried desperately to ignore. On earlier occasions he had always struggled hard to put it out of his mind. This morning, it would not budge. He must look at it candidly and acknowledge a truth he had long tried to deny.

His thoughts took him back to a day almost a decade earlier when he was one of the new boys who had come to live in Bishop Morton's household. Father Damien was a young priest whose duties called for comprehensive supervision of the boys he was charged with educating. After all of these years, Thomas could not clearly recall how the priest had looked. He remembered that he had a beard and dark hair which he wore long down to his shoulders; but he recalled nothing about the appearance of his face.

One afternoon Father Damien had asked Thomas to come with him to his quarters, where he had a tub filled for a bath. He disrobed and ordered Thomas to do the same. He stepped into the bath, sank down into the water to wet his back and then stood up and bade Thomas to soap his back. Once this was done he turned around and instructed his young helper to soap his chest, his abdomen and legs. Thomas recalled a mixture of curiosity, and reluctance to touch the priest as he observed the increasing turgidity of his male member.

Thomas was shocked when the teacher he respected and trusted ordered him to put soap on his now bloated penis and rub his hands back and forth along it. He shuddered, experiencing a feeling of revulsion. Something told him he was doing something that was not right.

'I can't!' he cried out. 'I won't!' he insisted as he dropped the soap and tried to scramble out of the tub to flee from the scene. Father Damien had different plans. He grabbed Thomas and held his thin squirming body next to him while his erection throbbed against Thomas's soft tummy.

Thomas's effort to call out and free himself were blocked when the priest grabbed him by his jaw and one of his arms. Overpowered, Thomas saw the futility and possible danger of further resistance.

Once he calmed down, Father Damien sponged the soap off both their bodies, dried them with a towel and dressed, bidding Thomas to do the same.

He then turned to Thomas and said, 'That was great. It was really fun, wasn't it?'

Thomas balked at the thought of agreeing.

Damien was not pleased and tried again, 'Well, it was not bad; it is something you will learn to enjoy. Remember we are friends and this is just a little secret we will keep between us. Won't we?'

When Thomas refused to answer him, he became abusive. 'Listen, you little snipe! You are not going to tell anyone about this, are you?'

By now Thomas knew he had participated in an evil act. He started to shake and quiver but did not cry. Damien too saw the seriousness of the situation. He could murder the boy to keep him quiet; but he had no desire to do him any harm. Still, he could not risk a charge being raised that might ruin his career.

He grabbed hold of his young charge as if to shake him

and said, 'If you want to leave this room alive, you must take a solemn oath to forget everything that has happened here and never speak of it to anyone.'

'Not even at confession?'

'Most certainly not at confession. Are you ready to take your oath?'

Thomas pleaded, 'Don't do this to me. I won't tell. Honest, I won't. I promise.'

'You will take the oath, or else!' Damien sternly demanded.

Thomas knew he was cornered. There was no other way out for him, so he nodded his reluctant consent.

'Then put your hand over your heart and repeat after me, I, Thomas More, swear and give this oath in good faith that I will do my utmost to put all memory of what happened this afternoon out of my mind, that I will never think of this experience, and that I will never mention it to anyone nor think of it in my prayers or confessions. I further swear that if I break this solemn oath I will surrender my rights to the salvation of my soul and will consign my soul to eternal hell.'

It was a crestfallen and disheartened Thomas who went back to his fellow students after the ordeal. An oath to him was something sacred, a declaration not to be violated. True to his word, he said nothing of the experience to any associates or teachers. No mention of it was even hinted in his confessions. With passing time, he succeeded in burying the memory so deep in his subconscious that it rarely surfaced in his thinking.

Perhaps some other student who had a similar experience with Father Damien reported it. Thomas did not know because no one at the house talked openly about such things. But he did know that Father Damien never called on him for a repeat performance, and that he suddenly disappeared from Morton's house a few months later without fanfare or any explanation being given.

The emergence of this half-forgotten memory from his past startled Thomas. For years he had fought to keep it submerged and had pushed it back every time it started to surface without ever considering its substance. He had long equated any revival of the memory with the breaking of a sacred oath, an oath intimately associated with the salvation of his soul.

This morning he had done the unthinkable. He had violated his oath by thinking about that experience. Somehow though, this violation did not seem a sin. What he had really done was to uncover the mind-wrenching basis for the troubling torment that afflicted him. This was not a perfect answer to his problem. But now that he recognised that his mental aversion to thoughts about sex had sprung from his horror at Damien's wanton behaviour, he could accept a more positive view of his natural self. He still had the problem of dealing with the violation of his oath. He probably would also still have erotic fantasies; but gone would be the disgust, dread, and terror he had usually felt in their aftermath. He could now live a more normal life.

Chapter Eighteen

Thomas felt he must talk to someone who could calm his troubled mind. Much of the misery and revulsion associated with his fantasies was washed away with his confrontation of that forbidden memory of sexual abuse. He could now accept his sexual being in a more wholesome manner. But by recalling that memory, he had violated an oath, and thereby endangered the salvation of his soul.

This was not a matter he could discuss with his father, nor with his parish priest. He thought of going to Father Gregory but decided against it. Gregory was filled with kindness and understanding, but this was hardly his area of expertise. After serious thought, he decided he should go to the prior of London's order of Carthusian monks. The prior was a saintly man who deserved his reputation for piety and wisdom.

Father Bruno was willing to see him and listened attentively as Thomas explained his problem. When he had finished, the good priest thought for a while before he spoke.

'You have done well to come here, my son. We Carthusians are sworn to lives of chastity as well as poverty and piety. You were abused when you were a helpless child by a man of the Church. That is a terrible crime, but it is his sin, not yours. Your only sin was in breaking your forced oath of silence. God can forgive you for that, but you must live a life of penance to be worthy of his forgiveness.'

'And what must my penance be?'

'That is not a matter for me to decide,' the prior told him. 'Only you can decide what it is you must give up once again to find favour in the eyes of God.'

The decision Thomas had to make was a hard one. What could he give up that would represent a valid but still acceptable act of self abasement. It was obvious that God did not want him to give up his eyesight or the use of an arm or leg. These were tools he must use in pursuing his mission on earth. Nor did he feel that God wanted him to become a priest when he already knew he could never be a good priest. No, his penance must involve giving up some comfort of life he had enjoyed until this moment.

Yes, his father had brought him up in a comfortable home, and as an unredeemed sinner he must now give up some of that comfort as his penance. For centuries ascetics had shown their piety by sleeping on bare planks with only a log for a pillow and only a light mantle to cover and warm their bodies. They wore horsehair shirts that pricked and irritated their skin. They scourged themselves with whips until blood oozed from the welts on their backs. He would do all of these things with a fervent prayer that God would forgive him and accept his soul for salvation.

With this decision made, Thomas took immediate steps to move from his father's house. John More discouraged his hurried decision, but agreed his son was an adult earning his own living, and that the time had come for him to move from the family household. He was surprised, however, at Thomas's choice of a new domicile. Instead of renting a house or a suite of rooms as he could well afford to do, he chose to live at the monastery of the Carthusian monks.

The Carthusian order had been founded in France some four hundred years earlier by St Bruno, a monk who sought peace and solitude for his followers. Their monastery on the outskirts of London had three sets of cells. A cluster of central rooms was reserved for the use of the prior and his assistants, a second block of cells was used by the monks, and a third block was occupied by lay brothers and penitents who lived with the monks for varying periods of time.

Thomas was assigned to a cell in the third blocks. His life there was devoid of luxury or adornment. The monks lived in perpetual silence, avoided contact with the flesh, ate only one meal a day, and wore a cilice, the horsehair shirt of piety. Their time was spent in silent prayers, and hours of manual labour, with virtually no recreation.

The simple life-style appealed to Thomas. He slept on bare boards with only a sheet to cover him, wore a cilice, prayed with the monks, and frequently joined them in eating their plain fare. But he lived a fuller life outside the monastery walls. He enjoyed the pageants, walks and scenery of London. He was engrossed in the promotion of his legal career and responded with enthusiasm when he was invited to become a part-time teacher by serving as a Reader of Law at Furnivall's Inn.

One of the most exciting experiences came with the parade and festivities that greeted the arrival of Princess Catherine and her party from Spain. Catherine was betrothed to Arthur, the sickly young Prince of Wales. Thomas had several opportunities to see her both on the street and up close at a reception. He was critical of the appearance and bearing of some of the party that had come with her from Spain. But his feelings for the Princess were decidedly different. She was very beautiful with her dark hair and flashing eyes. From his first view of her, he felt himself committed to her perpetual service.

His legal practice was concerned mostly with protecting and furthering the interests of merchants and traders. His father's connections brought him several of his first clients. Their favourable reports to others about his quick grasp of their problems and his ability to use the law for their benefit soon brought enough new business to keep both him and his father very busy. Thomas soon earned a reputation as an effective pleader in court cases. Most of his legal work, however, called for acting in his clients' interests in business negotiations. Here too, he acquired a superb reputation as a negotiator who could bring merchants and other businessmen with rival interests together by devising mutually acceptable solutions that would not tie up their funds in time-consuming court litigations.

One case that commanded his attention involved Richard Hunne, a well-to-do tailor. Hunne's infant son had died when only a few weeks old. He had taken the boy's body to his church for burial and the priest, a Thomas Dryfield, had demanded the child's christening garment as a mortuary fee for his service at the burial.

Payment of the mortuary fee was a controversial but long-accepted practice with the Church. It was treated in canon law as a symbol of the layman's subservience to the priesthood. Those who were anticlerical opposed the payment as a tool used by greedy priests to extract property from bereaved parents, for performing funeral services and providing spiritual consolation at a time of sorrow.

Hunne could well afford to pay the fee. He chose instead to stand on principle and refused the request for payment. When Dryfield sued him for payment, he countered with the argument that as a corpse could not own property under the common law, the raiment in which his child had been wrapped at his christening did not belong to the dead boy's body and thus could not be claimed as a fee for his burial.

Hunne came to Thomas to solicit his services as his legal representative. Thomas quickly discerned that this was a conflict between the canon law and the common law. If he took the case, he could soon be forcing clarification of an anomaly in English law. At the same time, he would be espousing anticlericism and its opposition to the special perquisites and privileges enjoyed by priests, which the prelates of the Church stoutly maintained were theirs by time-honoured right. Here was another assault against the privileges of the clergy that Bishop Morton had worked hard to protect.

Thomas favoured Church reform. As a humanist he favoured re-examination of Church doctrine to identify it more closely with the content of the original gospels. But he was a conservative Catholic on the matter in hand. His convictions supported the position of the Church. He tried to persuade Hunne to stop his fight. When Hunne demurred, he recommended that he find another lawyer to handle his case. When his father raised questions about his stand, he clung doggedly to the position that this was an issue on which the canon law should not yield to the popular demand for reform.

'How can you take that position?' his father asked. 'You are a liberal, almost a radical, when it comes to talk of Church reform. Yet you are defending a despicable practice that priests use to fatten their purses at the expense of the poor.'

'Simplifying the Church and cleansing its doctrines is one thing, but undermining the rights of the priesthood is another,' Thomas responded. 'I see this as a challenge to the authority of the Church. That is the threat I oppose.'

In addition to his law practice, Thomas found time to continue his pursuit of humanist studies. He met frequently with Grocyn who now was vicar of St Lawrence Jewry, and also with Thomas Linacre, a Londoner who had once lived in Greece and who had an interest in Greek manuscripts that touched on medical and scientific issues. Both of these men wished to further their knowledge of Greek literature. His meetings with Grocyn brought an invitation for him to give a series of public lectures in

Grocyn's church on St Augustine's *City of God*.

Thomas had long been an enthusiastic devotee of St Augustine. He found it hard to decide whether Augustine or Aquinas was his favourite saint. From frequent reading, he had almost memorised much of *The City of God*. He approved of the saint's defence of the Church against pagans and infidels, his condemnation of sensuality as evil, and his argument that it was a basic duty of governments to force their citizens to be good Christians. His well-organised lectures, delivered with his resonant speaking voice, stirred public comment and were well attended, even though his emphasis was more on historical and philosophical than on theological issues.

A few days after the fifth and last of his lectures, he stopped at the Chancery to pay an informal visit to Father Gregory.

The good father congratulated him. 'Several of your listeners have gone out of their way,' he reported, 'to tell me they found your comments interesting and instructive. Your lectures have earned respect for you and for your talent. I have also heard that more people attended your lectures than attended those Father Grocyn recently gave at St Paul's.'

Thomas thanked Gregory for his encouragement and passed on as quickly as he could to a discussion of other topics. While they were talking, Brother Bernard came into the room. Gregory introduced him and explained that Bernard was working at the Chancery now that his inspection assignment was completed.

Thomas had heard of Bishop Morton's decision to send inspectors out to examine church and shire records, but had an erroneous understanding of their purpose. Not knowing of their true nature, he jumped to the conclusion that Bernard had been sent out to find evidence of Richard's perfidy and misconduct. He therefore observed, 'I trust you found the evidence you sought of Richard III's cruel and heinous nature.'

'Heinous nature?'

'Yes, there must be eye-witness accounts out there of his depraved nature, of his willingness to rape and kill to gain power. Bishop Morton said he was a vicious monster, an ugly hunchback.'

Brother Bernard was astounded by Thomas's assertion. He yielded to a sudden pressing desire to leave the room rather than argue with this brash visitor. Later, after Thomas had left, he asked Father Gregory if there was any truth in Thomas's outburst.

'I do not really know,' Gregory told him. 'I never once had a close view of King Richard, and I have never been in a position to make sound judgements about his behaviour either before or after he became King. Bishop Morton knew him well. If that was what he said about him, it must be true.'

Bernard was confused. Something definitely was wrong. He knew from his inspection tour that King Richard had been popular in much of England, and that many people who had known him remembered him as an honourable leader who was interested in the welfare of his subjects. He also knew that Henry for some reason had ordered the destruction of recorded evidence of his popularity. Now he had met a close associate of Archbishop Morton who spoke of Richard's cruel and heinous nature. Thomas More was too young to have known Richard. Was his harsh impression a product of his association with the Archbishop? Could Morton and the King somehow have been involved in a plot to blacken Richard's otherwise good name? If so, why? These were puzzling questions for which he had no answers.

Chapter Nineteen

Brother Bernard was an amiable man who usually avoided controversy. He was troubled, however, by Thomas's claim that Cardinal Morton had described Richard as 'a vicious monster, an ugly hunchback'. Something was wrong. This was definitely at odds with the impression he had gained during his inspection tour. One view or the other had to be wrong. So aroused was his curiosity that he felt himself compelled to seek out the truth. In committing himself to this task, he realised he must be circumspect. It would not do for him or for Father Gregory to be identified as men who questioned King Henry's policies. At the same time though, it seemed important to him that someone determine whether Richard had been an evil and vicious monarch, or the victim of a conspiracy to make him appear so.

As a member of the Chancery staff, Bernard had ample opportunity to seek out and talk to a wide spectrum of people, including almost everyone who was now active or who in the past had been active at court. He soon found that it was easy to talk with most of them, and that the older courtiers were often eager to gossip about the good old days. After a few minutes of general conversation, he could sense whether they were willing to converse further, and if so, where their biases lay.

In an effort to canvass a wide range of opinions, he sought out several people now in their forties and fifties who were known to have supported Henry before he gained power. Many of them were critical of Richard for reasons of principle, some despised him for his action in seizing the crown; and some admitted they had hated him mostly because he was a champion of the House of York.

Lord Exeter said, 'My opposition to Richard had nothing to do with him as a man. He was probably as good a man as any in England; but my family and I had fought against the old Duke of York and his sons for twenty-five years. My father, my brother and two uncles were killed in wars with them. I opposed him on principle; but if you pressed me, I would have to admit he did England a good turn in getting rid of the Woodvilles and saving us from the reign of another boy king.'

Bernard was surprised to find that none of Richard's critics described him as being deceitful, monstrous, or ugly. On the contrary, many of them saw him as a reasonable, even praiseworthy, monarch who had been an unfortunate victim of circumstance.

He was also surprised when some of the people he talked to confided that they had been Yorkist sympathisers. Some of this group criticised Richard for crucial mistakes, such as the trust he had placed in Buckingham and the Stanleys, and thought he had been a good King at heart. They saw him as an honourable but often maligned man, who could have done much for England had his time not been cut short.

Lady Alice Bodwin was one of this latter group. Bernard decided to visit her when he learned she had been a young bride at Richard's court whose husband had had the good fortune of being on a trip to Antwerp at the time Henry seized power. Lady Alice and her lord had favoured Richard, but lost nothing at his death, and were able to maintain their position at court after a quick shift of allegiance to the new monarch.

Lady Alice was now a widow who lived in partial seclusion. She made no effort to hide or disguise her sympathy for Richard. In her view, he had been a good King, much better and more loveable than his successor.

'But wasn't he an ugly hunchback?'

'Ugly and a hunchback? Where did you get that preposterous idea? I only saw Richard once at court while King Edward was still alive. You can believe me when I tell you he was the most handsome man there. He wasn't as tall as his brother Edward, but he was erect and had a manly bearing. He was a good dancer and most of the women would have done anything to get him; but the Lady Anne was the only lady for him.

'You ask if he had a twisted back. I know for certain that his back was as straight and muscular as that of any man. I can say that because I saw his naked back. I was there in the Queen's party when Richard and Anne were crowned. At one point in the ceremony both of them were required to strip to the waist and walk in their bare feet through the cathedral to be anointed by the Archbishop.'

'You mentioned the Lady Anne who was Richard's Queen. Did he show an interest in any other ladies at court?'

'When it came to his love life, I should say his sex life, Richard was very different from his brother Edward. He lavished all his affection on Anne.'

'But wasn't there some scandalous talk about him?'

'No, Richard was one of the most strait-laced kings we have ever had. Every little thing that happened at court was soon bandied about in gossip. With King Edward, we knew the name of every woman he took to any of his chambers within hours of the time she went through the door. Everyone was watching to see if they could find something similar to report of Richard; but there was never anything to report. Oh, he danced with his niece, the Princess Elizabeth who is now our Queen, during the Christmas festivities one year. Some gossips tried to make a big thing out of it, and even suggested that Richard might put his wife aside to marry her. Those of us who were there, though, knew there was nothing to it except vicious gossip. Queen Anne was the only woman for him, and he kept on loving and honouring her memory after she died.'

'Was there any talk of him remarrying?'

'Of course. His son died a few weeks before Queen Anne did. Both of them suffered from the lung disease. Almost everyone at court wanted the King to remarry. He probably would have had he lived longer; but he was true to Anne's memory right up until he was killed.'

'Was King Edward popular with the ladies at court?'

'He had that reputation. I did not come to the court until the last year of his reign. By then he was fat and bulging. I cannot say I found him attractive. Several of my friends told me he had been a handsome Prince Charming earlier. Some of them even admitted they had encouraged his advances, as if he had ever needed encouragement.'

'What did the men think?'

'Some husbands and fathers took offence at the King's behaviour; but most of the men at court just tried to ignore it.'

'Is it true that Edward had affairs with several of the ladies at court?'

'No one made any secret of that. There were several women there like Kate Milford and Elizabeth Lucy who had borne bastard children to him who bragged publicly about their relations with him. It did not come as a surprise to us when we learned after his death that he had promised when he was a young King to marry Eleanor Talbot if she would go to bed with him. Everyone knew he gave the same promise to Elizabeth Woodville, who was then the widow of Lord Grey, and that she had held him off until he went through that secret wedding ceremony with her.'

'Didn't the Queen object to his affairs with other women?'

'He did not pay her any heed if she did. My friends said the Queen was willing to let him be a master stud as long as he kept showering her and her family with honours and benefices. She was an attractive woman and gave him two sons and four daughters. Some men at court called her "the King's grey mare" because she had been Lady Grey when he met her and because he rode her so often.

'I thought they were really unfair with their criticism. My husband said that in their hearts most of the men who were doing the criticising were really just envious of the King's ability to attract beautiful women and treat them like concubines in his private harem. Some of those same men set their eyes on Jane Shore when she came to the court. They were not too happy when she gave her favours only to the King, and a few other top men. They were the ones who were quick to call her a whore and a slut.'

With Lady Alice's reminiscences, Bernard felt he could put his questions to rest. He was surprised when she volunteered another lead.

'You were asking about King Richard. If you really want to hear what he was like, you should talk to my brother, Sir John Cowan. He was one of Lord Stanley's lieutenants. He saw Richard many times at court.'

'Sir John Cowan? I have not heard of him at court.'

'He isn't there any more. He turned away from the evils of the world three years ago and is now a lay brother at the Dominican monastery at St Matthew's.'

A week later Brother Bernard journeyed to St Matthew's where he asked to see Brother John Cowan. The old brother came to him with a very wrinkled face, and a grizzly beard, clothed in a simple friar's robe. He seemed pleased to have a visitor from the outside world, and particularly so when he found that Bernard had come at the suggestion of his younger sister Alice. When Bernard stated his desire to learn more about Richard, the old man beamed.

'That is a story I held back from telling for many years, and I have since given up hope that anyone would ask to hear it.'

'If you will grant me that honour, I would like to hear you out.'

Brother John began. 'When I was a young man I was an officer at the court of Edward IV. My father was a cousin of Lord Thomas Stanley, and I rose in his service until he selected me as one of his lieutenants. I first knew Richard when he came to court as the Duke of Gloucester. He was a man you had to respect, not only because he was a great warrior and the best military commander in the kingdom, but also because he was a man of high principles. He frowned on many things that went on under his brother's nose at court, and chose to live in the more wholesome countryside most of the time. The Woodvilles hated him for what he was. They also knew their influence would end if he ever came to power.

'Like many others at court, I had no love for the Woodvilles and the way they were bleeding England dry. I kept my feelings to myself, but I was not alone in thinking that it would be best for England if someone could do some house cleaning. Then Edward died, and we discovered he had picked his brother to serve as Lord Protector. Had I been independent, I would have jumped to his support. But Lord Stanley was My Liege lord, and it was my duty to serve his interests.

'There was a lot of confusion at court after Edward's death. The Royal Council acted as though Edward's will was an accidental mistake. Most of the members of the Council did not want Richard to rule, even temporarily, so they made plans to bring Prince Edward to London for an early coronation. Richard heard about their scheme and came south from his castle at Middleham with a small army. He captured the Prince's party and brought the Prince with him to London. That surprise threw everything into turmoil.

'Sir Thomas Stanley, who was on the Council, suddenly shifted to support Richard. As I think of it now I realise that he and his brother Sir William were both two-faced schemers who had no scruples. Neither of them saw anything wrong in promising their support to one party and then turning against it. Their only allegiance was to their own interests. Sir Thomas swore his support for Richard, and Richard showered him with honours, some of which spilled over to me.

'But Lord Stanley was somehow mixed up in that Hastings affair. He was knocked down and wounded in the brawl that took place in the Council Chamber when Richard accused Hastings of treason. Stanley was arrested with the other leaders of the conspiracy and detained in his own house. Richard released him after a few days, but he was inactive for weeks because of his wound. While he was recovering, I was on my own, and I was one of those who cheered Richard on and begged him to accept the crown.

'After Lord Stanley's recovery, we were public supporters of Richard. Stanley's wife, Margaret Beaufort, was already secretly conniving to advance the claim of the crown to Henry, her son by her earlier marriage to Edmund Tudor. I am not sure Stanley knew much about her activities that early on; but he started working with her a while later when he was pretending to be Richard's friend and supporter.

'When Henry's army invaded England, Lord Stanley took his army to support Richard at Bosworth Field. The Earl of Northumberland also had an army there and both were pledged to support their King. When the battle started, both of them knew where and when they were to send their men into battle, but both commanders ignored their orders and just held their forces back and waited.

'With half of his army just watching the fighting, the battle seemed to be going against King Richard; when he saw an opportunity to win by charging the hilltop where Henry sat in his saddle, well protected by his guard. Richard led that charge like a demon out of hell. I could see it all from where I sat on my charger next to Lord Stanley. If we had given Richard a few more minutes, he would have won the day. At that moment Stanley, acting like the Judas he was, ordered us to turn our might on the King's flank. Richard and the warriors around him were hacked to pieces and Henry was our new King.

'I have never been proud of that day, nor of our action in charging across that field to cut down King Richard and his brave men. It brought no honour for us. Lord Stanley saw his wife's son crowned as King. Henry made him the Earl of Derby, but aside from that he gained little profit from his treachery. His brother William bragged openly that it was he who led the charge that saved Henry's life, but Henry showered no honours on him, and even ordered his execution a few years later.

'I hated every day of my service with the Stanleys after Bosworth, and left their service after Sir William was charged with treason. His execution was not enough to wipe away my feelings of guilt for turning on the King we were pledged to support. I gave up the world out there at that point and came here for peace.'

'You said Margaret Beaufort was conniving to put her son on the throne. What did she do?'

'You probably know she was a daughter of the first Duke of Somerset, who was a grandson of John of Gaunt. That made her one of the few people of Lancastrian blood who were still at court. In addition to that, she had been married first to Edmund Tudor, the Earl of Richmond, who died before her son Henry was born; then to a brother of Buckingham's father; and thirdly to Lord Stanley. She saw a lot more of Buckingham, who grew up in her household at court, than of her own son who lived with his uncle in Wales. But she was still devoted to furthering Henry's career.

'She kept in touch with him both while he was growing up in Wales and later when he was hiding out at the court of the Duke of Brittany. There was not much she could do while Edward was King. She was a close friend of Edward's Queen, and made the best of her situation. After Edward's death she spent quite a bit of time with Buckingham, and then showed her true colours when she saw a chance for shifting the support the Woodvilles had among the nobility on to her son.'

'Weren't Edward's two sons still alive at the time?'

'Everyone assumed they were. But Lady Margaret was looking beyond that. She knew the two boys and Richard were all that stood between Henry and the throne. My wife was one of her women and from what she told me I was fairly certain the two princes were already dead or soon would be.'

'Do you mean she was plotting to do away with them?'

'I cannot be sure of that. After Hastings was executed and Rotherham and Morton were sent to the Tower, my wife heard Margaret tell Buckingham that he should cultivate Morton's friendship and get him out of the Tower because, she said, "He can help us get what we want." Neither of them wanted to see the Woodvilles in power again, so I assume what they wanted was for either Buckingham or Henry to be King.'

'Do you think Buckingham acted for her?'

'Again I cannot be sure. She was his aunt and he felt much closer to her than to any of the Woodvilles. I have often wondered if Buckingham didn't get rid of the two princes at her suggestion. With Richard going on progress that summer the way he did, he certainly had the opportunity.

'Anyway, Lady Stanley made such a nuisance of herself after Buckingham's death that Richard attaindered her estates. But he made a mistake when he turned them over to her husband on Stanley's promise that he would keep her under control and out of contact with Henry.

'She sent a message to Morton, who was then in France, about Richard's negotiations to bring Henry back from Brittany. Stanley may not have known what she was doing. In any case, he went along with Richard's conditions for accepting her estates, and then turned his back on his King when the time came for him really to keep his promises.'

Bernard was more than a little moved by Sir John's story. 'Peace be with you, brother,' he murmured as he embraced the old warrior and prepared to leave.

Chapter Twenty

Edward Barnes and John More were once again seated in the corner booth of the Grey Horse Inn where they now met almost every Friday to exchange news and professional gossip.

'What news do you bring from the court?' John asked. 'The accounts we pick up on the street are so rattled and twisted that one hears a different version around every corner. One of the best things about sharing a beer with you is that you at least have your facts straight.'

'Street news is eighty per cent imagination, John. With all the printing presses we are starting to get, one would think someone would start printing reliable news for us on a regular basis.'

'That would really be something, Ned, but we will never live to see it. A few people like us might be willing to pay a farthing for the latest news. Most folks though could not care less. With so few people able to read, or even concerned about the real news, there just is not enough market out there to make printing it a paying proposition.'

'Well, I am happy if I can bring you some titbits that are based on facts rather than just gossip. If what I tell you is better than what you get on the streets, it is only because my news comes from second or third hand rather than from thirtieth-hand sources.'

'Is it true that the King is finally going to name a new Lord Chancellor?'

'That is the rumour. I wouldn't get excited about it

though. It has been almost three years now since Bishop Morton died, and in that time we have heard rumours of several different people being appointed to the post.'

'With the Chancellor being the King's principal advisor, the post should have been filled long before now. Henry is pretty canny though. As long as he has Father Gregory handling the routine operations of the Chancery, I suppose he figures he can get along without extra advice.'

'That is probably true. From what I hear, he has been impressed lately with the service and advice he has received from Bishop Warham, and that Warham will be his choice for Lord Chancellor and also for Archbishop of Canterbury.'

'Warham, the Bishop of London. He'll make a good choice. If he gets it, we will probably see some changes.'

'It is past time for changes, John. Everything has been turned upside down at the court since Prince Arthur died. The King put a lot of stock by having his son succeed him, and seems to be pretty broken up about his death.'

'What really happened to Arthur?'

'You probably know as much as I do. I have it on good authority that he was a sickly lad for several years. We have not seen much of him here in London. Henry brought him here and paraded him around from time to time as though he was a strong young bullock. Truth is, he had him living at one of the palaces in the country most of the time in the hope that his health would improve. He was thin and had a cough. Some people who ought to know say he had the lung disease. If he did, you know how it affects people. Anyone can get it, and once they do, they may last only a few months or sometimes go on for several years before the cough causes them to spit up so much blood they just get too weak to live.'

'If he had the lung disease, I'm surprised Henry rushed him into marriage. He wasn't more than fifteen when he married the Princess Catherine.'

'It was a hurried affair all right. Oh, they had been planning the details for several months. It took time to work out a marriage contract with Spain and line up the big dowry the princess brought with her. I've heard though that Henry wanted to get his son married early because he had fears about his health and hoped he could get an heir to the throne before anything might happen to Arthur.'

'Why should he have done that? He had his second son, Prince Harry, to fall back on.'

'The word is he has never thought highly of Harry. It is hard to say why. The young Prince is a sturdy robust lad who has twice the energy Arthur showed. Some say he had a preference for Arthur because he was his first born and because he looked like his father while Harry looks more like a Plantagenet. People who have been at court for several years tell me that Prince Harry bears a strong resemblance to his grandfather Edward IV.'

'I have not heard that before. From what I have heard though, Edward looked a lot more like a King than our good King Henry ever has, so most of us will be happy to have Harry inherit his grandfather's looks as long as he doesn't inherit his sexual appetite as well.'

'I say amen to that,' Barnes observed.

'I can understand Henry's desire to get an heir who will set up the succession,' John went on, 'but maybe it is not too late. The Princess could be pregnant.'

'There has been plenty of speculation on that score. Arthur was old enough to have sired a child. Still, he was sick and tuckered out after the wedding, and he was only married for five months before he died. Catherine has not shown any signs of being pregnant. More than that, about half the people at court are willing to wager that Catherine's maidenhead is still intact.'

'Where does all this leave the King?'

'That is the rub. You know how Henry is with money. He is not only tight, he is downright greedy. Catherine brought a big dowry with her. If she goes back to Spain or is sent back, Henry will have to return the dowry, and he looks forward to that like I would to losing a leg or having all my teeth pulled.'

'Does he have any plans?'

'It is too early to say. He will not do anything about the dowry until the Spanish Ambassador starts making a noise about its return. Meanwhile, he has had his doctors examine the Princess. She says the marriage was never consummated. If that is true, Henry has a problem because Spain will want her back for sure. It is rumoured that Henry is considering the prospect of marrying her to his second son, Harry.'

'But isn't it incest if a man takes his brother's wife?'

'It would be incest and illegal if the first marriage was consummated. If someone can convince the Pope that it was not, then he could give a dispensation for Catherine's marriage to Prince Harry.'

'Our next Lord Chancellor will have his work cut out for him if he has to get that dispensation.'

'You are dead right on that. If he can get it, it will take time. By then Prince Harry will be old enough to marry, if he will consent to the marriage.'

'Are there any doubts about that?' John asked.

'I am not close enough to the royal family to know. People say he likes Catherine. She is a few years older than him and you know how most men feel about that. Then too, I've heard that he's a strong willed youngster who just might take it into his head to resist his father's wishes. Should he do so, Henry would have a problem.'

Their conversation shifted to other topics. Then as if he had just thought of it, Barnes said, 'By the way, I may have some good news for you. There is talk that Henry will soon name another group of barristers as Sergeants-at-Law. I have put your name in and think this time you have a good chance of making it.'

John thanked him. Yes, indeed, it would be good fortune for him if he were selected for the honour. The Sergeants-at-Law were an official body of legal experts. Names were added to the roster from time to time by royal command, and the members were looked to as legal authorities on the common law. It was an honour and a sign of recognition. Moreover, the crown usually picked judges for its courts from among the sergeants when it did not give first consideration to sons of noblemen.

'It is an honour you should have received a long time back, John,' Barnes continued. 'I am confident you will get it this time. It will be good for you and your practice. It won't hurt your son either. Incidentally, how is Tom doing? I have heard some mighty favourable comments about his lectures on St Augustine, and also about his teaching at Furnivall's Inn.'

'Thomas is doing well with his teaching, and with his legal practice. There are days when I think he knows more about the law than I do. Starting as my partner has helped him with his practice. It is surprising though how fast he has caught on. Some of my long-time clients are now asking for him rather than me.'

'I suppose we have to expect that kind of competition from these young bucks.'

'That is true. But I am sure I would not appreciate the competition as much if it was someone else's young buck. It is different with Thomas. I am proud of him. Of course, there are some things I wish he would do. He should find a wife and settle down. Right now he is living as a lay brother with the Carthusian friars.'

'Is he still thinking of becoming a priest?'

'No. I think he finally has that out of his blood. That

does not mean he has lost any of his piety or devotion to the Church. Maybe you haven't heard. That fellow Hunne asked Thomas to represent him in his defence against that priest who sued him when he refused to pay the mortuary fee. Thomas refused to take the case because he did not want to be a party to a challenge against clerical perquisites.'

'How is the case coming?'

'You have probably heard that the priest sued Hunne in the Bishop's court. As you might expect, he was found guilty under the canon law. Hunne is sufficiently well-to-do that he could easily pay the fine. He is a strong-willed chap though, and is determined to stand on principle. They have him in prison at Lollard's Tower. He has the option of appealing to Rome, but we both know what the answer would have been there. Instead, he has filed a countersuit under the Statute of Praemunire to have the case tried in one of our common law courts.'

'Praemunire!' Ned snorted. 'No one knows what that means. The law opens the way for our secular courts to handle non-spiritual cases that might otherwise be referred to the pope. So little use has been made of it that we do not have a lawyer or a judge in the kingdom who knows what its limits are.'

'That is Hunne's point. He argues this is not a spiritual matter like a charge of heresy. He knows full well that most of the people are on his side when he questions special privileges of the clergy. Most people don't give a damn about the mortuary fee, but they resent the way churchmen lord it over us and use this fee business as a symbol of our subservience to them.

'If Hunne can get the crown to refer the case to one of our secular courts, he will probably succeed in his challenge against special privileges for the Church. The bishops know it, and they are fighting tooth and nail to prevent any yielding of jurisdiction to our secular courts.'

'How do you and Tom feel about it?'

'I am a neutral bystander on this one. If I had to rule on it, I would probably turn it over to our common law courts. Thomas takes a totally different stand. He is four square for defending the position of the Church. For him, it is heresy to question the authority or status of the Church.'

'Tom is a bright lad. But he is wrong and just does not speak for the people of London on this issue. I dare say nine-tenths of the people support Hunne's position. If this case came before my bench and no more convincing evidence were presented favouring the Church's case, I would rule for Master Hunne. More than that, I would rule that our civil courts have full jurisdiction in all save spiritual cases, and that no cleric should be immune from prosecution for civil law violations simply because he is a cleric.'

'I am trying to stay neutral,' John observed. 'But I am inclined to agree with you. The case is interesting because it pits the rights of people under our common law against the rights claimed by the Church. Men like us who are trained in the common law see the situation one way whilst the clerics who live under the canon law see it differently. As long as the bishops can keep the jurisdiction of the case in their courts, they can and will ride roughshod over us. If the King would just nudge the case over into our common law courts we could get a decision that would rock the foundation of many of the special privileges the priests have claimed since way back when.'

'Speaking of court decisions, John, have you heard much about Sir John Tyrell's trial and execution?'

'I understand that he was tried for treason, and that he confessed shortly before they took him to the block that it was he who murdered the two young princes in the Tower. Who was he anyway?'

'Tyrell was one of King Richard's lieutenants. He came from a good family up North and apparently had a commendable record of service in the army. Richard made him Captain of the garrison at Guisnes Castle at Calais. He was there helping to guard Calais from France when Henry invaded England and won the crown at Bosworth. Henry attaintered some of Tyrell's estates but left him with his post at Calais. He apparently satisfied Henry about his loyalty because the King restored his estates and showed him signs of favour. He had no troubles until a year and a half ago when someone accused him of supplying aid to the Earl of Suffolk.'

'Suffolk? Isn't he the younger brother of the Earl of Lincoln, who Richard III named as his heir after his son died?'

'Yes. The Earl is Edmund de la Pole, the son of one of Richard's sisters. He swore allegiance to Henry after Henry took the crown and was allowed to go his way; but the King has never really trusted him because he sees him as the most important surviving heir of the House of York. Something or other caused the Earl to flee to the Continent and ever since Henry has been trying to get his hands on him.'

'His life won't be worth much if Henry catches him?'

'No one will dispute that. Well, back to Tyrell. All was going smoothly for him at Calais until someone accused him of providing aid to Suffolk, who stopped at Calais on his way to one of the German states. Tyrell denied the charge, but the King sent out orders for his return to stand trial.

'Tyrell apparently got wind of what was happening and refused to leave his post at Guisnes Castle. Henry ordered the army at Calais to besiege the castle. Tyrell held out successfully for several months until he was lured out with the offer of a safe conduct guaranteed by the Privy Seal to do some negotiating on shipboard. As soon as they had him on the ship, they ignored the guarantee and arrested him and his son. They were brought to the Guildhall where Tyrell was found guilty of treason and beheaded four days later on Tower Hill.'

'What did they do to his son?'

'Oh, he received the death sentence too. Not that he was guilty of anything, but he was the son of a convicted felon. The really unusual thing about Tyrell's case is that his execution was carried out without ceremony. None of the witnesses who were there reported hearing any public confession of guilt from him. Yet after it was over, it was reported that Tyrell had made a written confession for the relief of his soul before he was taken to the block.

'According to the confession, it was he who murdered the two Princes. He described how he and two scoundrels named Forest and Dighton went to the Tower on Richard's orders, located the two young princes, smothered them, laid their naked bodies out for positive identification, and then buried them under a pile of debris under a staircase at the Tower.'

'At least one good thing came of it,' John observed. 'That confession finally solves the mystery of what happened to the two Princes, doesn't it?'

'I think it raises as many questions as it answers,' Barnes replied.

'Are you suggesting that the confession was fabricated?'

'Well, you must admit it leaves some questions unanswered whilst it opens up some new ones,' Ned responded. 'I wonder what Sir Francis Musgrave, God rest his soul, would be telling us if he were here.'

'If I remember Sir Francis, he would be sniffing the wind and suggesting that the confession was all part of a conspiracy of some sort.'

'That is just the point. Sir Francis would say that Henry has finally got around to the realisation that he must come up with a murderer he can link to Richard. Tyrell looked like a likely prospect. At least he was a former associate of Richard's. Then a trap was set to catch Tyrell and make him appear guilty. Tyrell goes to his execution without making any confession of guilt. Afterwards, a confession signed with what is supposed to be his signature is presented as evidence that the murders have been solved.'

'As long as he confessed, there should be no problem accepting the account,' John argued.

'But did he in fact confess? I have yet to hear of anyone who witnessed the confession or who has even seen it. If there was a signed confession, what evidence is there that it was his signature? And if he signed, did he do it voluntarily? He could have been tortured and forced to sign; or he could have been given a choice at the last minute of signing and being beheaded or of going to the gallows where he would be hanged, cut down while he was still alive, his clothes ripped off, his private parts mutilated, his belly ripped open, his guts spilled out before his eyes, and then quartered.'

'So you have your doubts?'

'Yes, and that is not all. It seems odd to me that no one has started a search to find those fellows Forest and Dighton, who were supposed to have been Tyrell's confederates. If they are still alive, their confessions could be important.

'Then there are two other details that bother me. I wonder whether Tyrell's son was executed because he was guilty of some crime, or rather because he could have proclaimed his father's innocence of the murder charge. I also question the casual way in which King Henry treated the confession. If this was the long-hidden truth, why hasn't he proclaimed it throughout the land instead of passing it off like last year's news?'

'There is nothing I can tell you that would still your doubts, Ned. You will probably go on thinking that Henry is guilty of trying to place the blame on Richard until the end of your days. As for me, I am happy that the mystery about what happened to the two princes has finally been solved. One of the best things about it is that people will no longer place the blame on Bishop Morton.'

Chapter Twenty-One

Queen Elizabeth, wife of Henry VII and daughter of Edward IV and Elizabeth Woodville, died in childbirth in 1503. All London mourned her death. It was her marriage to Henry that had brought the Houses of York and Lancaster together and ended the long war between them. Though seldom seen in public, she was far more popular with the people than the King, and her death was deeply felt. It was said that she had suffered from declining health in the months before her death and that this had been caused by concern over the illness and demise of Prince Arthur. Whether this was a cause of her early death, no one could say.

Almost everyone in London turned out for her funeral. Moved by the occasion, Thomas More composed twelve verses that were read at the funeral. His verses voiced the sentiment of a Queen who was bidding her family farewell. In one verse, he wrote:

> If worship might have kept me, I had not gone,
> If wit might have me saved, I needed not fear,
> If money might have helped, I lacked none.
> But O good God what availeth all this gear?
> When death is come, thy mighty messenger
> Obey we must; there is no remedy
> Me hath he summoned, and lo now here I lie.

The fervour with which Thomas supported the Queen did not spill over into solid support for her husband. Like his father, he thought poorly of Henry VII. As the weeks passed after the Queen's death, he visited the Chancery only infrequently. Most of his attention was centred on his legal practice; but he was also blossoming in the fame he had attracted with his lectures at St Lawrence Jewry. His reputation as a speaker brought numerous invitations for him to talk to different groups on topics of theological and civic interest.

Two items of family interest added indirectly to Thomas's growing prominence. His father was one of ten jurists selected by the King to serve as Sergeants-at-Law. A public dinner, attended by the King and several noblemen together with the Lord Mayor of London, was held in their honour at Lambeth Palace. Two days before the dinner, Sir Thomas Granger, Thomas's maternal grandfather, also was honoured by his election to the post of Sheriff of London.

In the speech he was asked to give at the dinner, Thomas recited a comic ballad he had written called, *A Merry Jest of How the Sergeant Learned to Play the Friar*. What the story, told in doggerel verse, lacked in quality and substance, was amply made up for by the style of Thomas's presentation as he told a merry tale of a lowly police sergeant, not a Sergeant-at-Law, who disguised himself as a friar to gain entry to a house where a debtor who was wanted by the law was hiding. The sergeant found his man and made his arrest but his disguise was discovered by the women of the household who proceeded to attack and soundly beat him as they laboured for the debtor's release.

Almost without his realising it, Thomas's life was shifting in a new direction. He enjoyed periods of solitude and was a pious person by nature. Yet he enjoyed fame. He tried to practise humility, but he was a gregarious person who craved recognition and the respect of others.

After months of living with the Carthusian friars, he was finally convinced that that was not the life for him. He would be a sincere servant of the Church for the rest of his life. He would continue to sleep on bare boards, wear a cilice, and whip himself as penance for his sin of breaking his oath. But he wanted more than a life of poverty and silence. He did not covet wealth or power for their own sake; but he wanted to live in some comfort. He knew he had been blessed with talents, and that he should not be deluded into hiding beneath some bushel.

While Thomas was still living with the Carthusian friars, a call went out from Henry's court for the election of a new Parliament. Seven years had passed since the election of the last Parliament. The man who had represented Thomas's borough was now dead. Thomas paid little heed to the election at first. It was brought suddenly to his attention when some of his fellow lawyers asked him to stand for election. To his surprise, a group of businessmen who looked to Thomas and his father for legal advice also requested that he be a candidate for the vacant seat in the House of Commons.

Election to the House was a perfunctory exercise in most of the more rural areas of England, where the choice of whom to select was usually decided by the local noblemen and leading landowners. It was different in London where the nobility had little influence on the views of the voters. Election here depended upon popularity among the electorate.

Thomas agreed to stand for election with full knowledge that he would have competition and that he would have to speak to crowds of people and be willing to respond to their sometimes irritating and embarrassing questions. He found the challenge exciting, and soon demonstrated with his keen wit and oratorical skills that he was a match for anyone. The campaign was brief. The two men who stood against him were older and more experienced, but otherwise ill-equipped to run against him. In the end, he won with a clear majority of the votes.

The new Parliament met in early 1504. Like most Parliaments, it was called into session because the King needed, or thought he needed, an additional subsidy from his subjects. When the new Parliament met, Henry's ministers requested the passage of two subsidies. By custom and long practice kings were entitled under the rules of fealty to a subsidy on the knighting of their eldest son. Henry was now asking for a subsidy for the knighting seven years earlier of the now deceased Prince Arthur. A subsidy also was requested for the marriage of his eldest daughter Margaret to the King of the Scots.

Henry with his usual desire to fatten the royal purse indicated that a subsidy of three 'fifteenths' – about ninety thousand pounds – would be appropriate for Margaret's marriage, and that a comparable grant should be made for Arthur's knighthood. The requests received a mixed reaction in the House of Commons. Burgesses who represented noblemen and landowners who had benefited from Henry's reign supported the proposed grant. Many others dissented.

Thomas More was one of the dissenters; and it was he, 'a beardless youth' as he was reported to the King, who took the lead on the floor in opposing the requested taxation. In the end, the King got his subsidies, but the total amount was pared down to a total of about forty thousand pounds, a quarter of which the King was later persuaded to remit to his subjects.

About the same time that Parliament met by which time it was three and a half years that the position of Lord Chancellor had remained unfilled, Henry finally appointed William Warham, the Bishop of London, to the post and also made him Archbishop of Canterbury. No significant problems had arisen at the Chancery in the absence of a Lord Chancellor. Father Gregory had continued in the capacity he had served in under Morton, and he had made certain that the wheels of Henry's government trundled along as usual.

One of Warham's first acts after taking on his new post was that of asking Father Gregory to stay on as his executive assistant. Warham would advise Henry VII on his domestic and foreign policies, but it would be his assistant who handled the book work and supervised the selection and direction of the many minor officials, clerks and scribes who kept the government functioning.

Father Gregory accompanied the new Lord Chancellor on a tour of the Chancery offices and explained the types of activities handled and administered in each of the various offices. Warham saw no reason to recommend changes. His only important suggestion came when he was shown the rooms Bishop Morton had used. These rooms had been sealed off, out of respect for his memory, since the Bishop's death. Warham reasoned that they should be used for some more pressing purpose, and directed that steps be taken to catalogue Morton's papers and dispose of his personal effects together with those files that were no longer needed at the Chancery.

Father Gregory delegated the responsibility for carrying out this order to Brother Bernard. Bernard was instructed to assemble and catalogue all of the late Bishop's furnishings, mementoes and other personal belongings and arrange for the sale of those items that could not be used elsewhere in the Chancery. He was then to assemble all of Morton's mountainous file of letters, papers, manuscripts and books, examine every item to determine which items should be retained for the Chancery files or be given to libraries or other interested parties, and discard those items of no value.

Aside from occasional visits to Father Gregory, Thomas

had little reason to be concerned about what was happening at the Chancery under the new Lord Chancellor. With his responsibility as one of London's burgesses, he decided that the time had come for him to leave the monastery, find a wife, and settle down.

When he asked his father for advice on how to find a proper wife, John More told him to go out and meet women. When Thomas asked how he could be sure he chose the right wife, John chuckled.

'There is no foolproof test or formula for that. Many men marry women they love and make good matches. Some make dreadful mistakes. Choosing a good wife is much like a blind man putting his hand in a sack filled with nine snakes for every eel. If you want to pull out an eel, you must first take a chance and put your hand in the bag.'

Thomas took his father's advice. He attended more functions at which women were present. He spent more time talking to young ladies and acting the role of the eligible bachelor. Some of his colleagues and friends noted his marital eligibility together with his rising status in the city. Invitations came his way to attend gatherings at which he could meet their daughters or sisters. His new life was a heady one, but Thomas took care not to lose either his head or his heart.

His quest reached a peak when John Colt, a long-time friend of his father, invited him to spend a weekend at Colt's estate in Essex. Thomas accepted the invitation half expecting that he would spend his days walking through the woods, perhaps trying his hand at some angling, or maybe even hunting with his host.

Somewhat to his surprise, he was greeted on his arrival at the estate by Colt's three lovely daughters. Jane, Kate, and Bess were eighteen, seventeen, and sixteen and each of them a picture to behold. Thomas had no need to choose between them. All three hovered around him like honey bees around a succulent blossom. They waited on him and did their best to provide merry company and make him feel completely at home. Thomas drank it in without complaint. This new experience had an intoxicating effect on him. It was not at all like life at the monastery. Their laughter and singing, their brightly-coloured gowns, and their radiant smiles contrasted greatly with the sombre attire, sober faces, and subdued silence of the monastery.

The weekend passed all too quickly. The three young ladies ate with him, played games and danced with him on the green, took him on a picnic and delighted him with their conversation. There was no discussion of serious topics; but Thomas was pleased to converse with them and listen to their questions and their enthusiastic babbling about each other and their life in the country.

As the visit approached its end, he began to sort out the characteristics of the three girls. Jane was lovely to look at, quite spirited, but still the most calm and sedate of the three sisters. Kate was the most attractive in his eyes. She was more impetuous and impulsive than Jane, more forward in her actions, and more inclined to do little things that teased him. Bess, the youngest, had had the least experience in attracting men; but she was a coquette whose charming demeanour made him want to take her in his arms and squeeze her.

Thomas hoped for an invitation for an early return to the estate, which was graciously offered to him both by his host and the three charming mistresses of the house as he mounted his horse for his return to London. As he rode away, his thoughts were filled from time to time with erotic fantasies not unlike those that had bothered him in earlier years. He realised now though that his sexual drive was normal and that his fantasies were not a design of Satan's to ferret him out for damnation. He had two new problems to perplex him now. He must decide first whether he might be willing to marry one of Colt's daughters, and if so, which one.

Colt obviously had invited him to his estate for the sole purpose of meeting his daughters. He had been a gracious and indulgent host; but he had turned the full responsibility for entertaining the guest over to the daughters. Thomas was sure he had been picked out as a future son-in-law. He had no inkling, though, as to which of the daughters he was supposed to marry. They had all impressed him as being competitors for the honour, if one could indeed consider it an honour.

He had no misgivings. What Colt had done was what most fathers would do for their daughters. Anyway, how could Thomas complain. He was looking for a wife, and here was a man of good family and reputation who was offering him a choice of three eligible brides.

Thomas was still totally undecided as to which of the girls he preferred when he returned to the Colt estate two weeks later. The first day there, they hiked along a stream through the woods and then played ball and danced on the green. Rain forced them inside on the second day. Left alone without supervision, Thomas found himself trapped into playing a kissing game. The weekend ended, and as he returned to London, he decided it was Kate he wanted. She was more lively and aggressive than her sisters. Jane's ardour seemed subdued, whilst Bess was a bit too young. He had had no signal from the girls, at least none he recognised, that told him what they thought of him.

A third visit to the Colt household brought a revival of the fun of his earlier visits and this time more open courtship on the part of the daughters, than he had experienced earlier. Thomas thoroughly enjoyed the attention that was showered on him. His opportunity for further comparison of the three sisters definitely supported his choice of Kate.

One little detail bothered him. It rained on the second

day and the young people spent the day indoors where the sisters did their best to entertain him. They were all on their best behaviour, and he was feted like Prince Charming himself until Kate started to tease him about some trivial matter. The teasing continued until Jane ordered her to leave him alone. The incident might have annoyed him, had he not found it amusing.

John Colt rode back to London with him. After some general conversation he asked Thomas which of the three daughters he preferred. Thomas was not prepared to answer such a direct question. His first impulse was to ask what right Master Colt had to ask it. He was annoyed because the father was talking about his daughters very much as a merchant might ask him to choose between three bags of flour. On second thought, he realised that by now Colt had every reason to assume he must be interested in pursuing a romantic attachment to one of his daughters.

'You have three attractive daughters and I love them all,' he answered. 'I think, though, that Kate is my choice.'

'So you want the perky one? Well, I can see why. I hate to see this happen to Jane though. She is the eldest and should be married first.'

Colt's comment troubled him. He recalled Jane's effort to protect him from Kate's teasing comments, and suddenly he was back re-evaluating the perceptions he had of the three girls after his three visits to the Colt estate. He did not consider the details of his courtship any of his father's business. But he did tell John More about Colt's comment concerning his eldest daughter. John's reaction was more humorous than serious.

'So he is like father Laban in the Bible story of Jacob's romance? He wants you to take the eldest daughter first. In the Bible story Jacob had to marry Leah and then work seven more years to get Rachel. If it were not for our laws against bigamy, you could plan to marry both of them.'

Thomas brushed aside his father's jest. On his next visit to the three sisters though, he found himself provoked by Kate's pert jauntiness and decided he should revise his earlier thinking. The more he thought about how his life might fare with Jane and with Kate, the more certain he became that Jane should be his choice. Without asking Jane how she felt, he went to Master Colt and asked his permission to court his daughter Jane.

The courtship that followed lasted for several weeks. Jane was pleased with his choice. Thomas found himself travelling almost every weekend to the estate in Essex. The young couple found they were comparable. Neither knew for sure if they were in love. Thomas heard no ringing of bells, no clashing of cymbals. As he tried seriously to evaluate the situation, he knew he liked Jane, and that she seemed to meet the standards he had set in his thinking of what he considered an acceptable wife. He was not sure he loved her; but he had never been in love and so had no standard for comparison.

Jane too had qualms about accepting Thomas as her husband. He was handsome, witty and definitely a good prospect; but he was so talented and smart she wondered if she could really measure up to his standards. She too had never been in love before, and she wondered if the feeling she had for him was really love, or just a romantic acceptance of this friend of her father's who showed such promise of having a successful career.

Kate and Bess took their disappointment at Thomas's choice of their elder sister with good grace. Kate told herself she was looking for a more ardent lover who might sweep her off her feet. Bess concluded that she still had plenty of time to find the man of her dreams.

Six months after they met, Thomas More and Jane Colt were married and started their wedded life together.

Chapter Twenty-Two

Thomas and Jane's first year of married life should have been a time of budding happiness for them, and particularly for the young bridegroom who was free of many of the anxieties and fantasies that had haunted his earlier years. There were many things for which Thomas had reason to be thankful. His legal business was thriving. His public speaking and his success in paring down Henry VII's requested subsidy endeared him to the people of London. Much of the satisfaction he derived from this rise in public esteem was dampened, however, by a new and unexpected struggle he felt he was losing.

His marriage to Jane Colt had promised to provide such a logical and workable answer to his personal problems. The first short weeks of honeymoon had been pleasant – exciting and enjoyable. It was a totally new experience learning how to live with another person in his life, in his house, in his bed.

Jane had been sweet, loving and co-operative. His sampling of the secrets of their sexual union had proved satisfactory, even though it was in a way disappointing. Somehow after months of waiting and what had seemed like years of abstinence, he had anticipated a more exciting and thrilling experience than the consummation of their union provided.

He had gone to the well of his expectations, but the water there was neither as plentiful nor as satisfying to his taste as he had anticipated. More than that, he harboured a feeling of guilt. St Augustine, who had been his guide in so many ways, had viewed the sexual act with loathing as a sign of depravity. Yet, while he had not found it as exciting as he had expected, he felt he was letting his favourite saint down both by enjoying it and by looking forward to its repetition.

He was still learning new things about Jane and her body. He thought that perhaps she could help him improve his service if she were not so passive. But concern about his sexual prowess was not a major problem. He could seek satisfaction of that appetite on a frequent basis as long as his goal was procreation, which it was. Once Jane became pregnant a different situation would arise; but there was no need to face that issue just yet.

Thomas's problem was that those first happy weeks of honeymoon were turning into wormwood. Jane respected him and he knew she loved him as he did her. Behind or beneath her surface behaviour though, he was finding that she was a different Jane from the one he thought he had married. Their conversations during their courtship had dealt mostly with everyday concerns and with frivolous matters such as their preferences in food and clothing. She had been charming and, he thought, intelligent. Now he found that he had paid more attention to the smile on her face and the way she flashed her eyes at him than to the substance of what she said.

Thomas chose a house in the Bucklersbury area of London for their first home. In his estimation, the house was adequate and possessed all the basic features they needed. Jane saw the house through different eyes. It was already old and its rooms were dark. And she disliked the narrow winding streets, the abundance of noisy neighbours, the dirt and filth of London. She pined for the open space, the trees, and greenery of the estate she had grown up on in Essex.

Her ideas about what were adequate furnishings clashed with his. Thomas was satisfied with the bare essentials and expected to sleep on bare boards. Jane was used to and insisted on furnishings that were more lavish and stylish with a big plush bed, cushions for their chairs, tapestries for the walls and good pans and pottery for cooking and eating.

Jane had grown up in a household which had a cook and maids who handled the housekeeping and cleaning. Neither she nor her husband had mentioned or even thought of this detail before they were married. Once they were in their home, he found that she knew virtually nothing about buying food or cooking it. Her first meals were near disasters, but she gradually learned how to do better; how to strike bargains with the local butchers, bakers, and grocers, and how to prepare tasty meals. She learned how to wash their linen and clean the house. Thomas was of little help with any of these tasks as he spent long hours with his legal work, and most of his spare time was spent at meetings or in his endless studying.

Thomas had not expected great things from his wife as a cook or housekeeper. True, he wondered why she could not shower him with the cakes and sweetmeats that had helped to make his visits to the Colt estate so delightful. But he overlooked this culinary mystery because his long stay with the Carthusians had accustomed him to simple fare and minimal housekeeping.

Jane's major shortcoming as he saw it was the abysmal state of her education. She would go to mass with him, but she could not carry on a decent conversation about theology or any other serious subject. She could read, but spent no time reading. He slept only four or five hours a night. She wanted to sleep for eight or nine. She spent hours in pointless pursuits such as primping her hair or putting lotions on her face, time he felt could be better spent in studies to improve her mind.

Thomas saw it as his duty to initiate Jane into a rigorous programme for expanding her intellect and making her the accomplished companion he mistakenly thought he had married. He saw no reason why she should not respond to this challenge and become a brilliant and knowledgeable conversationalist who could spend long hours talking to him about a wide spectrum of topics.

With the simple objective of making her over as a more perfect wife, he tried to interest her in taking music lessons. He bought books for her that he insisted she read and discuss with him. He showed her his favourite sections of St Augustine's writings and bade her read and memorise them. He found several sermons he felt she should learn by heart.

The campaign Thomas began with such earnest hope ended in frustration and near disaster. Jane tried for a while to do his bidding. She tried to cut back her sleeping hours and rise with him at dawn, but soon found that she could not function effectively on less than eight hours of sleep a night. Thomas was willing to overlook this weakness of the flesh. After all, he understood that most men and women customarily slept for that long. What he could not understand was her seeming inability or unwillingness to handle the reading and memorising tasks he assigned her.

All too often, Jane simply broke down and wept when he asked if she had done the day's readings. Her answers to his prodding about what she had read were disjointed and often meaningless. If she was reading the material at all, she certainly did not understand it. When he pressured her to work harder, to do better, she cowered and broke into tears. When he became more insistent, she finally rebelled and told him she had had enough.

Thomas was not a violent man. He could never strike a woman or even think of beating her. He did not want to so much as raise his voice with her. Yet what was he to do to correct this obstinacy? Surely what he was doing was right. There was no room in his thinking for an admission that he could be wrong. That would amount to a confession of defeat.

He decided to discuss the problem with his father-in-law, whom he had come to regard as a reasonable man with an abundance of common sense. John Colt was indeed a man of the world who had experience in many areas. He was perplexed when Thomas told him of Jane's resistance to his tutelage. His only advice was, 'Exercise your rights as her husband. If she refuses to obey, then beat her.'

'I could never do that!' Thomas responded. 'What I want is for you to use your authority as her father to get her to do as I ask.'

John Colt saw more humour in the situation than Thomas did. He liked his son-in-law and wanted the marriage to continue on a more amicable basis. He agreed to talk to his daughter, and told her in private that he was going to give her a stern lecture after which she should beg for her husband's forgiveness. Then, in Thomas's presence, he put on a dramatic performance in which he shouted and castigated her and threatened to send her to a nunnery if she did not submit to her husband's desires. Poor Jane did as she was instructed, broke down in tears, fell on her knees before Thomas, begged for his forgiveness and promised her future co-operation.

Thomas was quick to question the effectiveness of this reconciliation. He wanted Jane to do as he bid, but he did not want to alienate her affections. He decided to discuss the problem with his father.

John More listened to his recital and told him, 'It is as I have often said. There is only one contrary wife in this world, and every man I know is married to her.'

He then gave Thomas a sound bit of advice. 'You have lived pretty much to yourself for too long in a world where you have made the rules. You are married now. One of the first lessons you must learn as a married man is that Jane cannot change you into the man of her dreams, and that you will have little success in trying to change her into your idea of a perfect wife. When two people get married, they should take each other for what they are. From then on, they should work together, each partner accepting the give and take of married life. If you really love your wife, you will let her help you make decisions, and you will accept her for what she is.'

Thomas seriously considered his father's advice. He certainly had no desire to lose Jane. For all of her shortcomings, she had his interests at heart. Maybe he should accept the fact that she would never be the brilliant conversationalist he had hoped she might become. Yes, he should take the advice he had often given his clients. He should forget about his pride, and the loss of face which might come with backing down from his earlier position.

He should focus instead on what he could gain through compromise. If he refused to budge, he could lose his wife and that was the last thing he wanted. By compromising, he could still have half a cake, even more than half, and that was far better than no cake at all.

It was a new day for Thomas when he finally realised his marriage had much in common with the contracts he arranged between his business clients, and that just as compromises were often needed to keep two businessmen working together, they also had their place in ensuring successful marriages. He decided that hereafter his marriage would be based on mutual trust. From that day on, his feelings about his marriage improved for the better. Jane was a good wife. As he looked at the marriages of his colleagues he realised he was lucky to have a wife like her. Their marriage was certainly better than most.

Thomas had hardly settled into a comfortable new routine with Jane when Erasmus came to London on his second trip to England. His command of English was no better than it had been six years earlier, but he was now a famous scholar. The collection of noteworthy quotations from Greek and Roman authors he had published as his *Adages* was now one of the most popular books in circulation.

Another book, *Enchiridion*, also called *The Dagger of a Christian Knight*, was widely read but controversial because of its arguments for toning down the Church's emphasis on ceremonies, pilgrimages, and the veneration of saints. It also argued for purification and simplification of the liturgy. Thomas argued with him about some of the statements made in *The Enchiridion*. He was willing to simplify the Church's liturgy, but disagreed with Erasmus's view that God looked with equal favour on members of the priesthood and on laymen.

Erasmus could now read and write Greek as though it were his native tongue. He had used this ability to assemble and restore the gospels to their original form in his Greek version of *The New Testament*. He had a manuscript copy of this literary achievement with him and glowed with pride as Thomas and his English colleagues showered him with admiration and praise.

With his usual inquisitiveness, Erasmus wanted to learn all he could about Thomas's adventure in matrimony and his attempt to train his wife. Thomas was more interested in talking about his humanistic interests. As an outgrowth of these discussions, he took time off from his other activities to work with Erasmus in preparing a Latin translation of selections from the dialogues of the Greek satirist Lucian.

In a conversation on the eve of his departure, Erasmus again raised the question of Thomas's writing career. 'There is nothing wrong with your translations from Pico and Lucian. We need efforts like that to give people a window on the wondrous literature of the classics. But you, Thomas, must go farther. You must start putting your thoughts on paper for others to read. What you really need is a break in your present routine. You should go to Paris or Rome, and while there give your attention to some serious writing.'

Only a week after Erasmus left, Thomas learned that Richard Foxe, the Bishop of Winchester, Lord Keeper of the Privy Seal, and a member of Henry's Privy Council, wanted to talk to him. He hastened to comply because Foxe was a man of considerable power and influence. When they met, Foxe quickly told him that the King had expressed annoyance about Thomas's actions in the House of Commons, and particularly about his success in holding down the amount of the subsidy voted to the crown.

'If you will be ruled and ordered by me,' Foxe told him, 'I will labour on your behalf to win the King's favour for you.'

The next day, while he was still considering the reasons for Bishop Foxe's offer, he had a surprise visit from Richard Whitford, a friend of his who served as Foxe's chaplain. Whitford explained that he had learned of Foxe's offer and that, while perhaps he should not get involved, he was concerned about Thomas's welfare.

'My advice,' he warned, 'is that you avoid seeing the Bishop further on this matter. Bishop Foxe is a capable man but in this instance he is not trustworthy. He is so dedicated to pursing his good standing with King Henry that he will endeavour to get some confession from you.'

'I have nothing to confess,' Thomas protested. 'I have done nothing wrong. The stand I took as a burgess in Parliament is protected by law.'

'That is not the point,' Whitford assured him. 'The Bishop will try to ferret out some weakness from your past, a time when you said or even thought something critical of the crown. With that admission he will have something to take to Henry that can be magnified into a formal charge against you.'

Thomas suddenly realised there was more truth than fancy in his friend's warning. The perilous nature of his position bothered him. He decided to seek counsel from his father. After telling John of the two conversations, Thomas lamented, 'I am in the position of the offending virgin.'

'What do you mean by "offending virgin", son?'

'It is an example from Roman literature,' Thomas answered. 'There was once an Emperor who decreed that death should be the penalty for a particular crime, but who also decreed that no virgin should be executed for any crime. When the first offender to commit the crime turned out to be a virgin, the Emperor was puzzled by the conflict between his two decrees. A logical answer was suggested by a councillor who advised him first to deflower her so that he might then devour her.'

'And you fear that the Bishop would deflower you so that Henry might devour you.'

'That is precisely my concern,' Thomas answered.

'Then you must tread your path with care,' his father advised. 'Before you do anything rash, you must check with your friends at the Chancery to see how serious your predicament is.'

With that purpose in mind, Thomas went to the Chancery where he found Father Gregory talking with Brother Bernard.

'You will be interested in what Bernard is doing,' Gregory told him. 'Bishop Warham has asked us to catalogue Bishop Morton's personal effects and papers, and dispose of any surplus we can not make room for or do not need here at the Chancery. It has turned out to be a major undertaking. You will recall that the Bishop was a regular pack rat. He saved copies of almost every scrap of paper that crossed this table.'

Thomas was quick to ask about the plan for disposing of those papers that would not be deposited in the Chancery files. When he learned that the surplus papers would be available as gifts to interested parties, he promptly asked if he might select those documents that might be of interest to him.

'I have not much more than started my examination,' Bernard told him. 'I expect to prepare a detailed catalogue of the papers, and I will be pleased to make it available to you when we are ready to dispose of the surplus materials.'

'That would be wonderful,' Thomas answered. 'As you know, I did some reading for Bishop Morton during that last year before he died. He told me about many of his experiences and observations of the past. I am especially interested in any papers you may find that have a bearing on events during the years when Richard was Lord Protector and King.'

After Bernard left, Thomas told Father Gregory of his meeting with Bishop Foxe, and his concern about Henry's possible plan to punish him. He asked if Gregory had heard anything on the matter. Gregory confirmed that Bishop Warham had mentioned the King's irritation. Warham had tried to smooth matters over.

'If this were just a matter involving the Archbishop and the King, I doubt you would have any reason for concern. Unfortunately, Warham is not in the best position right now to protect you. As you probably know, Henry is set on seeking a dispensation from the Pope that will free Princess Catherine to marry Prince Henry. Warham opposes the idea, whilst Bishop Foxe is encouraging him to go ahead. As long as this conflict continues, you are in a perilous position.'

'But I have committed no crime. Members of Parliament have legal immunity against charges for how they vote or what they say in Parliament.'

'That is true, Thomas. But do not be so rash as to overlook the fact that you are dealing with Henry Tudor. He has made it a point to draw more and more authority to himself. No charge will be made against you for what you did in Parliament. Any other possible charge can serve the King's purposes just as well. Whitford was right, you must steer clear of Foxe's trap.'

'What advice then do you give me?'

'Warham likes you and will do what he can to protect you. My personal advice is that you go to the Continent on business for a few months until our current storm blows over.'

Thomas was on edge when he left the Chancery. What Gregory had said disturbed him. All his life he had regarded the King as his liege lord, as an authority sanctioned by God, whom he should respect and obey, if not love. In return for his loyalty, he expected the King to provide him with protection and with the opportunity to pursue a normal life as long as he abided by the King's laws.

Was King Henry doing what he ought? A tyrant thinks of his subjects as slaves, Thomas thought, while a king treats them as his children. In my case, I wonder if my King is not crossing the line into tyranny.

Thomas was well aware of the bitter fate suffered by many people who had stood in Henry's way. He had no desire to be a martyr, or even worse, just another statistic. Facing the hard reality of his situation, he decided it would be best for him and his family if he accepted Father Gregory's advice.

Chapter Twenty-Three

Paris was a larger city than London. Thomas enjoyed being there for a while, at first as he visited the churches, palaces and major attractions in the role of tourist, and then spent hours exploring the city's book shops as a serious student. But the strange surroundings and the sickening smell of the streets repulsed him. When he was finally ready to start writing, he found himself uninspired, and was unable to write as well as he knew he could. He was not sure whether his disability sprang from his disgust with the city, or from homesickness. Whatever it was, he decided after two months to move on to Louvain where he found the environment more to his liking.

He was still homesick at Louvain. He pined more than he thought he would for Jane, who was pregnant and living with her family on the rural estate she loved. He could have gone home. Father Gregory, however, still advised against it. To keep himself busy, he went to a library where he found several old manuscripts that attracted his attention.

After a few false starts, he finally found himself in the mood to write and penned off two drafts, one in English and one in Latin, of an account he called *The History of Richard III*. Here at last was the book he had promised Bishop Morton he would write. In keeping with his promise to the Bishop, he made little mention of Morton in the narrative and gave him no credit for authorship, though he would have admitted to anyone that the text was based almost entirely on what Morton had told him, together with some additional details from Tyrell's confession.

Thomas sensed an inner glow of satisfaction as he put the final touches to his narrative. He was sure it was the best writing yet that had come from his pen. It was with pride that he showed the Latin version to Erasmus when that now prominent writer came to Louvain. Erasmus was impressed and insisted that he turn it over to a printer for publication. When Thomas demurred, Erasmus demanded an explanation.

'My reason is simple enough,' Thomas told him. 'I have no love for King Henry. Publication of the history could ingratiate me with him; but more than that, it would make him look like a far better king than he is. I have no desire to glorify him.'

'But you consider him a better king than Richard III don't you?'

'True, but that does not make him a good king.'

'Good king, bad king, what is the difference?'

'A good king is like a watchdog that is the guardian of his flock. By his barking, he keeps the wolves away. A bad king is the wolf. King Henry is more of a wolf than a trusty watchdog.'

'So you have no plans for publishing either text?'

'Not at the moment. Sometime later, when Henry is no longer King, the situation may be different.'

Erasmus turned away from him in disappointment. 'If it were me,' he opined, 'I would play my cards while they still have value. What a waste of talent! It is a pity too, because this could be a perfect piece to pair the sketch I am planning to write on the education of a good prince.'

Thomas's misgivings about Henry VII peaked a few days later when he received a letter from his brother. His father had been caught between the prongs of Morton's fork. Henry's agents had levied a fine of one hundred pounds against him. John More did not have enough money available to pay the fine, and was accordingly clamped into debtors prison, there to stay until the fine was paid.

Thomas was upset by the news. He felt indignant. There was no question in his mind but that his father had been arrested and sent to prison because the King resented his action in opposing Henry's interests during the Parliamentary debates. He knew now how many an English landowner felt when he was fined for what appeared to be no valid reason, and was forced to make a contribution to the crown to regain his freedom. There was no justice here if royal agents were allowed to extort random payments from the King's subjects.

Thomas returned to England less than six months after his departure. He had two manuscripts in his possession, which, once published, could be worth far more to Henry's reputation than a mere hundred pounds. He was willing to show them to a few close friends, but he was determined not to show them to Father Gregory or anyone else in the King's employ. The manuscripts, valuable and informative as they were, would remain hidden from the world until he was ready to release them, and that time definitely would not come while Henry VII still lived.

His first action following his return to London was to seek out some of his father's well-to-do clients and secure a loan of sufficient funds to secure John More's release from prison. The two Mores, father and son, then set about restoring their legal practice to its earlier prominence. With John More's fine paid, Henry's agents lost interest in pursuing further action against the Mores.

Jane More gave birth to a daughter, whom they named Margaret, a few weeks after his return. With the mother and daughter moved back to the house in Bucklersbury, Thomas started a new phase of his life, that of being a doting parent. Baby Margaret was the apple of his eye. With her in his arms, he now knew what true love was. Like his father, he had never had great respect for women; but with little Margaret that situation changed. He would train her and tutor her so that she could become the charming and polished conversationalist he had hoped Jane might be.

Meanwhile other things were happening. Father Gregory informed him on his return that Henry had commissioned Polydore Vergil, an Italian priest and writer who had originally come to England as the Pope's collector of St Peter's pence, to prepare a history of Henry's reign. Vergil was already at work collecting information from various sources. He had started his research by exercising a grant of royal authority to insist that selected source materials be sent to him from libraries throughout the kingdom. Most of the requisitioned materials were single copies of manuscripts which the prelates had up till now refused to relinquish for use outside their libraries. Vague promises had been made about their return; but many priests already feared that they would never see the borrowed manuscripts again.

The bizarre drama at Court concerning Henry's dealings with Spain was continuing to unfold. A formal request had been sent to Rome for a dispensation that would permit Princess Catherine's marriage to Prince Henry. Spain wanted to separate the issue of Catherine's marriage from its demand for repayment of the dowry. King Henry meanwhile had no intention of releasing the dowry. When the Spanish ambassador persisted in his demand for its return, Henry offered himself as the royal bridegroom for the remarriage of his son's widow.

Queen Isabella of Spain was horrified when she heard of Henry's proposal. Instructions were immediately sent to her ambassador in London to forget the dowry and get Catherine back to Spain. The negotiating parties then came to terms and agreed to a marriage contract between Catherine and Prince Henry, the dowry remaining in the hands of

Henry VII.

While these negotiations were still underway, a ship carrying Archduke Philip, the husband of Princess Joanna, who was the daughter and heir of Ferdinand and Isabella, was driven by storms to a refuge on the English coast. While in England, the Archduke was fêted royally by Henry at his court. He died quite unexpectedly shortly after his return to Spain. King Henry promptly offered himself as suitor for the hand of the widowed Princess Joanna, as the marriage would have given him a future claim to the crown of Castile. The Princess, who was said to be insane, declined the offer. King Ferdinand, however, promised Henry that his offer would be considered if Princess Joanna by chance decided to marry again.

Like many Englishmen, Thomas thought this succession of events bordered on insanity itself. 'It is utterly ridiculous,' he said to a friend. 'It makes about as much sense as milking a he goat into a sieve.'

In another part of the city, the Richard Hunne case reached a tragic climax. Hunne had been imprisoned at Lollard's Tower for several months because of his continued refusal to pay the mortuary fee as dictated by the Bishop's court. He was finally interrogated by the Bishop of London, Bishop Fitzjames. There was little doubt that his continued imprisonment had become a matter of increasing embarrassment for the Church.

Two days after his interrogation, Hunne's body was found hanging from a peg on the wall of the cell to which he had been returned. A coroner's jury considered the reported suicide in the context of the other facts of the case, and found ample evidence to support the conclusion that Hunne had been strangled in his bed, and that his body had been hung on the peg to give the appearance of suicide.

Bishop Fitzjames was outraged by this refusal to accept his assistant's report of Hunne's suicide. He called the jury a pack of 'false, perjured caitiffs'; insisted that Hunne had taken his own life, and attempted to strengthen the Church's case against him by accusing him of heresy.

Even though he was not officially involved with the case, Thomas went out of his way to defend the Church's position in comments he made to various friends and groups. He argued that Hunne had been wrong from the beginning; that he had in fact killed himself; and that the popular outcry in the city against the arrogance and authority of the Church was not justified. Three members of Bishop Fitzjames's staff were formally charged with the murder. The question of their guilt, however, never came to trial, as the indictment against them was quashed at the Bishop's request.

Activities of a very different nature were taking place at the Chancery where Brother Bernard was uncovering hidden secrets as he reviewed and catalogued Bishop Morton's papers. Morton had left a small mountain of correspondence, along with piles of notes and manuscripts. Bernard wondered what intention he had had regarding them, or if he had had any at all. Had he expected that someone would sometime plough through them looking for details that could enhance his reputation? Had he planned sometime to sort them out for preservation or disposal? Or might he have saved everything out of habit with the expectation that his successors would feed them to the Chancery's fires?

Most of the letters and reports he found were easily cast aside, as they dealt with matters which were no longer relevant. But there were a surprising number that Bernard felt had historical value. Amongst these, he particularly looked out for materials that could cast light on Morton's programme for cleansing all official records of any favourable mention of Richard III.

As he half expected, he found a series of letters to various priors, bishops, and town and shire officials, instructing them to expunge favourable references to Richard from their records. His curiosity was aroused when he found an old letter that identified the Bishop as having been in the Duke of Buckingham's service. Two other letters, one to and one from Margaret Beaufort, who was then Lady Stanley, seemed to implicate her in some early conniving with Bishop Morton to bring her son to the throne.

Bernard's big find came when he opened a packet of papers, all written in Latin in the Bishop's handwriting, that described the life and character of Richard III and ended with an account of the murder of Prince Edward and his brother in the Tower. Bernard studied the papers with particular care. After reading them, he read them again and carefully noted item after item which seemed to show a very different Richard from the one his own research had revealed. The overall picture they painted was so damning that he felt repulsed; not so much by the supposed character of Richard, as by the author of this pack of distortions, half truths, and lies.

Knowing he would have accepted the account as accurate had he not already established a very different picture of Richard from his conversations with people who knew him, he wondered what Morton's purpose was in writing the account. To the best of his knowledge, the account had not been published or even shown to anyone. Had the Bishop planned to publish it, or to leave it in his files to be discovered and published after his death?

This last option appeared plausible. Yet if the Bishop had planned for it to be published, why did he leave it in a mountain of files he himself would have asked some clerk to cart off and burn? The account had numerous corrections and inserts. It was obvious its author had given more than just passing attention to its preparation. But for what purpose? Overall, it looked like a draft for some lectures the

Bishop might have given to some group or other. Yet Bernard was reasonably sure Morton had never talked in public on the topic. What private group or person, he wondered, could Morton have talked to?

Bernard was also disturbed by what appeared to be an attempt to blacken Richard's reputation. Why had Morton undertaken this vicious vendetta against Richard? Had he had a legitimate grievance against him? Was he acting on Henry VII's orders? Might he have been in league with the King and possibly others in a conspiracy to discredit a monarch, now dead, whose reputation during his lifetime had been almost as white as the rose his family took as its emblem?

Chapter Twenty-Four

Bishop Morton's commentary on Richard III was not something Bernard could ignore or simply set aside. It stirred up a fire storm in his thinking that threatened to destroy the admiration and respect he had long had for the Bishop. He had known for months that Morton, as Lord Chancellor, had administered a project of purging England's records of any favourable mention of the late monarch. That he could accept; but the deliberate and vile charges brought against Richard in the commentary were too much.

He had always thought of the Bishop as being an honest and fair-minded man. Now he had reason to wonder where the truth lay. Here was evidence that Morton had participated in a deliberate and vile plot to destroy the reputation of a man Bernard had come to admire and respect as an honourable ruler who was loved by his people. The more he thought about Morton's disquieting charges, the more he saw them as a foreboding puzzle, the truth or falsity of which he must determine.

Almost in self-defence, he marked several items in Morton's account which he was almost certain were false. The disgusting picture he painted of Richard's birth, and his appearance, describing him as having a repulsive face and a hunched back; of his greed and lust; of the crimes he committed against his wife and brothers and sisters: all of these were lies, deliberate distortions of the truth. He suspected that the Bishop's account of what had happened at court when Richard rode into London as Lord Protector was self-serving. His description of Richard's decision to kill the young princes was vivid and chilling but incomplete, almost as if he had written it before he had decided what the final details were.

Bernard's conviction that the Bishop had deliberately twisted and altered the facts made him want to know more, much more, about Morton's activities at the courts of Edward IV and the Lord Protector. He wanted to learn more about Morton's shadowy dealings with Buckingham. He was satisfied that Richard had not killed Prince Edward at the Battle of Tewkesbury, but he wanted to know more about what he did after the battle and if he could have been the one, as Morton stated, who killed old Henry VI in the Tower where he was kept as a prisoner.

Finding answers to these questions called for some hard-headed prying for information together with a dash of ingenuity. He could not share his findings, and his suspicions about Morton's account with Father Gregory, at least not yet. Gregory was too committed to Morton to be willing to consider that the Bishop had been engaged in a conspiracy to blacken the reputation of Richard III. But Gregory could tell Bernard much of what he wanted to know about Morton's activities at the courts of Edward and Richard. When he broached the subject, Gregory told him substantially the same story he had told Thomas half a dozen years earlier.

He was surprised when Gregory assured him that Morton had never really stopped supporting the Lancastrians. He had supported Edward and Richard of York only because he had no other viable options at the time. After his arrest, he shifted his support to Henry of Richmond because he was the most eligible remaining prince of the Lancaster line.

'Why did he tie up with Buckingham?' Bernard asked.

'I asked him that question once,' Gregory replied, 'and never did get a straight answer. I suppose the reason was simple enough, but I was never able to look into the Bishop's mind and discover just what happened.

'Before you consider their relationship, you should know that Buckingham had a claim to the throne that was almost as good as those of Richard and Henry. All three of them were descended from sons of Edward III. Buckingham helped Richard when he was Lord Protector, and was as responsible as anyone for getting the people to offer the crown to him. Richard recognised his assistance and heaped honours on him. The trouble was that Buckingham had more ambition than common sense. Instead of repaying Richard with loyalty and respect, he started to itch for an opportunity to replace him.

'Bishop Morton was a prisoner in the Tower when Richard was crowned. From what he told me, he had small hopes of being released. Then Buckingham, who had an office in the Tower, came by one day to see him. The Bishop knew what kind of a man Buckingham was, and saw him as a possible means for getting out of prison. He turned on his charm, as he always did when he wanted to impress people, and flattered Buckingham. The Duke liked it and came back on other visits. A few weeks later Buckingham had the Bishop released into his custody, and arranged to have him taken to a castle in Wales.

'The Bishop never admitted it in so many words to me, but I assume that he had advised Buckingham about his prospects for leading a successful uprising that might put him on the throne.'

'Did Bishop Morton really plan for Buckingham's success?' Bernard asked.

'That is a hard question to answer. I've heard him answer both "yes" and "no" to it. He probably gave his complete support to the Duke at first. He certainly went through the motions of doing so; and right up until the end, Buckingham thought Morton was working for his interests.

'Some people say Bishop Morton was in league with Margaret Beaufort to gain the throne for her son even before he was sent to the Tower, and that they plotted with Buckingham in order to further their interests. Some think he made his first contact with Henry's party after he got to Wales, and that he worked thereafter for Henry's cause. Others say he was Buckingham's man until the Duke used his report of the murder of the two princes to gain the support of the nobility who had favoured the crowning of young Edward V. Still others say he did not shift his allegiance to Henry until it became obvious that the noblemen who were in revolt preferred Henry to Buckingham as their candidate for the crown.

'Whatever the circumstances were, it is pretty clear that Bishop Morton tried to get the Duke to come out for Henry before he was captured and executed. He had enough contacts among Henry's friends by then to be able to rely on them to smuggle him to the coast and then over to France where he could work openly for Henry's success.'

'While he was making arrangements with Buckingham for leaving the Tower, did he and the Duke discuss the fate of the two Princes?'

'If he did, he never mentioned it to me. They probably talked about them, but I have no idea what was said. I know that the Bishop assumed from comments made by guards that the princes were still alive when he left the Tower. To be honest, I must confess I thought for a long time that Buckingham arranged for their murder after he sent the Bishop off to Wales. He had ready access to them; he knew they would always stand between him and the throne; and he was the first to announce their death. But Tyrell's confession showed that I misjudged him.'

Bernard knew he could not stop his inquiries at this point. To satisfy his curiosity, he had to know more about Richard's activities as Lord Protector and King. When Father Gregory said that he had never been close enough to the court to know what was going on, Bernard asked if Gregory knew of any chronicles that might have been written about the period.

'No,' Gregory replied. 'No one to my knowledge has written a history of that time and unfortunately most of those who were in a position to know the details are now dead. However, there is a chap over in Seal's, a man named Strachey, who was an assistant to Archbishop Rotherham, who can probably tell you what happened about as well as anyone.'

When Bernard found Edmund Strachey in the office of the Lord Keeper of the Privy Seal, he met a greyed and wrinkled minor official, now in his late fifties, who had spent a third of a century in government service. Strachey walked with a limp caused by a wound received at the Battle of Barnet. The second son of a minor nobleman, he had planned to pursue a military career until that aspiration was dashed by a chance blow from some warrior's lance. King Edward had recognised his valour and found employment for him in his Lord Chancellor's office.

When Bernard told him of his desire to learn more about what had happened during the hectic two-month period following King Edward's death, Strachey chuckled.

'You have probably come to as good a source as can be found,' he said. 'I am one of the few men who are still alive who were very close to those events. I was more an observer than a participant; but from my position in Bishop Rotherham's office I did have a close hand view of what was happening. Where should I start?'

'Why not start with Edward's death?'

'King Edward died in April. He knew he was dying and

added the codicil to his will that named his brother as Lord Protector just hours before he died. In the ten days that followed, the court was in turmoil. Queen Elizabeth and her eldest son, the Marquis of Dorset, refused at first to believe that they were not in charge. They knew Richard's appointment would mean the end of their glory days.

'They called the royal Council together and insisted that its members ignore the codicil and issue orders for bringing Prince Edward, who was being educated along Woodville lines at Ludlow castle, to London for an early coronation. Richard, of course, knew nothing of these proceedings as he was living at Middleham up near the Scottish border.'

'At Middleham?' Bernard interrupted. 'I understood he was at court when his brother died.'

'Whoever told you that had his facts muddled,' Strachey replied. 'Richard had visited the court a few months earlier, but he was two hundred miles away at Middleham when Edward died. If the Woodvilles' plan had worked out as they wanted, his protectorate would have been over before he ever learned of it.

'After King Edward was buried on 20th April, Dorset set 4th May as the coronation date. Word was sent to Lord Rivers, Queen Elizabeth's brother, to bring Prince Edward to London by 1st May. Another of her brothers was named Commander of the Fleet to fight off some French raids that were expected along the channel coast. He used his appointment to strip the Tower of most of its store of armaments, and also to appropriate a good part of the royal Treasury. Dorset and his mother, Queen Elizabeth, divided what was left.

'Lord Hastings, the Duke of Norfolk, and Bishop Russell were the only members of the royal Council who wanted to wait until Richard could come to London. Hastings took it on himself to send a message to Richard urging him to come quickly. Meanwhile, the Woodvilles thought they were firmly in control and went ahead with their plan for keeping the government in their hands.

'Their coup was foiled when Richard, the Duke of Buckingham, and Lord Rivers all arrived with their armies at Northampton on 28th April. Richard and Buckingham joined forces and arrested Lord Rivers and the Queen's second son, Lord Gray, who had ridden out from London to meet Rivers. Richard then marched on to London with Prince Edward.

'News of Richard's coming reached London just before midnight on 30th April. It was a madhouse around here for the rest of the night and all of the next day. Dorset and the Queen tried frantically at first to raise an army to go out and challenge Richard. When hardly anyone flocked to their banner, the Queen moved her family and all the wealth she could assemble to Westminster Abbey where she claimed sanctuary. They had to tear down part of a wall at the abbey to get all of her loot in before Richard arrived.

'The situation gradually settled down during the next four weeks. It was obvious to observers like me that trouble was brewing. Richard took charge. I must say I admired him for the way he handled himself. He started right away to clear up the mess the Woodvilles had left. The prelates of the Church were suspicious of him but most of the nobility were pleased. His biggest mistake was the trust he put in Henry Stafford, the Duke of Buckingham. Buckingham had provided him with valuable aid at Northampton and had advised him to take quick action in arresting Rivers and Gray. We wondered if he did that to gain favour with Richard, or more because he hated the Woodvilles who had lorded it over him and forced him to marry the Queen's sister while he was still a boy.

'Richard showered Buckingham with honours and leaned heavily on him for advice. This upset the others in the Council. Bishop Russell and Norfolk were neutral, but

Bishop Rotherham was resentful as were Bishop Morton and Lord Stanley. Lord Hastings was the one most upset. He had been Edward IV's closest advisor and seemed to think he should play the same role with Richard. Richard gave him several honours, but apparently not enough. Hastings saw Buckingham as moving in on his territory and did not like it at all.

'The conflict in the Council came to an end in June. I was never in on the details. But it was apparent from little things Bishop Rotherham said that there was a move afoot to push Richard aside and make Prince Edward king, with Hastings, Rotherham, Morton and Stanley as his principal advisors. Some friends of the Woodvilles who were still around apparently had a plan for working with Rotherham and Hastings to rule through Prince Edward. I have never been sure where Morton and Stanley stood. Both of them were wily schemers with agendas of their own.

'Whatever the details were, Richard and Buckingham learned of the plot. Richard called a special meeting of the Council on 13th June, informed those present of what he had learned, and set up the cry of "Treason!" that caused his guards to come in and arrest Hastings, Rotherham, Morton, and Stanley.'

'Is it true that the guards took Hastings out and beheaded him with his neck on a log without waiting for a trial?'

'No, that was just another wild rumour spread by Richard's enemies. Hastings had his trial, was found guilty, and was executed later that week. His death put an end to the Woodvilles' conniving at least for a while. Queen Elizabeth came out of her sanctuary without a fuss. Then Bishop Stillington came up with his charge that Edward IV's marriage to Elizabeth Woodville was bigamous because he had previously been affianced to Eleanor Talbot. Parliament accepted his evidence, declared Edward's children illegitimate, and offered the crown to Richard.'

'Was Queen Elizabeth among those who plotted against Richard at the time of the Hastings incident?' Bernard asked.

'She probably knew about the plot. Her family must have known of it too, because Lord Rivers and Lord Gray were put on trial about ten days later and executed for their complicity in it. But the Queen was still in the Abbey when Hastings was executed. She gave up her sanctuary three or four days later. I can be positive about that because Bishop Rotherham was in prison at the Tower, and I went as a representative of his office to see her out of the Abbey.'

'Did you agree with the manner in which Richard handled the conspiracy?'

'I had no influence on that. If I had been in his place though, I would have done what he did, and probably gone even further in weeding out the malcontents.'

'You would have arrested others?'

'I would have preferred a charge of treason against some of them. Hastings, Rivers and Gray were the only big names who were executed. Richard let Rotherham, Morton, and Stanley off with no more than a slap on the wrist. From what I saw, they were probably as guilty as Hastings was. Richard's decision to free them soon after their arrests merely left them free to plot against him on a later day.'

Bernard had the information he had come for, but before leaving, he asked one more question. 'You had a courtside opportunity to observe Richard's actions as a ruler. What did you think of him?'

'I suppose I should have been critical. After all, I was one of Rotherham's assistants. But like most of the other young men in government service, I liked Richard and what he was doing. In my view, the Archbishop was more concerned with protecting his own perquisites and those of the priesthood than with the welfare of the kingdom. Richard had some worthy objectives. He was willing to make tough decisions and make them fast. I only wish he had had more time to carry out his reforms.'

'You mentioned his strengths. Did he have any weaknesses?'

'Every man has weaknesses. His biggest one was pretty apparent. He put his trust in more than one false friend who was only waiting to sink a knife in his back. Had he been a better judge of character, he never would have trusted men like Buckingham and Stanley any further than I could jump with my feet tied to this chair.

'The chief complaint we heard about him at court was that he chose too many northerners for his posts. I would also fault him for being overly generous. The Woodvilles had drained the Treasury dry. Instead of waiting until he had some wealth back in it, he gave away too many of his family estates, estates he should have kept to provide him with future income.'

Strachey's willingness to talk prompted another question. 'Are you satisfied with Tyrell's confession?'

Strachey looked searchingly at Bernard before replying. 'With most people I would refuse to answer that question. But you are a Grey Friar whom I trust, so I will speak in strictest confidence. I am suspicious of the story the court has handed us. Somehow the details do not match up with what I know of what happened. I rather doubt that Richard had anything to do with the princes' disappearance.'

'If not him, who?'

'I am not pointing any fingers. It is quite possible they were still alive after Bosworth Field. My wife's cousin was one of the guards at the Tower who were turned out of their jobs the day Henry arrived in London after the battle. He and a fellow guard were killed in a mysterious tavern brawl later that week. As far as their families know, neither of them ever so much as hinted that the princes disappeared while they were guards at the Tower. Going beyond that, if it is true that the princes were murdered during Richard's reign, I would want to know a lot more about the activities of Margaret Beaufort, Bishop Morton, and Buckingham.'

'I am not sure I am following you,' said Bernard, intrigued.

'What I am saying is that Lady Stanley with her machinations to bring her son to the throne and Buckingham with his personal ambitions had more reason for wanting the two princes dead than Richard had. Both of them knew that as long as either of the princes lived that they would block their plans. They also knew that if the princes disappeared while Richard was King that the blame would fall on him if he so much as admitted that they were gone.'

'How do you implicate Bishop Morton with them?'

'Bishop Morton and Lady Stanley had friendly ties that went back for many years. They shared a loyalty to the Lancasters that probably bubbled over in their conversations after Edward died. She could very well have told Buckingham, who was her second husband's nephew, and whom she had raised in her household, to go to Morton for advice. One can easily believe that either she or Morton might have advised Buckingham to get rid of the two boys while he could.'

'But the Archbishop was a priest, and what you suggest implicates him in their murder.'

'I am not accusing him of carrying the knife. Ordering the execution or murder of this man or that was never beyond the Archbishop during his years as Lord Chancellor. Why would it have been worse in the case of the princes if murdering them would have helped him get his way? The thing that bothers me with this scenario is that I am not sure whether the good Bishop was working at the time for Henry or for Buckingham. Later, when Buckingham's plot began to fall apart, it was easy for him to claim he had been Henry's man all along.'

Bernard's visit with Strachey left him with the feeling that he now had nearly all of the missing pieces of the puzzle concerning Richard's life and character in his hands. He still had no answer as to what had happened to the two Princes, and he wanted to check out the details regarding Tyrell's confession. One other confusing piece of the puzzle troubled him. He needed more information as to Richard's whereabouts after the battle of Tewkesbury. Could he have murdered Henry VI and his son, as Morton had charged, or were these two more lies told to undermine the reputation of an otherwise honourable man?

The quest for more information about Richard's activities at and after Tewkesbury turned out to be easier than he had expected. London had an old soldiers' home, a place where veterans of the country's wars, most of them men who had lost an eye or an arm or leg, could live and work out a meagre existence. Almost three and a half decades had passed since Tewkesbury, but there were still a few old warriors living at the home who had fought with Edward's army.

Bernard found two wrinkled old veterans who remembered the battle. At the offer of beer and cakes, both were eager to share their memories with a new audience. One gave him a vivid account of how Richard's charge had broken the back of Somerset's army at Tewkesbury. With the victory won, Richard had turned his attention to caring for his wounded soldiers. His brother George had sent out a troop to round up the remnants of Somerset's army. One squad found Prince Edward hiding in some woods and killed him when he resisted their demand that he surrender.

Both of the veterans had fought with Richard. Both praised his leadership as a warrior, and as a commander who showed concern for his men. After the victory at

Tewkesbury, Richard went to London with King Edward. He was dispatched the next day to march with part of the army to Kent, where they subdued a remnant portion of the Lancastrian army led by Lord Fauconberg. Bernard's informants were with Richard on this march, and both agreed that it was not until after their return to London that they learned that Henry VI had died of grief over the loss of his son and his crown while they were fighting in Kent.

Chapter Twenty-Five

Father Gregory was sharing a simple meal of bread, cheese, and beer with his nephew. They had been discussing the possible significance of one of Bishop Morton's letters when Bernard asked, 'Did you ever have any problems in working with the Archbishop?

'No,' he replied. 'Well, very few anyway. Most of the time he was pleasant and good-natured. He was cordial in his dealings with his staff, but at the same time had a manner that commanded our respect. The fact that we had been friends for most of my life made it easy for me to get along with him. When he asked me to do something, he usually explained what he wanted and why, so I had no apprehensions about what I was doing. There were a few times though when he was a real bear. On those occasions, he could press those he was working with pretty hard. He could be very demanding and let it be known he wanted what he wanted quick and without questions or explanations. Fortunately, that did not happen very often.'

'Did he ever ask you to do something you thought of as unreasonable or mysterious?'

'What he asked mostly made sense if you thought about it. He did make an unusual request once, though, during that plague we had in London in the summer of 1499. For some reason I never understood, he asked me to find the bodies of two boys for him.'

'Two boys? Why on earth did he want two bodies?'

'He never told me what he wanted them for, and it was

one of those days when I felt it best not to ask him for an explanation. All I remember is that he wanted us to get the corpse of a boy who would have been around twelve or thirteen, and another of a boy who would have been about two years younger. Because of the plague, we had no trouble finding the bodies he wanted. Families all over London were putting their dead out on the streets for the city to pick up and bury. We could easily have found two dozen dead boys of those ages for him.'

'That was a strange request if I ever heard of one. Do you think he may have been working with some doctor who was looking for a cure to the plague?'

'That is a possibility, but if that was his reason he probably would have told me about it.'

Later that day, Thomas paid a visit to the Chancery and asked to see Brother Bernard. He had come to see if Bernard had found any manuscripts or materials that might interest him. Bernard showed him a pile of surplus materials and told him to help himself to any items that seemed of value to him. Before Thomas could start his examination, Bernard went on to tell him that he had found several letters and papers relating to Richard's reign that were being held back for deposit in the Chancery files.

The two men spent the next few hours examining and discussing Bernard's findings. Thomas was surprised to see Morton's letters to local officials and priests in which he ordered the expunging of commendatory references to Richard from their records. Bernard told him of his inspections and of his experiences in talking to people who had known Richard. He showed him the letters that proved Morton's involvement with Margaret Beaufort and with Buckingham, and finally Morton's file of comments on the character and life of Richard.

'I probably should not be telling you this,' he said. 'I know you worked for the Archbishop and think highly of him. For years I too have looked up to him. But these papers make me wonder, because most of the things they say about Richard are simply not true. They build up a totally misleading picture of Richard's character. Were they not in the Archbishop's handwriting, I would dismiss them as forgeries.

'Do you have any explanation for them?' he went on to ask. 'Could they be a copy of someone else's comments? Or might he have drafted them as an example of some charges the King's party could use to destroy King Richard's reputation?'

The weight of the evidence that Bernard paraded before him came both as a surprise and a heavy blow to Thomas. He had been so confident that the details he had heard from Morton were true. Now Bernard was telling him that the entire account was false. Moreover, he had shown him a narrative in Morton's handwriting which appeared to be an outline of what the Bishop had told him.

Shocked though he was, Thomas was not yet ready to abandon his trust in Bishop Morton. Bernard could be wrong. It was possible that it was Bernard, not Thomas, who had been misled. Whatever the situation, Thomas drew on his courtroom experience to retain his composure as he observed, 'That is a grave charge, Brother Bernard. The Bishop was an honourable man and one of the best I have known. I find it hard to believe he lied to anyone about anything.'

'That is the way I feel too. The Archbishop's friends at the Chancery and in the Church love him and his memory. Still, we have this evidence in his own handwriting which runs counter to everything I have been able to discover about King Richard. What use, I wonder, did Cardinal Morton plan to make of these papers? He did not publish them during his lifetime and it is only because Bishop Warham asked us to examine them that we found them before they could have been taken out and burned with a lot of other stuff he left in his office.'

'At first glance, they look like idle scribbling to me,' Thomas remarked. 'Do you see anything unusual about them?'

'I have thought of that. From what I have seen, I'd say he put far too much effort into writing the account for it to have been just a wild fantasy. The numerous corrections and inserts show that he must have spent a lot of time editing and improving this draft of his account.

'There are two other things about them that are unusual. The ending is incomplete, and the fact that he did not have a scribe write a finished copy suggests that he still expected to make more corrections before finishing his narrative. Overall, I have the feeling the papers are a draft of a speech or lecture he was planning to give to some group.'

'To the best of my knowledge he did not give any lectures I know of in the months I worked with him,' Thomas observed.

'Do you think he might have used the account as the basis for a conversation with King Henry?'

'That is possible,' Thomas replied. What he was not saying was that he remembered Morton telling him essentially all of the details enumerated in the account before them. Another thought about the papers occurred to him. He asked to see the final section again. He wanted to know what the Bishop had written about Richard's complicity in the murder of the two Princes.

Thomas reread the final portion of Morton's account. Yes, this was the way Morton had told him it had happened. Responsibility for ordering the murders was pinned firmly on Richard. The details, even the episode about one of the King's pages recommending his cousin for the assignment, were there. Three of Richard's henchmen had gone to the Tower where they smothered the two boys and hid their bodies under a staircase at the Tower.

Tyrell's name and the names of his two confederates were missing. And yes, he remembered that Morton had not given him Tyrell's name. He hadn't given it to him because he did not know it. How could he have known it? After all, Tyrell's identity was not known until he confessed to the crime, and that confession came almost three years after the Bishop's death. But hadn't Morton told him he did not remember the name and that he would give it to him once he recalled it?

As he was about to leave, Thomas turned to Bernard and said, 'Thank you for taking me into your confidence by showing me these papers. I am really at a loss to know what to make of them. What you have told me and shown me calls into question so much of what I have been told by others. I will concede that the Bishop may have overworked his negative description of Richard's appearance and character. However, the evidence still points to his complicity in the murder of the two Princes. Tyrell's confession proves that.'

'You have a good point there,' Bernard admitted. 'Yet I'd like some explanation of how the Archbishop was able to report so many details about the murder, when he apparently did not know who the murderers were.'

Thomas's mind was a-whirl as he left Bernard and prepared to leave the Chancery. Quite by accident, he met Father Gregory in the passageway, and fortunately had the presence of mind to exchange friendly greetings. Gregory had just come from the Lord Chancellor's office and was bubbling over with excitement.

'I have some exciting news. At least it will be exciting for many people when it is announced to the public tomorrow. We have just received a dispatch from Rome. The Pope has finally granted the dispensation for Princess Catherine to marry Prince Henry.'

'I understood that you had reservations about that.'

'What I thought does not matter, but you are right when you refer to Bishop Warham's feelings on the matter. This whole affair has dragged on for so long, though, that it is good to have it over and done with so that we can get back to our normal operations.'

'Speaking confidentially, Father, do you think the Pope's action is a good thing?'

'It reflects politics more than religion, that is for sure. King Henry has reason to rejoice tonight, because this action guarantees his hold on Catherine's dowry. I have an eerie feeling that it may not bode as well for England and the Church.'

Thomas realised as he walked toward his home that he probably should be thinking about the Pope's dispensation and its implications for the future. His thoughts, however, kept dwelling on Brother Bernard's findings. He wanted desperately to believe what Bishop Morton had told him, but felt that the foundation for his blind acceptance of Morton's revelations was crumbling.

He had no answer to the logic of Bernard's parting observation. How indeed could the Bishop have known as much as he had told him about the details concerning the murder of the Princes? It seemed impossible that the Bishop could have fed him a stream of misinformation. He loved and trusted the old man, and had believed Morton felt the same way about him. He could not believe he had been gulled into a scheme devised by Morton, or perhaps by Henry VII to have him prepare an account that would have the dual purpose of discrediting Richard III and giving a righteous note to the roles Henry and Morton played in seizing the crown for the last remaining prince of the House of Lancaster.

As he analysed the situation, he had to admit he had accepted Morton's account as the truth without making a serious attempt to find substantiating evidence. He knew more evidence would have been needed in the courts he practised in if he expected a jury of twelve men to bring in a verdict of guilty. Yet he hated to admit he could have been deceived and used by a man he had come to love.

He could see why Morton might have wanted to use him in this way. The old Chancellor had had a feeling for history, and was concerned about what future generations might think. This was a consideration he could understand. The manuscript he had prepared as *The History of Richard III* had a much greater potential for shaping the thinking of future generations than for affecting the views of people now living.

Yes, Thomas's mind was a-whirl as he tried to decide which of the two conflicting explanations that made up his dilemma was right. Had he written a truthful account of King Richard, or had he been duped into writing an unfair and disreputable history that discredited the record of an honourable monarch? Tyrell's confession provided the one convincing bit of evidence that supported his belief that he was not the victim of a vicious strategy. The confession was an uncontested bit of evidence. The fact that it substantiated Morton's account of the death of the princes gave credence to the rest of the Bishop's charges.

Bernard was totally unaware of the mental anguish his discoveries had stirred up in Thomas's mind. He saw Thomas's reluctance to accept his findings at their face value as the natural reaction of one who had worked with and esteemed the Archbishop, and who had placed his memory on a higher pedestal than it perhaps deserved.

As he proceeded with his examination and cataloguing of the Bishop's remaining files, he found little things that substantiated his overall view of Morton as an active and powerful Lord Chancellor. It was clear he had a commendable record on most counts, but it also seemed to be true that he had a penchant for discrediting Richard III.

Bernard was nearing completion of his cataloguing some ten days after Thomas's visit to the Chancery when he found an unexpected document. It was a draft of a confession written in Morton's handwriting. The confession was that of some officer in the King's army who had once served as Richard's lieutenant. It told of how the officer had acted on Richard's orders, going with two colleagues to the Tower, where they had found Prince Edward and his brother Richard asleep in their cell, had smothered them, and then disposed of their bodies.

Bernard was shocked by his discovery. The confession matched the details of what he knew of Sir James Tyrell's confession. Before taking his finding to Father Gregory or anyone else, he decided he must first validate what he suspected was the truth. He took a copy of the confession with him to the government records office, where he used his status at the Chancery to get permission to examine Tyrell's confession. The clerk who searched for it came back to him with the report that the original confession was nowhere to be found. All they had on file was a scribe's copy. This copy lacked Tyrell's signature. Comparison with the copy he carried with him showed the two copies to be word for word alike.

How, Bernard asked himself, could the Archbishop, who died two years before Tyrell's arrest, have had an exact copy of the confession in his files? Only one conclusion was possible. He must have drafted it no less than two and a half years before Tyrell was tricked into leaving his fortress at Calais so he could be tried for treason. The confession was a bogus product. No wonder there were no reports of him proclaiming his guilt before witnesses at the time of his execution. There was no need now to question the validity of his signature on a written confession; no need to ask if torture, or threats of torture or of a more gruesome death had been used to secure his confession. One might ask now whether he ever saw or was told of his supposed confession.

Bernard pondered what he should do next. He did not want to take the evidence to Father Gregory. Yet he felt he must share his discovery with someone. More than anything, he needed competent advice. Knowledge of Morton's draft of the confession could prove dangerous. King Henry would think nothing of destroying one more thorn that threatened his side. Thomas More was a man of the law, a man who already knew a lot about Morton's papers, and a man whose judgement he could respect.

Bernard went to Thomas, and soon was fighting back tears as he explained his predicament. Thomas too was stricken with bewilderment when he learned of the confession.

'What you have told me shocks me to the core,' he admitted. 'I would never have thought that the Bishop could have prepared a confession a man was to sign, while that man was still serving the crown as a free man, uncharged of any crime.'

The last pillar on which he had based his pride in his *History of Richard III* crumbled away. He now knew Morton had used him. Whether the decision came before or after they became good friends was not important. He had been duped. Yet the trap which had been so carefully baited had not yet been sprung. True, he had written the history, but few people had seen it, and it still was not published. It could very well be the best writing he would ever do, but he could destroy the manuscript or file it away unpublished.

With his best professional manner, he asked Bernard who else, if anyone, knew of his discovery. When Bernard told him he had talked to no one but him, Thomas said, 'You came here for advice. I wish I could tell you that you should tell the world of this dastardly act. But you and I both know that that would place a noose around your neck, and probably mine as well. The Chancery needs good men like you, and I do not want to see your life imperilled. My personal advice is that you go back to the Chancery and burn that copy of the confession before someone else learns of it and reports it to the King's men.'

Bernard thanked him for what seemed a reasonable and sensible recommendation. As he was about to leave, Thomas turned to him with a questioning look.

'Brother Bernard,' he said. 'There is something I have been wanting to ask you. You have shown far more interest in Bishop Morton's papers than most workers at the Chancery would. Is there some reason for the special interest you seem to have in him and his papers?'

'Yes, it is true. I do have a special concern for him. I fear his soul is trapped in purgatory, and that it is up to me to right some of his wrongs so his soul can pass on to its reward.'

'That is a big responsibility for any man to take on for another. I think you are side-stepping my question though. There is something about your face that reminds me of Bishop Morton. Might your interest in him stem from the possibility that you are in some way related to him?'

'My interest in the Archbishop is natural enough. It involves a detail we never talked about. He was my father.'

'Your Father? You mean he was your priest?'

'No, my flesh and blood father. In plain crude every day English, I am Cardinal Morton's not-so-holy bastard.'

Afterword

For five hundred years the question of what happened to the two young princes in the Tower of London has stood as one of English history's most intriguing mysteries. Were they murdered on the orders of the vile Richard III described by Thomas More and William Shakespeare? Or should their disappearance be charged to someone else? If this second alternative be true, as many historians believe, then it can be assumed that King Richard's memory may well have become the unfortunate target of a carefully crafted conspiracy, a plot designed to blacken his reputation, whilst removing a tarnish from that of his royal successor.

This book fleshes out the bare historical possibilities that have come down to us to tell how Bishop Morton, Henry VII's closest advisor, spun a self-seeking web of conspiracy to discredit Richard in the eyes of future generations; and of how he induced Thomas More, a pious and gifted young man of emerging promise who was just entering the second season of his career, to write his damning *History of Richard III*.

Apart from Father Gregory, Brother Bernard, Sir Francis Musgrave, and Isabel Swanton, all of the leading characters in the story, and several of the supporting characters too, were real people who lived in fifteenth-century England. Henry Tudor, Bishop Morton, Erasmus, and John More are pictured very much as historical accounts describe them.

The same is true of Thomas More, the central figure of the story. He is depicted here as his biographers have described him: a brilliant, pious and talented young man, whose thoughts were haunted by a gnawing fear that his erotic fantasies foreshadowed the damnation of his soul. The author has gone a step further than the biographers in this respect, suggesting a rational explanation for Thomas's obsessions and also for his later life-long commitment for wearing cilice and practising self-flagellation.

In the absence of historical evidence, it is assumed that Thomas More worked for a while in Bishop Morton's Chancery. Whether he did or not, it is known that he lived in Morton's household as a boy and that Morton supplied the information he drew upon for his *History of Richard III*.

The story told here follows the chronological sequence of events known to have taken place during Thomas More's early manhood. One and possibly two events have been moved back in time for narrative effect. The Hunne affair happened later in More's life than the period dealt with here, but is reported as is because it illustrates More's attitude about the rights of the clergy. Questions might also be raised as to whether More wrote his *History* when here reported rather than in later years.

This account only deals with an early phase of Thomas More's life. Ahead were the years when this man for all seasons authored his *Utopia*; was knighted for his service to the crown, served as Henry VIII's Lord Chancellor; and finally chose to endure martyrdom in 1535 rather than accept Henry as the spiritual head of his Church.

It is not known whether More had plans to ever publish his *History*. He made no attempt to do so during his lifetime; and his work might easily have been lost had his son-in-law not found it among his papers and published it in 1557, some twenty-two years after his death. Does the fact that More did not offer his book for publication indicate, as some have suggested, that he had doubts about its veracity? No one knows.

Two other events of dramatic significance for this tale occurred long years after the demise of its characters. Workmen engaged in the repair of the north wall of the Tower of London in 1674 found the skeletal remains of two bodies at the base of a stairwell. Positive identification was not possible, and no one could say for how long they had been hidden. Many people, then and since, have accepted their discovery as proof that the two princes were murdered and buried where More had reported.

A second event came in 1935, four hundred years after his death, when Pope Pius XI elevated Sir Thomas More, who had long been venerated by his Church for his martyrdom, to sainthood.

The House of York

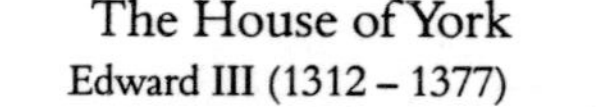

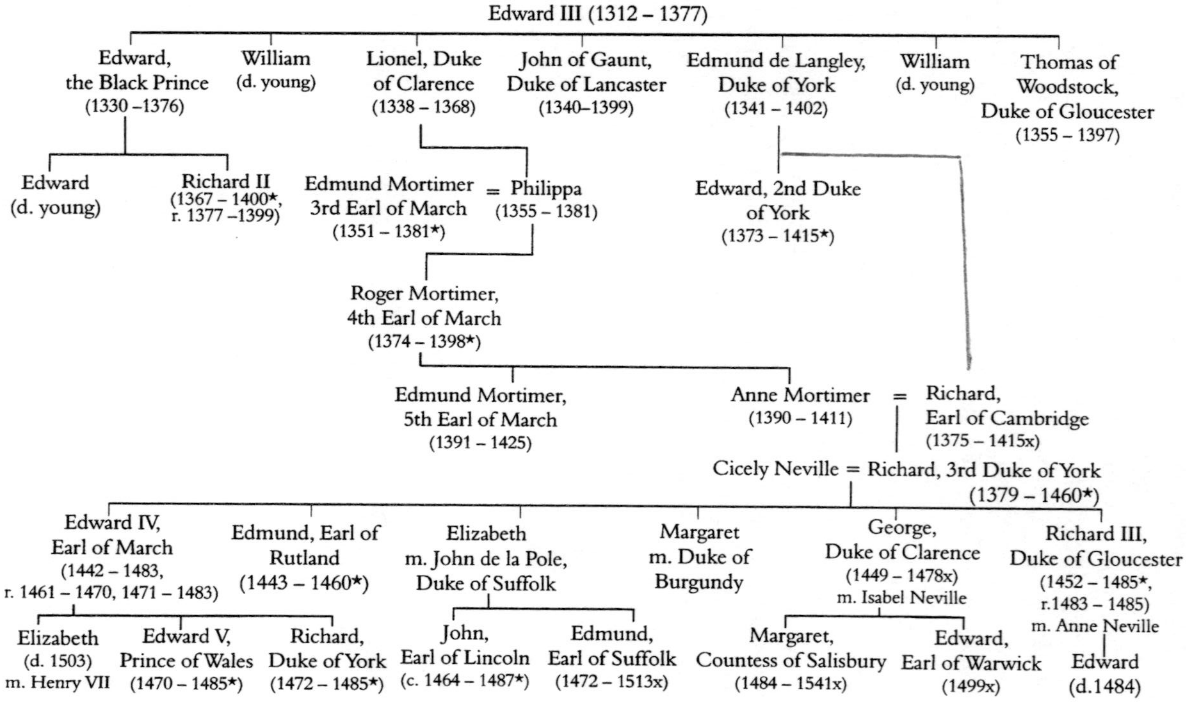

Edward III (1312 – 1377)

- Edward, the Black Prince (1330 –1376)
  - Edward (d. young)
  - Richard II (1367 – 1400*, r. 1377 –1399)
- William (d. young)
- Lionel, Duke of Clarence (1338 – 1368)
  - Philippa (1355 – 1381) = Edmund Mortimer 3rd Earl of March (1351 – 1381*)
    - Roger Mortimer, 4th Earl of March (1374 – 1398*)
      - Edmund Mortimer, 5th Earl of March (1391 – 1425)
      - Anne Mortimer (1390 – 1411) = Richard, Earl of Cambridge (1375 – 1415x)
- John of Gaunt, Duke of Lancaster (1340–1399)
- Edmund de Langley, Duke of York (1341 – 1402)
  - Edward, 2nd Duke of York (1373 – 1415*)
  - Richard, Earl of Cambridge (1375 – 1415x)
- William (d. young)
- Thomas of Woodstock, Duke of Gloucester (1355 – 1397)

Anne Mortimer = Richard, Earl of Cambridge

- Richard, 3rd Duke of York (1379 – 1460*) = Cicely Neville
  - Edward IV, Earl of March (1442 – 1483, r. 1461 – 1470, 1471 – 1483)
    - Elizabeth (d. 1503) m. Henry VII
    - Edward V, Prince of Wales (1470 – 1485*)
    - Richard, Duke of York (1472 – 1485*)
  - Edmund, Earl of Rutland (1443 – 1460*)
  - Elizabeth m. John de la Pole, Duke of Suffolk
    - John, Earl of Lincoln (c. 1464 – 1487*)
    - Edmund, Earl of Suffolk (1472 – 1513x)
  - Margaret m. Duke of Burgundy
  - George, Duke of Clarence (1449 – 1478x) m. Isabel Neville
    - Margaret, Countess of Salisbury (1484 – 1541x)
    - Edward, Earl of Warwick (1499x)
  - Richard III, Duke of Gloucester (1452 – 1485*, r.1483 – 1485) m. Anne Neville
    - Edward (d.1484)

The House of Lancaster

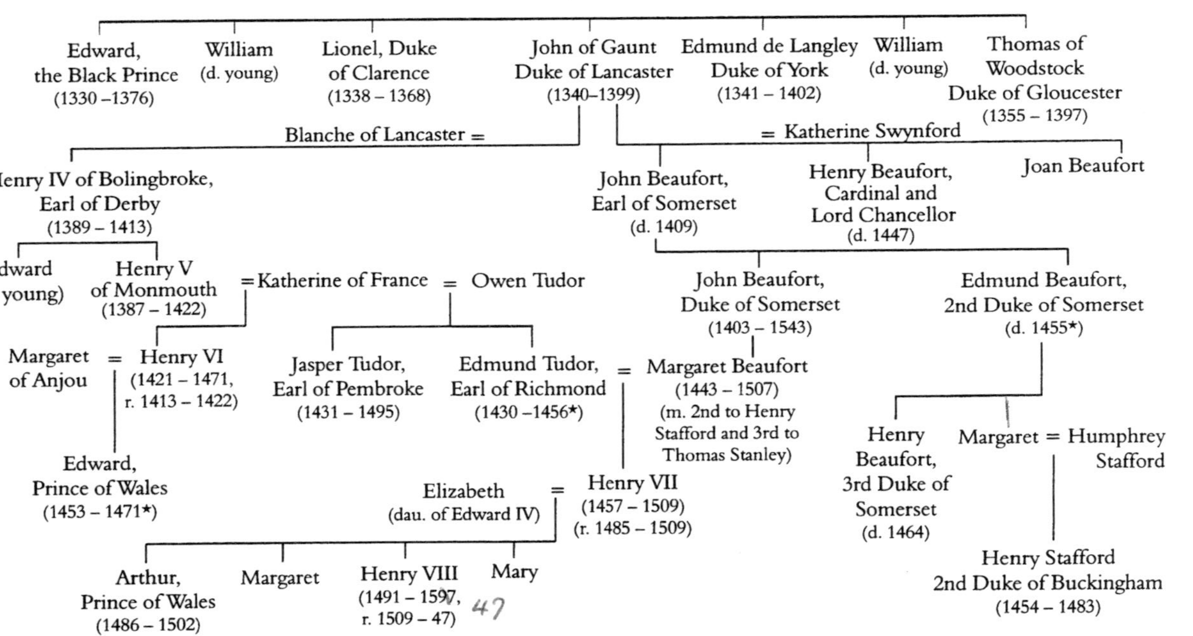

The House of Buckingham

Edward III (1312 – 1377)

Edward,
the Black Prince
(1330 –1376)

William
(d. young)

Lionel, Duke
of Clarence
(1338 – 1368)

Katherine Swynford = John of Gaunt,
(3rd wife) Duke of Lancaster
(1340–1399)

Edmund de Langley,
Duke of York
(1341 – 1402)

William
(d. young)

Thomas of Woodstock,
Earl of Buckingham and
Duke of Gloucester
(1355 – 1397)

John Beaufort,
Earl of Somerset
(d. 1409)

Edmund Beaufort,
2nd Duke of Somerset
(d. 1455*)

Humphrey,
Earl of
Buckingham
(1381 – 1399)

Edmund Stafford, = Anne = Wm. Bouchier,
5th Earl of (d. 1438) Earl of Ewe
Stafford

Humphrey Stafford,
Duke of Buckingham
(1402 – 1460*)

Thomas Bouchier,
Cardinal and Lord
Chancellor

Henry,
3rd Duke of Somerset
(d. 1464*)

Edmund,
4th Duke of Somerset
(d. 1471*)

Margaret = Humphrey Stafford
(d.1455*)

Henry Stafford,
2nd husband of
Margaret Beaufort,
mother of Henry VII

Catherine Woodville = Henry Stafford,
2nd Duke of
Buckingham
(1454 – 1485x)

Edward Stafford,
3rd Duke of Buckingham
(1478 – 1521x)